THE
RAGNAR STORMBRINGER
TALES
VOLUME I

Also by Stephen Zimmer

The Rising Dawn Saga
The Exodus Gate
The Storm Guardians
The Seventh Throne
The Undying Light

The Fires in Eden Series
Crown of Vengeance
Dream of Legends
Spirit of Fire

The Faraway Saga
Dream of the Navigator

Hellscapes
Hellscapes, Volume 1
Hellscapes, Volume II

Chronicles of Ave
Chronicles of Ave, Volume 1

The Ragnar Stormbringer Tales (eBook only)
Depths of Night
When the Cold Breathes
Altar of Gods
Tears in the Snow

The Rayden Valkyrie Tales (eBook only)
Blood of a Queen
Winds of War
The Sun's Caress
Across Desert Plains

THE
RAGNAR STORMBRINGER
TALES
VOLUME I

Stephen Zimmer

 SEVENTH STAR PRESS

Cover art: Olivia Pro Design
Cover art in this book copyright © 2018 Olivia Pro Design & Seventh Star Press, LLC.

Editor: Holly Marie Phillippe
Published by Seventh Star Press, LLC.

ISBN Number: 978-1-948042-69-7

Seventh Star Press
www.seventhstarpress.com
info@seventhstarpress.com

Publisher's Note:
The Ragnar Stormbringer Tales, Volume I is a work of fiction. All names, characters, and places are the product of the author's imagination, used in fictitious manner. Any resemblances to actual persons, places, locales, events, etc. are purely coincidental.

Printed in the United States of America

First Edition

ACKNOWLEDGEMENTS

I cannot thank my readers enough. Your interest, support, and encouragement mean more to me than you might realize. An author is nothing without readers. It is a very special and unique bond that I take very seriously. Readers deserve the best work possible from an author, and I want my readers to know that I give every effort on my part to always honor that.

A heartfelt thank you to Holly Marie Phillippe for her hard work and scrutiny working as an editor on these novellas. Her understanding of the world that Ragnar inhabits and his character have been so beneficial in watching my back to be sure that I am delivering my readers the best quality of work possible. An author must trust the editor of their work to identify anything that may need more attention, and I can say without hesitation that Holly has my full trust!

Deep gratitude to Olivia, of Olivia Pro Design, for such wonderful covers on the Ragnar Stormbringer novellas in both eBook format and for this compendium. Olivia's attention to detail and maintaining consistency is exceptional and she has really shined in her design work on the covers of of these releases.

I would like to thank my family and friends who are family for all of their help in taking this often difficult road that I am on. From the time you have given working alongside me to the regular encouragement and support you extend, I salute you! A special shout out in this area to Eric Jude, Kylie Jude, Diana Wieczorek, David Sheridan my sister Courtney Zimmer, Martin and Mindy Roberts, and our sweet and loving cat Dubious!

Last, but not least, I would like to thank my community of friends and creatives for all of the support you have shown, from helping me to raise awareness of my projects to stepping up to help me when life's storms arise unexpectedly. You are an amazing and wonderful bunch, and I carry you always at heart!

DEDICATION

To the One Who gives me the strength to stand alone when what is right is at odds with what is popular.

To my mother and father, who taught me to never follow the crowd and trust to my own heart in finding my way along life's journey.

To my beloved Holly, who is that rare kind of person who will stand with you against all odds to fight the good fight.

To my sister, who has shown a true kind of courage in rising again and again when great storms have tried to shake her world.

DEPTHS OF NIGHT

A RAGNAR STORMBRINGER TALE

STEPHEN ZIMMER

DEPTHS OF NIGHT

The sleek northern vessel crested the rolling wave and glided downward. Low to the water, the longship cleaved through the sea with elegant grace.

At any other time, Ragnar would have taken pleasure from the smooth motion of the vessel, the view of gentle waves sparkling in the rays of the sun, and the salt-tinged breezes coursing through his long locks. At the moment, his thoughts and eyes were locked on the dark, triangular shape cutting through the water to the right of the bow.

The tall black fin belonged to a massive hunter of the deep. The close presence of the creature sent a deep unease rippling through the longship's crew, most of whom plied at their oars, pulling the vessel closer and closer to the shore now in sight ahead.

Four other vessels of similar size and shape traversed the undulating waves in the near vicinity. Though continuing to work at their oars, the men and women aboard the other longships were well aware of the great fin slicing the water.

Their heads turned incessantly in the direction of the ship carrying Ragnar. Monsters from the oceanic depths always a source of fear and concern for seafarers, chagrin and trepidation reflected from every face.

Stephen Zimmer

"So close to land!" a stocky man to Ragnar's left exclaimed, vexation emanating from his terse expression. His long, braided beard of gray and brown whipped about as he looked fast from the fin to the shoreline.

The leader of the raiders and a veteran of the seas, Strala exhibited much less anxiety than all but Ragnar, but a heated frustration could be seen within his eyes. Loosing a torrent of curses, he pounded his right fist down on the edge of the highest strake.

"And now this!" he shouted.

"We have not far to go," Ragnar said, his ice-blue eyes remaining on the dark fin drifting slow through the water.

"Where there is one of those brutes, there are bound to be more," Strala said, eyeing the sea predator.

Behind them, those laboring at the oars pulled the vessel though the water at a regular pace. A cadence guided them, called by a man set near to the main mast, its square sail now furled.

Cries broke out on the other longships. Ragnar looked back to them and saw the cause of the commotion. Near the last vessel in their group, two more fins had broken the surface.

"What is their purpose? " Ragnar asked, glancing back to Strala. "Curiosity? Or a hunt?"

"I do not know," Strala replied in a low voice. .

Loud cracks of wood and cries ringing out answered Ragnar's question a few moments later. Timber pieces exploding into the air within a great spray of water, a massive black and white form slammed into the side of one of the other longships.

The violent impact cast a number of men and a couple of women into the sea. Shouts and cries rife with fear carried to Ragnar's ears. Those in the water flailed and thrashed about, as tall, dark fins converged toward them.

"The bastards knew damn well what they were doing!" Strala said, loosing another series of curses.

Depths of Night

The crippled longship floundered in the water, all oars having come to a stop. The others continued forward.

"Use archers, and swing this vessel about, we do not abandon our own," Ragnar told Strala.

"Have you lost your wits? We can do nothing against those brutes," Strala said.

"We can only do nothing if we do nothing!" Ragnar thundered, anger brewing in his eyes. "Turn this vessel around!"

"You forget yourself, this is my longship!" Strala retorted.

"We do not abandon our own," Ragnar said in a firm voice. "Act now, before others are cast into the waters."

The look on Strala's face, a mix of fear, anger, and shock, told Ragnar that his meaning had not been missed. Glaring at Ragnar, Strala's jaws tensed.

A moment later, Strala gave the commands to turn the vessel about. Several of the rowers were then told to cease and take up weapons, but enough remained at the oars to maneuver the vessel well and propel it along the surface at a fair pace.

Those with bows positioned themselves wherever one of the sea hunters drew closer, readying to shower the beast with arrows should it make a move to attack the longship. For the moment, the creatures did not threaten the vessel.

Many gathered at the bow with Ragnar and Strala, and looked toward the other longship now languishing in the waves. Nothing could be done when some of their comrades bobbing in the water began vanishing beneath the surface.

Carried high upward, and face contorting in agony, a man screamed within a great explosion of water. The lower half of his body held within the jaws of a black and white monstrosity, the hapless man was dragged below a moment later, as the great bulk of the predator fell back into the sea with a tremendous splash.

Seeing the threat in their midst, those stranded in the waves began swimming toward the damaged longship. Making slow progress, a few more disappeared from view, falling victim to the leviathans roaming among them.

"The bastards are playing with them!" Strala exclaimed.

Ragnar could not dispute the man. Not far away, an ill-fated man was tossed out of the water, falling into an area hemmed in by three of the huge beasts. A hot, bitter-laced furor came over him, seeing that the monsters did not kill the man outright, but rather humped and tossed him about.

"Swim to the ship!" Ragnar roared at those still in the water.

When Strala's vessel drew alongside the other longship, Ragnar and others worked fast using bearded axes, ropes, and other implements to hold the two ships close.

Many on the other longship began climbing over into Strala's vessel, while a few remained on the stricken vessel to help pull survivors out of the water. Boarding the other longship, Ragnar joined in the effort, lifting a couple of men up and into the vessel as they reached its side.

When Ragnar turned back toward the water, after helping the second man aboard, he recognized a dark-haired woman named Thorsalla swimming toward the longship. Near to her, a man went down suddenly, engulfed in the maw of one of the sea hunters.

"Make haste!" Ragnar shouted at her.

The woman needed no encouragement, striving hard to cross the last few body lengths remaining between her and the vessel. Kicking hard and arms churning fast, she covered the distance in swift fashion.

Reaching down, Ragnar grabbed Thorsalla's forearm, plucking her up and out of the water with a single, great heave. Soaked and cold, Thorsalla landed heavily on the deck. Getting her feet underneath her, she stood up.

After catching her breath for a moment, Thorsalla said to Ragnar, "I thought you wolves would flee to the shore."

"You know little of me then," Ragnar replied, with a trace of irritation. Looking back to the water, he eyed another man making his way along the surface toward the longship. "I do not abandon my comrades."

"I am not so sure of the others," Thorsalla said, looking away to where the other three longships continued toward the shore.

Keeping a watch on the incoming swimmer, Ragnar glanced toward her. "All that matters is I am sure of myself. And you are alive."

"You did save my life, and I'll let you know more of me ... later," Thorsalla said, with a lusty glint in her eyes that echoed in the grin she gave him.

"First, get yourself out of here!" Ragnar told her in a raised voice, irritated at her banter and indicating Strala's longship. "This is no time for talk!"

"Being close to death makes one hungry for life," Thorsalla replied with another grin, though she heeded his words and strode toward the other vessel, her long dark locks dripping seawater.

Ragnar paid her no more attention. The man he had identified in the water had drawn close.

Ragnar shifted his position over to the spot where he gauged the man would reach the vessel's side. Grabbing him by his tunic and one arm, Ragnar pulled the man upward. Looking half-drowned, the man slumped onto the deck,

"No time to slumber, get aboard Strala's ship now!" Ragnar commanded the man, a warrior many years older than him.

Ragnar continued until he had pulled six more men from the blood-filled water, all of whom made it over to the deck of the other ship. Not long afterward, everyone but Ragnar had boarded Strala's longship.

Eyes searching the water's surface, Ragnar took one more survey of the area in the hopes of finding other surviving comrades. Walking to the bow of the longship and casting his gaze all over, he could see no sign of anyone else left out in the waves.

A couple of tall fins passed close, spurring Ragnar to take his axe out of the loop at his belt. Should one of the monstrosities surface right next to him, he wanted to get one good strike in for what they had done to many of his comrades.

"Get back here, Ragnar! There are no others left out there!" Strala yelled at Ragnar from the other ship.

Ragnar turned away at last, and took one stride toward the other vessel.

A loud splash of water broke out farther behind him.

Rising from the depths, the enormous beast surged high out of the water and tilted its body, bringing its bulk slamming down close to the stern of the crippled longship. Tilting the end where Ragnar stood, the force lifted him far out of the water and separated the vessel from Strala's longship.

Whirling about at once, Ragnar swung his great axe and hooked the extended, lower part of the head over the edge of the top strake, close to the bow. He had used that lower extension to hook and pull many shields away from enemy warriors. Now, clutching onto the haft of his axe, with all his strength, the precarious grip of iron upon wood weighed his life in the balance.

The weight of the beast swung the vessel about, causing the longship to take on more water and taking it a little farther away from Strala's ship. Hanging from Raven Caller's leather-wrapped haft, arms bulging with muscles holding him fast, Ragnar looked downward.

A nest of veritable daggers lining a gaping maw set in position beneath Ragnar, the beast stared back at him. He could read nothing beyond a promise of death in the creature's solid black eyes.

A couple moments passing, the beast remained in place, seeming content to keep the other end of the vessel pressed down, waiting for Ragnar to tire, slip, and plummet into jaws large enough to swallow him whole. He knew he could keep his hold for a little while longer, but he could not withstand forever.

"I'm no damnable seal, you hellspawn, and this is no ice floe! You'll not get me this day!" Ragnar shouted at the creature, angry defiance brimming in his face and voice.

Dangling from his axe, he looked over to the warriors on the longship close by. He then glanced back to where the beast was positioned.

A thought came to his mind.

Twisting his weight, and risking dislodging the axe, he swiveled his end of the vessel over a little more, giving those on the other vessel a clear view of the monster holding the stern end down.

"Now, you fools!" Ragnar shouted at them. "What do you wait for? Send arrows into the beast! The brute is exposed!"

Arrows whistled through the air moments later, several lodging deep into the flesh of the huge sea creature. Riddled with feathered shafts, the beast erupted with a number of high-pitched cries. Sliding back into the water, the creature released its hold on the longship.

The end Ragnar held onto fell downward fast, slamming back into the water with a large spray of water. Ragnar grunted, his body hitting the deck hard. Freeing Raven Caller from where the iron had bitten deep into the wood of the strake, Ragnar got to his feet without delay.

"To the bow!" he yelled to the other vessel.

Maneuvering the steering oar set near to the stern, and with vigorous rowing, the other longship made a sharp turn. Lurching forward, the vessel then glided on a course bringing its side close to the bow of the doomed ship.

Ragnar slid the haft of his axe into the loop at his belt, and took a few deep breaths. Judging the distance between the longships, he waited until the last possible moment before bounding forward and leaping from the bow of the sinking vessel.

Hurling himself through the air, Ragnar landed with a heavy thud onto the planking of the other ship.

Looking around, he could see no sign of the monster that had been anticipating Ragnar sliding down into its gullet a handful of moments before.

"Make for the shore! Now!" Strala called out.

With every oar being used, a rapid cadence, and the rowers putting all the strength they could muster into the effort, the longship hastened toward the shore at a pace Ragnar had never experienced on the seas. A misty, salty spray dampening his face, Ragnar eyed the shoreline, drawing closer with every moment.

Looking back, Ragnar watched as the abandoned longship behind them finally sank beneath the waves.

Moving in a cluster, several dark fins headed northward; the tallest of them at the lead of the sea-roving pack. The sight of the creatures heading away drained the tension in the air at once. Looks of relief passed among the longship's occupants as the word spread among them.

"You gave me a few scares, you big lout," Strala told Ragnar, joining him at the bow. "That was some chance you took swinging at the end of your axe."

"I had little desire to meet death in the belly of some sea creature," Ragnar replied.

Strala turned head and watched the crew at the oars.

"You were right," he said in a lower voice. "We could not leave our own to those brutes."

"You'll need every warrior now," Ragnar said, turning his attention back to the nearing shore. "Many were lost."

"Enough remain to do what we came to do," Strala said. "You counted among them. We will discover the mettle of the Petranni for ourselves soon enough."

Thoughts of solid ground beneath his feet sounded welcome enough, but a good fight would give vent to a lot of things following the harrowing encounter with the sea brutes. At least the one that had beset Ragnar had been made to pay a price, incurred in the form of several arrow shafts now stuck in its flesh.

Wherever the thing swam, it would carry tangible reminders of Ragnar at every moment.

Keeping his eyes on the shore, Ragnar grinned.

***

Pulled onto the shore with the other remaining vessels, Strala's longship rested upon the sand. Around the vessels, the surviving northern raiders set about making their encampment for the night.

Descending into the ocean to the east, the sun cast a beautiful display of red and purple hues across the skies. Shadows lengthened all around with the encroachment of darkness.

No signs of the Petranni had been seen, but the raiders kept a constant lookout for the land's inhabitants. A watch was organized for the duration of night.

After gathering some wood, the raiders set a few fires and prepared meals. The evening's fare was bolstered from a couple of deer, found just off the shore in the woods, brought down close to twilight by arrow. A little fresh meat came as a boon to many among the raiders after the meager provisions endured at sea.

Savoring every bite of his portion of the deer, Ragnar sat with Strala near one of the fires. Warm and dry, he looked forward to a good night's rest, doubting that the Petranni would cause any disturbances. It would take them a little time after assessing the strength of the raiders to muster enough warriors to present a threat.

"Make no mistake, those brutes out there are hunters of men," Ragnar said, casting a glance toward the sea. "They have gained a taste for our kind, and they are not swayed by a longship. The one lout wanting me in its belly treated the vessel like it was a piece of ice. The big bastard looked at me like I was a seal, trapped to fill its cursed gullet."

"You know the bastards hunt up and down long coastlines," Strala said. "When we depart, we will have to trust to chance at some point. It is possible to run into them again."

"Who knows if we will survive tomorrow, Strala?" Thorsalla interjected, taking a long draught of ale and taking a place next to Ragnar. "What we have is today. Let us make the most of it."

Ragnar grinned, catching the silent promise for later within her piercing eyes.

"I found some more clothes that fit, so I'm no longer soaked, but I might yet be a bit salty from the sea water," she said with a playful air, eyeing Ragnar with an intent gaze.

"Go to your tent, if you wish to rut," Strala grumbled.

"You should have pulled me from the water," Thorsalla replied to Strala with a chiding air, a wry grin on her face.

"I keep my senses. It is how I have remained alive all these years of seafaring and raiding," Strala said. He looked over to Ragnar and shook his head. "One can be reckless when favored by the gods."

Ragnar chuckled. "That favor might have been fleeting if you had left me hanging from my axe at the bow of that ship."

"Do not feel too much affection, Stormbringer," Strala said. "I did not want to lose your axe for this raid."

"You still have my axe, and you also have the weapons of many others because we returned to that longship," Ragnar said. After pausing to take another bite of deer meat, he asked, "How many fell among the other ship's crew?"

"Seventeen are unaccounted for," Thorsalla said.

"And the loss of a good longship," Strala said. "Less room remains to take plunder and thralls."

"Four vessels and well over a hundred warriors is enough to gain and transport a lot of plunder," Ragnar said.

"You better not take a Petranni woman," Thorsalla told Ragnar, smiling. "It would be unfortunate for a thrall to fall overboard at sea."

"You know I have no desire for thralls of any kind," Ragnar said. "That is something for others to concern themselves with."

"I am not much for thralls," Strala said. "Always causing headaches on the seas with the need to be fed, guarded, and tended to. Though it is said there are some beauties among the Petranni."

A wistful look crept into the older man's eyes.

"Why would you think of Petranni women? Unn and Marta also survived today, and might yet have hungers tonight," Thorsalla told Strala, a mischievous grin on her face. "Do not give up so soon."

Ragnar chuckled, thinking of the other two women who had joined with them for the raid. Both stalwart warriors like Thorsalla, they possessed a bawdiness that rivaled the most libidinous of the men. Both were also quite attractive. As with Thorsalla, Ragnar had availed himself of their carnal attentions and inclinations more than once, to his extreme pleasure.

"Those two?" Strala said, his face taking on an incredulous expression. "I would rather wrestle an elk in our homelands than spend a night getting clawed up by one of them. I have heard enough tales from my warriors."

Ragnar laughed. "You just need to learn how to tame that which is wild."

Strala shook his head. "I have already said I am not one to be reckless, Stormbringer."

Ragnar nodded and smiled. "Yes, you have."

"Do not forget we have a promising raid before us," Strala said. "A day's march inland from here it is said to be well-inhabited. Temple sites, large homesteads, and other sites with loot for the taking."

"What of strongholds, or the dwellings of tribal chieftains," Ragnar said. "These are a tribal people, yes?"

"They have a Great King, above lesser kings, who are above the tribal chiefs," Strala said. "Sometimes there are two Great Kings. I should mention these Great Kings are chosen at a gathering of their men of highest rank. Those who can be chosen come from the bloodline of the women. It is enough to make your head churn trying to understand it all."

"Such an order creates fertile ground among them for alliances and strategy," Ragnar said, thinking upon the complex system. "But for our purposes it would be better if we encounter no kings of any kind. We have a strong raiding force, but it is not an army."

"We will be careful and scout any area we go into," Strala said.

"We must appear where we are not expected, and give them no time to gather a response," Ragnar said. "We can take a small fortress if we are diligent."

"That is my intention," Strala said. "A large temple site is not far from here. If we catch them unawares, the plunder could be rich."

"I am in for any chance of rich plunder, but I grow weary of talk," Thorsalla stated, her eyes and words directed toward Ragnar. "I desire some action."

"Which you will have soon enough," Ragnar said, quaffing more ale and rumbling with laughter.

"Neither of you are speaking of raiding a temple site," Strala said in a gruff manner. "I did not get where I am from being naive."

"What about a temple site?" Thorsalla riposted, laughing, in an air of jest.

"There is nothing remaining to discuss here," Strala replied. He shook his head and then continued in a dismissive manner, "Go on, get out of here, you two! Just be sure not to tire yourselves out too much before tomorrow. We have a raid to undertake."

"I make no promises about him, when I'm done," Thorsalla said, getting to her feet with a smile on her face. "But I'll be ready to wield my blade, Strala. Rest assured of that."

A smirk on his face, Ragnar stretched and got up. "Raven Caller will be ready when dawn's light arrives."

Leaving Strala by the fire, Ragnar and Thorsalla stepped away, heading for a tent he had set up a short distance away. More than a few eyes watched them from the surrounding tents and fires.

Ragnar slipped his arm about Thorsalla's waist, and hugged her close to him. "It is now time for me to collect on that promise."

"Spoken like you have a choice, Ragnar," Thorsalla said. "I would have you tonight, whether you pulled me from those bleak waters or not."

"You'd have found no argument from me," he replied, leaning over and kissing her deep, his tongue finding hers and intertwining.

Her eyes dancing with lust, Thorsalla raked her fingers through his beard and traced down the contours of his pronounced chest muscles and midsection. Flashing him a lascivious smile, and running her tongue across her teeth, she ran her hand lower and placed a firm grip, one that kindled a heat within him.

"That's mine for tonight, Stormbringer," she told him in a husky voice.

Well-aroused and grinning, he guided Thorsalla her into his tent when they reached the triangular opening, his trousers and under-breeches already being pulled down before he was fully inside. With a smooth upward motion, Ragnar lifted her tunic off, watching her hair tumble back down over well-toned shoulders and firm breasts.

Shedding the rest of their clothes, they continued to kiss and run their tongues along each other's neck and ears. Maneuvering Ragnar onto his back, Thorsalla straddled and guided him into her.

Rearing up and gazing downward, Thorsalla began to undulate her hips. In a breathy tone, she declared with a smile, "All mine."

***

After the light of dawn broke night's dominion, a handful of warriors were assigned to ward the vessels. Ragnar deemed the number inadequate, knowing that every warrior possible would be needed for the raid, a matter of increased importance after having lost seventeen on the previous day to the sea monsters.

The best scouts in the group were sent ahead of the main column marching through the woods and heading deeper into Petranni lands. The thick forest canopy sheltered the warriors when some rain fell a little later, cooling the air.

Ragnar walked near the front of the loose column, keeping his eyes out for any hint of an ambush. The undergrowth was not so dense that it offered concealment for large numbers of warriors, but he could assume nothing when trespassing upon the territory of another people.

Midday arrived, and the column halted for a short rest. A couple of the scouts returned to report their findings, though to everyone's dismay no viable sites had been found yet. A few small, fortified homesteads and simple woodland dwellings, all abandoned, had been all the scouts had found.

The absence of the inhabitants gave rise to the thought that word had been spread of the raider's presence, but the scouts found it strange that many things of value, and easy to carry, had been left behind while all livestock had been taken. Though most warriors dismissed the scouts' concern, Ragnar took their observations to mind when the group resumed the march.

In a world rife with dangers, raiders were not the only threat that could drive people from their homes.

***

Concealing the sun, and casting the land below in a dismal pall, an unbroken sea of gray spanned the skies to the far horizons. A light drizzle falling in a steady cascade, the drab, cold atmosphere mirrored the pensive looks on the faces of the raiders still marching through the wooded, hilly terrain.

After two days had passed, no treasures had been gained, and nor had the raiders come across any of the Petranni who dwelled in that land.

Again, and again, the raiders had come across deserted homesteads. Devoid of livestock, the walled sites contained small amounts of valuables that should not have presented any difficulty for the occupants to take along with them.

Ragnar's doubt increased with every homestead they searched that tidings of the raiders explained the dearth of Petranni. Rather, he found it much more likely that another kind of threat caused the people to flee their homes.

The long days of marching and absence of a propitious target to loot spurred a growing, irritable disposition among the raiders. Eating light and taking short rests, Ragnar and the others covered a large expanse of ground, finding themselves deep into Petranni lands when at last they came upon a welcome sight in the distance; a place with active signs of Petranni inhabitants.

A pair of massive rises loomed high above the rolling, woodland terrain. Both of the great hills crowned with timber palisades atop earthen ramparts, the roofs of many structures could be seen beyond the defensive barriers.

Lower areas on the other faces of the hills visible to the

raiders displayed similar defenses of palisades and ramparts. Positioned behind them were a number of conical, thatch-roofed structures.

"We have found where they have all gone to," Ragnar declared, eyeing the huge stronghold.

The place teemed with activity. Tendrils of smoke from a large number of fires and the smoke-holes of many buildings wound their way into the sky. A few pens visible on the lower levels looked to be packed with livestock.

"We do not have nearly enough warriors to take those mounds of rock," one of the other raiders exclaimed.

"I imagine there is silver and gold a plenty in there," another added.

"What has driven all of them in there?" Ragnar asked. Sweeping his gaze across the land surrounding the stronghold, he could see no signs of a besieging army.

"Maybe they have heard of us landing on their shores," Thorsalla quipped, with a lighthearted grin.

Her remark brought a smirk to Ragnar's face.

"That's one explanation," he replied. "But it is not one I find likely."

"Maybe the Warrior Queen marches upon them, and now draws near," Strala commented with a grim expression, keeping his eyes fixed toward the fortress.

"She is not said to desire these lands," Ragnar said, thinking of the tales he had heard of the renowned queen's exploits. Ruling the warrior tribes to the south; she reigned over lands that no band of northern raiders would now dare to venture in. "And I do not think the Petranni to be foolish enough to seek war with her. It would be an invitation to their own doom."

"Whatever it is, we must discover whatever drove the Petranni from their homes and into this place, before it discovers us," Strala said.

"We will have to scout the surrounding countryside," Ragnar said. "And keep an eye on the movements near this stronghold."

"Then we find a place to make camp, close to here," Strala declared, looking to Ragnar.

It did not take long to find a suitable place to serve as a main encampment, one that would give them access to water and the ability to keep a watch on the stronghold. The band of raiders then divided themselves into several parties, to begin scouting the land on the following day.

***

The night passed without incident, and the various parties set out just after dawn. Aside from coming across more homesteads, the party that Ragnar accompanied found no answers to explain the concentration of Petranni in the stronghold.

Regrouping at the encampment when night approached, a deep concern took root, growing into a harvest of anxiety and apprehension when one of the scouting groups did not return.

***

Shortly after dawn, Ragnar, Thorsalla, and a few other warriors who had volunteered to go with them headed in the direction the missing party had taken the previous day. Determined to gain answers, Ragnar had declared the foray when morning arrived and took the lead with Raven Caller in his hands.

In the early afternoon, passing between some low hills, they came to the top of a rise looking out over a narrow valley. A cleared swathe of land in the center of the valley grabbed their attention and brought them to a halt.

A shallow ditch and low timber fence bordered a square plot of ground that contained a unique-looking structure at its center. Open on all four sides, and supported on twelve stout timber posts, the large, thatch-roofed construct sheltered what looked to be some kind of pit beneath it.

On two opposing sides of the structure, in the open ground, rose a pair of tall wooden posts. Just beyond one of the posts were a couple of small, empty pens.

Several bodies lay strewn about the ground before the central structure, on the side facing the entrance to the enclosure. Even at a distance Ragnar could tell that they had been killed in a brutal fashion, or scavengers had already gotten to them. Clothing and weapons had been scattered all about the bodies, many of which had been dismembered. Limbs, heads and torsos dotted the area.

"Answers will be found soon," Ragnar told the others, starting down the other side of the rise and heading toward the compound. The others followed close behind, weapons drawn and in hand.

When they reached the compound, Ragnar, Thorsalla, and the other warriors crossed the short wooden bridge spanning the ditch. Creeping through the entrance, with weapons at the ready, they looked about the ground inside.

Coming to an immediate halt that brought a stop to the advance of the others, Ragnar braced himself.

Whether killer or scavenger, a strange figure crouched among the extensive carnage.

What looked to be a human, though one emaciated in appearance, with long, narrow limbs and leathery skin, bent low over the remnants of a man's torso. The severed head of Ubba, one of the warriors Ragnar had pulled from the sea only a few days prior, cast the rheumy stare of death from where it lay a few strides away.

Like a rope of knots running from the base of the neck down the length of its back, the figure's spine protruded in a grotesque manner. Drawn taut, the layer of skin covering the knobby line exposed each of the being's thin ribs.

Light sloshing and ripping noises came from the figure, whose head still remained lowered, and out of view. Ragnar suspected the nature of the sounds. The thought filled him with disgust and anger.

"Stand and face us, you scavenging wretch!" Ragnar addressed the figure in a booming, commanding tone.

The figure hunched over the remains of Ubba whipped about at the sound of Ragnar's voice.

Breath stilled in Ragnar's throat at the sight of a crow's visage looking back at him.

A loud, piercing screech emitted from the crow-headed being. Blood dripped from its thickly-coated beak, along with a tattered morsel of flesh gleaned from the grisly feast Ragnar had interrupted. Slowly, the thing rose up to its full height, exposing the rest of its repulsive, starved-looking appearance.

Instead of fingers, the creature possessed elongated talons, lathered in gore. Staring at Ragnar, it began moving them in a restless manner, as if eager to bury the talons into new flesh.

More talons extended from the elongated feet at the end of the being's narrow, bony legs. A thin membrane of skin spanned from each arm to the thing's sides, forming wing-like appendages.

"You think to interfere with a goddess?" the thing spoke to Ragnar in a rasping, grating tone. Sweeping its right arm outward, talons extended, it indicated the remains of dead raiders littering the open ground. "Fool, you will meet the fate of these men, who now fill our gullets."

"What kind of goddess needs crow-headed runts like you?" Ragnar chided. "Come, if you want to meet a bitter fate."

Shrieking, the enraged creature charged Ragnar. Moving much faster than he anticipated, the thing closed the distance between them in a couple of heartbeats.

Ragnar stepped forward to meet its advance. Spreading

his grip on Raven Caller, and holding the weapon firm in a horizontal alignment set in front of his body, he lifted the long axe upward and shoved hard. Putting the power of his shoulders, back, chest, and arms into the strike, he slammed the haft deep into the spread beak of his attacker.

The tremendous force of the blow lifted the creature off its feet and sent it hurtling backward. Flailing and emitting high-pitched screeches, it crashed hard onto the ground. Dazed and unable to open or close its beak, the creature struggled to gain an upright position.

It did not see Ragnar's axe blade rushing downward, cleaving the crow head from the crone-body in one vicious strike. A putrid stench filling the air in moments, the head rolled to a stop a few paces away, beak still open and black eyes dull, and void of life.

"Keep your eyes open for more of these miserable devils. I have a feeling this one was far from the last of them," Ragnar said, casting his gaze about. He glanced toward Thorsalla. "What manner of goddess has creatures such as this? You know of these lands."

"A goddess of death, most likely the one known as Macharriga," Thorsalla replied, eyeing the corpse of the thing Ragnar had just slain. Her grip tightened on the hilt of her blade. A look of astonishment spreading on her face, she pointed down with her free hand. "Look, Ragnar! It changes!"

Though decapitated, the corpse had begun to change. Talons retracting and malleable flesh shifting about, some power worked to transform the body to a more human-like state. The membranous skin beneath the arms started to merge back into the arms and sides.

The process slowed and halted, with a few of the talons and stretches of the wing-like membranes left in states of mid-transformation.

Nearby, the severed crow head remained unchanged.

"Death prevented it from finishing," Ragnar said.

"A shape-changer," Thorsalla remarked, continuing to stare at the corpse.

"A harder thing to kill," Ragnar said. "Unless you take their heads off."

Though faint, the caws of crows sounded in the distance.

The cries drew Ragnar's gaze upward, toward the skies. Though still far from the temple site, several dark shapes headed in their direction.

"Under the roof! All of you!" Ragnar shouted, starting for the structure at the center of the grounds. "It will force the bastards to land if they want to come at us."

Thorsalla and the others ran close behind Ragnar, jumping over the corpses in their way. A few moments the raiders had all taken shelter beneath the thatched roof.

A cursory glance at the pit revealed a large number of bones strewn within. While most were those of animals, a few unmistakable human remains lay among the skeletal pile.

Taking up a position at the edge of the shelter, Ragnar peered outward, keeping his eyes on the incoming shapes.

"Keep a mind on that damnable pit behind us," Ragnar warned the others. "It will do you no good to fall into it, while fighting these hell-cursed things."

Membranous wings spread wide, several creatures of the slain one's ilk glided into the sight of all beneath the structure, before alighting on the ground. Five in all, they paid no heed to the mutilated human corpses lying all about them.

Looking between the body of their felled comrade and the warriors gathered under the pit-sheltering roof, they began walking forward in a staggered line.

"You will pay a terrible price for this!" the one at the center declared in a shrill, rasping voice.

"Or you will make a terrible mistake, bird-head!" Ragnar

said in a mocking tone.

The creatures drew closer, step by step.

"This hour has been given to us!" the creature on the far left said.

"Not by me, or by those who stand here at my side!" Ragnar retorted, an icy grin on his face. "Your friend lying dead there learned that much."

His responses annoyed the creatures further. Flexing their talons in and out, and emitting screeching cries, they angled toward Ragnar and continued their approach.

"Do not think to take all of them by yourself, Stormbringer," Thorsalla said.

"Make sure you take their heads clean off," Ragnar replied to her, keeping his eyes locked on the advancing creatures.

"If I take more heads than you, then I get my way with you later," Thorsalla riposted. "You have your way with me if your count is greater."

"My count already stands at one," Ragnar answered, with a smirk. "A foolish wager, but one I will take."

With piercing shrieks, the creatures hurled themselves at the warriors.

Lowering his weapon and thrusting forward, Ragnar caught one of the charging creatures square in the chest, knocking it backward. A short, two-handed slash followed, crippling one arm and wing, but Ragnar gritted his teeth in the throes of a searing pain, as the creature raked the tips of its talons down his right arm.

Enraged and bleeding, Ragnar sent a heavy back-fist crashing against the side of the thing's head. Then, he brought Raven Caller across with his left arm, in a one-handed strike that bit deep into the side of the creature's right knee.

Crumpling to the ground, with two broken limbs and dazed from the hard blow to its head, the creature mustered no defense to the strike that took its head off a moment later.

Looking around, he saw Thorsalla standing over the headless body of another creature. Sword dripping blood and a battle-maddened smile on her face, she looked for her next opponent.

Bleeding from a multitude of savage wounds to face, neck, and mid-section, one of the other warriors who had come with Ragnar lay dying a few paces from Thorsalla. She wasted no time in attacking the warrior's assailant, who was crouched over its victim, beak buried in the still-breathing warrior's innards.

Blade flashing in an upward arc, she beheaded the creature, the blow sending the thing's head plopping onto the ground to the side of the dying man. She barely had time to look back to the maimed warrior when he shuddered and breathed his last.

Ragnar charged toward another warrior sprawled on his back in mortal peril. Face contorted, the man strained with all his might to hold back the talons of the creature pinning him down. Slowly, he gave way, bit by bit, bringing both talons and the beaked head of the creature closer to his flesh.

Blood gushed onto the man's face when Ragnar's axe took the creature's head off from the side. Gagging and spitting, he shoved the rest of the creature off his body.

"I am in debt to you, Ragnar," the man said, looking up to his liberator.

Ragnar extended an arm, grabbing the man by the forearm and pulling him to his feet. "Get your weapon in hand, this fight is not over."

One of the creatures remained, and two more of the warriors with Ragnar had fallen.

Lunging forward, the creature opened the throat of another warrior, whirling to face Thorsalla as she rushed upon it. The creature ducked her sword slash, grabbed her with one arm, and threw her off her feet.

She landed hard on her back. The creature sprang atop

Thorsalla, holding her to the ground. Clutching its narrow arms, her quick reflexes saved her from being shredded by the creature's talons. Strain showing all over her face, she grappled with the creature, locking her legs about it in a manner that hindered its movements.

Racing across the ground, Ragnar hurried to come to her aid. Raising his axe, he unleashed a heavy downward blow, aimed for the middle of the creature's back.

At that moment, Thorsalla used her hips and legs to roll the creature to the side, bringing her own body within a wisp of Ragnar's axe blade. The axe head buried deep into the ground with a prominent thump.

Unable to break free of the creature's grip or sustain her momentum, Thorsalla struggled and foundered. The thing lurched to the side, rolling Thorsalla onto her back once more, and immobilizing her beneath it. Ragnar had no time to pull the axe free of the ground and strike again.

Letting go of the haft, Rangar moved fast. Hooking both of his arms under the creature at the shoulders, he yanked it off Thorsalla before it could strike at her with its beak.

With harsh cries, the creature thrashed and flailed, exhibiting a great strength that tested Ragnar's own to the limit. Clenching his jaws, and veins standing out across his forehead, he kept his hold on the creature.

Regaining her feet, Thorsalla took up her sword and hacked the beak off the creature. She brought her sword back, poised to strike.

"Release it and get back fast!" she told Ragnar.

Letting go of his hold, Ragnar jumped backward. Thorsalla's sword arced down an instant later, sending the creature's beak-less head toppling to the ground. The thing's body flopped over a moment later, dark blood leeching out from the opened neck into the soil.

Thorsalla grinned. "That's three for me."

Ragnar returned the smile. "I should share in that kill ... and I had already taken three. That gives me the advantage."

"The killing blow was mine," Thorsalla declared, giving him a wink. "Three kills for me. Three kills for you.".

"We will have to resolve this later," Ragnar said, regaining his breath and looking around.

Nothing stirred on the ground or in the skies. Walking over, he pulled his axe from the ground and wiped the blade off using the edge of his own tunic.

The warrior Ragnar had saved trotted over, and another emerged from beneath the shelter.

Ragnar eyed the last warrior with a simmering ire, seeing no blood or signs of any injury. "Did you not see your comrades in peril?"

The shame filling the man's face told Ragnar all he needed to know. He did not wait for the other's reply.

Ragnar's right fist thundered into the other's jaw, spinning him about before he hit the ground, unconscious.

"Let him gain some courage in finding his way back to us by himself," Ragnar said with an edge of repulsion. "We do not need any who are so craven as to abandon comrades under attack."

"You are more merciful than I," Thorsalla said, spitting on the inert figure and giving him a hard kick to the groin. "That will give him something else to wake up with."

"Let us return to the camp," Ragnar said. "Maybe when one of the others hears of these creatures, and what happened here, they can make sense of everything else."

"Do you have any idea of what is happening?" Thorsalla asked.

"I only know that those creatures are part of the reason why the Petranni take refuge in their fortress," Ragnar said. "My instincts tell me we will face much worse before we leave these shores. Let us waste no more time here, and bring what we know to the others."

Thorsalla and the other warrior met his ominous words with silence, before following him out of the compound and back toward their encampment. Ragnar had little to say on the journey.

Immersed in his thoughts, Ragnar knew a grave danger stalked the lands of the Petranni. Their eerie cries sounding from fresh memories, images of the hideous, crow-headed beings echoed in his mind. Corrupted abominations, the creatures represented something malefic and cruel.

Whatever goddess they served, Ragnar had no doubt it wielded great power and harbored a wicked nature. One of the vile things had even claimed with an indignant tone of having been given the hour at hand, as if it had been acting within its rights.

Thinking upon that boast, the notion that death itself had been given reign over Petranni lands rose up again and again within his thoughts. If that were indeed so, he had no idea how he could possibly confront it. The things of sorcery had proved confounding many times before, but Ragnar sensed he was now pitted against something far beyond his understanding.

Chill, damp winds rushed over Ragnar, whistling through the trees like whispers of sepulchral emptiness. Listening to the footsteps of the two behind him, and drawing some consolation from the axe held secure in his hands, he marched onward.

***

"You slew six of them?"

Illuminated in the firelight, Strala's face carried a balance of fear and astonishment at Ragnar's telling of the encounter that day. The older man shook his head, brows creasing with lines signifying a deepening worry in him.

"Crow-headed ... bodies of crones ... form changing ... eating from corpses," Strala murmured, clasping his hands between his knees, where he sat to Ragnar's right. "These are dire tidings indeed."

To Ragnar's left, her countenance somber, Thorsalla listened to them in a brooding silence. From time to time, she broke off a little piece from a twig in her hands, and flicked it into the fire before them.

"You are no coward, Strala," Ragnar said, surprised at the veteran warrior's troubled demeanor. "Why do you react this way?"

"Now I know why these lands have emptied out, and a great many warriors remain huddled together behind the walls of that hill fortress," Strala replied. He took a deep breath, paused, and looked Ragnar in the eyes. "You have killed all but three of the Witches of Night."

"Then we should hunt down the last three of those wretched things and finish them off," Ragnar said, a memory flitting through his mind of the crow-headed thing hunched over the body of Ubba, tearing at the fallen warrior's flesh.

"You have killed six of Her nine greatest servants," Strala said, his voice low and thick with concern. "I know what we are now up against."

"Her?" Ragnar replied. "You mean the goddess one of those things mentioned?"

Strala nodded. "Macharriga, the Lady of Death, a goddess who prowls these lands."

"Then what must be done?" Thorsalla asked. "What are we to expect now?

"We need to abandon these lands at once," Strala declared. "And pray to our own gods that we leave these borders behind before She catches up to us. She will seek vengeance."

Strala's words left Ragnar uneasy, but far from cowed.

"The gods and goddesses of this world have their limits," Ragnar said. "Or a goddess like this would place everything in darkness."

"That is true," Strala said, nodding. "But there is no way to contend with Macharriga that is known to me. When She chooses to emerge from the depths of night to stalk these lands, and give all of her servants authority to roam and hunt at will, the people flee their homes and do not interfere. It is a curse the Petranni have long endured."

Ragnar thought again of the repulsive forms the witches had assumed. "I would never let such wretches travel at will in my homeland ... no matter who gave them authority. At least let me find the last three, and I will put an end to them too."

"Your spirit outshines your brain at times, Stormbringer," Strala replied, shaking his head again. "It is not the witches I fear. It is Macharriga. She is another threat entirely, Ragnar."

"We do want to return to our homelands, Ragnar," Thorsalla added, breaking her long silence. Her voice carried no trace of her usual confidence and swagger, and her eyes conveyed a deep unease. "I will raise my sword against any man, woman, or beast ... but a goddess? What blade can harm a goddess? And this goddess being Macharriga, the Lady of Death? Death is her abode."

"I have run afoul of gods and goddesses before," Ragnar answered. "Every time a way has been found to defeat their intentions. Some petty, others cruel, many vain, and a few easily provoked, and none of them proved to be all-powerful. I do not think this Macharriga will be any different."

Strala and Thorsalla both stared at him with worried expressions. He knew they recoiled from his brazen views of the realms of gods and goddesses, but he stood by his words.

A true god or goddess, in Ragnar's perspective, would be omnipotent, without blemish or weakness, beholden to no limitations within the world; a transcendent being capable of changing the underlying rules governing life and all creation itself. Every one of the deities he had come across during his years had their fill of flaws and weaknesses, even if they wielded tremendous powers and could transgress many of the rules governing the world.

He often wondered whether they were something else, and a true deity existed farther beyond. What the gods and goddesses of the world really might be, Ragnar could not say, but he suspected Macharriga had limits, flaws, and, most importantly, weaknesses.

It was just a matter of discovering them, before getting slain.

"I have no desire to find out, one way or the other," Strala said. Getting up to his feet, he looked to Ragnar. "I have told you before, I am not reckless. I have set my mind, and I intend to get what rest I can tonight. I counsel you to do the same. Dawn will come soon enough."

Strala walked away, leaving Ragnar and Thorsalla to themselves by the fire.

"We do not need to seek trouble," Thorsalla said, staring toward him with a pensive look.

"I do not plan to go looking for it," Ragnar said. "But a couple day's march stands between us and the ships. If dark things have been set loose upon the land, as it seems from what we have seen this day, then we must prepare ourselves to meet any threat ... including that of a goddess."

"A goddess named Macharriga," she replied, in a voice just above a whisper.

Thorsalla looked upward, to where slivers of moonlight filtered down through the dense tree cover above. Flames reflecting from the surface of her eyes, she remained quiet for many moments.

Listening to the wood hissing and crackling in the fire,

Ragnar studied her face, wondering what thoughts ran through her mind. At the present, she did not resemble the woman who would charge headlong into a mass of enemy warriors, while shouting a war cry at the top of her lungs.

Thorsalla had faced witches and the power of sorcery before. She had never shown the kind of hesitant, fearful disposition that had come over her when Strala identified the nature of the crow-headed beings and the goddess they served.

Bringing her gaze down, she turned to Ragnar. "It is one thing to prepare, but it is another thing to provoke. Be careful, Ragnar. I share Strala's position. I have no desire to find out whether or not this goddess is like others you have contended with."

Without another word, she got up and strode away, leaving Ragnar alone at the fire. Turning his gaze to the depths of the flames, he sat in silence for a little while longer.

Dismayed at what he saw in Thorsalla and Strala, rest did not come easy that night.

***

The following morning, at Strala's insistence, the raiders started back for their longships. Though disgruntled from the lack of plunder, none of the warriors other than Ragnar voiced objection to the decision. With no desire to face an angry goddess, the warriors had turned their minds to leaving the shores of Petranni lands.

Brooding and incensed at the other warriors, Ragnar broke away from the main column and traveled alone. Having already bloodied the nose of one warrior who had tried to argue with him, and cracked the rib of another, he had no desire for any company on his walk.

After a little early morning rain, the weather cleared, letting the sun break through to shower the forest with golden rays. A light wind stirred the boughs of the trees, but for the most part a silence reigned within the forest.

Ragnar kept his axe in his right hand. Once or twice, he had a sense of something watching him, but nothing emerged to impede his march. His anger simmering down, he kept his mind from thinking of the others.

He paused only once, to take a drink from a narrow creek, filled with glittering water running over moss-covered rocks. Splashing the cool water on his sweat-beaded face, he savored the refreshing touch of a breeze that flowed over him.

Continuing onward, he maintained a solid pace as the sun climbed higher. Insects flitted about, and a couple of startled deer bounded off, but a tranquil atmosphere prevailed, further cooling his irritated state.

He thought of the others again. A part of him wondered if he had been quick to judgment on Thorsalla and Strala. Both had proven their courage again and again in the time he had been with them.

A goddess was formidable enough as an adversary, but one steeped in an aura of death represented something unique. All living things, save those using or gifted with an unnatural power, were on a path toward death.

A goddess of death embodied a fate inevitable to all mortals; a doom that no amount of resistance could overcome.

Ragnar could understand how such a goddess could instill heightened fear in a warrior such as Thorsalla, who otherwise showed no fear of death.

For his part, Ragnar had no change in his estimation of Macharriga. She might have tremendous powers, but She was still just another deity of an imperfect world; and some means of resisting Her existed.

Keeping to his eastward path, he followed the course of a broad, shallow stream. The break in the tree cover afforded him a greater view of the hill summits around him, and it was on one of these that a strange sight met Ragnar's eyes. Moving a couple paces into the trees and crouching by some brush, he took in the bizarre scene.

Around thirty spear-bearing men and women stood in place near the top of a rise on a rocky outcrop not far from Ragnar's position. Making no effort to conceal themselves, the figures displayed mutilations that all of them held in common.

Each one had a right arm and left leg, but all were missing the other corresponding limbs. Further, the men and women bore the signs of prominent wounds about their right eyes. From what Ragnar could tell at a distance, all of the figures had only one eye intact.

Screeches in the air drew his eyes upward. High above the rise, three forms circled about, gliding with membranous wings spread wide.

His ire burning hotter in his veins at the sight of the three crow-headed beings, Ragnar gripped his axe tighter, wondering at their purpose; as well as that of the men and women on the rock outcropping beneath them.

His chances of having been undetected stood low, and he wondered why the three flying beings made no move toward him. If anything, it seemed as if they wanted to be seen.

***

"You came to raid people who had no quarrel with you. Why should you not expect death to come for you?"

Ragnar whirled about at the low, feminine voice coming from a few paces behind him. A woman in a long, brindled cloak that descended to the top of her sandaled feet stood to the side of an ancient, majestic oak tree. A curling bounty of lustrous black hair tumbled about her shoulders.

Her elegant neck exhibited a golden torque crafted to have

the look of small, intertwined ropes, with both ends culminating in smooth-surfaced orbs. Hanging down from a thin leather cord, an egg-shaped amulet rested mid-chest.

A circlet woven of leaf and vine around her head, the woman had a sharp nose and soft, full lips, but her eyes commanded Ragnar's attention from the moment he set his eyes upon her. At first, he wondered if the scattered light beneath the tree boughs was playing tricks with his vision, but the more scrutiny he gave exposed that she had multiple pupils in each eye.

The strange revelation heightened Ragnar's wariness and his breath came slow and steady.

Keeping eyes on his surroundings and holding his axe up, with hands spread apart on the haft, he asked her, "If you are the goddess, make yourself known."

The woman smiled, revealing teeth white as a fresh snow. "Goddess? I am no such being, though my concerns in this moment of time involve one of their kind."

A squirrel scampered up to the woman, jumped onto her cloak from the side, and climbed up to perch on her left shoulder. Settling back onto its haunches, the squirrel fixed its dark eyes upon Ragnar.

The woman brought up her left hand and stroked the creature's back with a light touch. The squirrel remained settled on her shoulder, displaying none of the skittishness that marked the usual examples of its kind.

"Then who are you? And if you are not a goddess, do you serve the goddess Macharriga?" Ragnar asked.

A frown darkened her countenance. "I would never serve the things of death and the abyss. I am merely a guardian in these lands, for all who dwell within it ... known to the people as Grianna."

"A sorceress?" Ragnar asked.

"In a manner of speaking," she replied. "Some call me a

healer, and others a seer. I use my gifts however I can, to bring light into darkness."

Her answer did nothing to lesson his caution, but he did not sense an inkling of hostility or deception in her. Nevertheless, Ragnar kept his axe at the ready, listening and looking out for any hint of an ambush.

"You speak my language well, for one who dwells in these lands," Ragnar stated.

"I have learned more than one tongue during the time I have walked in this world," she replied. After falling silent for a moment, she asked him, "Why do you travel apart from your comrades?"

"They have inflamed my ire," Ragnar said with a dismissive air. "Yet perhaps it is good that they did, as the path I took gained me a clear eye on our adversaries."

"You have seen witch and warlock alike," Grianna told him. "Several of each, yes?"

"The disfigured ones gathered on the top of the hill, each missing an arm, leg, and eye?" Ragnar asked, thinking of the eerie assemblage he had just witnessed.

She nodded. "The price each of them paid to learn the mysteries of Macharriga's dark arts."

"A heavy price, I would say. What fools they are to reduce themselves in such a manner," Ragnar retorted in a gruff tone. "What reward is it to gain power but lose so much of yourself?"

"To forfeit the everlasting spirit to gain temporal power in this world is one of the greatest acts of foolishness," Grianna said. "Macharriga does not hesitate to bind such fools to darkness. But make no mistake, though fools they are, they wield powerful magic during their mortal lives."

"I did not think they intended to fight us as warriors," Ragnar said. "What will they conjure against us?"

"They will combine their strength and call for a hunt, this

very night," Grianna told him. "You, and all of your comrades, are the prey."

"I did not see how three of the bird-heads and a few mutilated men and women would be a danger to over a hundred warriors," Ragnar said, not surprised at her declaration. "Unless they wielded powerful sorcery."

"They will conjure forth the Dark Host," Grianna said. "The spirits of wicked men and women who are cursed to roam the world of the living, for age upon age."

"Are not the spirits of those who are evil claimed by the Abyss?" Ragnar asked.

Grianna nodded once more. "Yes, they are ... but for whatever unknown reason, these spirits are barred from the black depths. They are left to suffer with a hunger that does not cease, and rove the lonely, desolate places in this land. Decay and disease are signs of their presence, as much as they are their essence. They shun the things of light, life, and love, and seek isolation wherever they can find it."

"And this Dark Host," Ragnar said. "I am guessing this conjuring draws all of these spirits together."

"From every bog, ancient forest, barrow, hole in the ground, and far flung haunt they inhabit ... into a host that comes like storm clouds in the night," Grianna responded. "They are given power, and able to assail the living in a way they cannot at other times."

"How can warriors fight against spirits? What weapon can any warrior wield against something that is not flesh and blood?" Ragnar asked, concern filling him at Grianna's explanation.

"There is a way," Grianna said, looking Ragnar in the eyes. "Your weapons can be anointed using the magic of an ancient, powerful ritual. Then, your blades can wound them."

"What good does wounding them do? If they are already dead, then how can they be slain?" Ragnar asked. "Could not they restore themselves, to pursue their hunt again?"

"I do not know what may happen," Grianna replied. "These spirits are barred from the other worlds, even the Abyss itself. But this ritual offers the only chance that you and your comrades have to survive the coming night."

Ragnar looked into Grianna's unusual eyes, finding them both enchanting and a visible caution. He could not allow himself to think of the being before him as a normal human being. In Grianna, he sensed great power, and the kind of presence that had witnessed ages of time.

Grianna could not be underestimated, even for a moment.

"Then why have you not helped the people of these lands rid themselves of these fell spirits, in the places where they can be found?" he questioned her.

"Few would be willing to subject themselves to the trial, where judgment is made on the blood needed for the ritual," Grianna said.

"What blood? A sacrifice?" Ragnar asked, his mood darkening. Few things in the world he loathed more than blood sacrifices.

"A life is not taken in this magic, the blood is given willingly, but a sacrifice of blood empowers the ritual," Grianna said. "Blood is life, and only the strongest of blood can enchant blades to cleave through the essence of a spirit."

"Where is the blood taken from?" A sense of unease began rippling through Ragnar. "And how is it given willingly?"

"A mortal of great strength," Grianna said. After a pause, she added, with a pointed edge to her tone, "And know that strength can be measured in many ways. Many who are strong of limb are riddled with weaknesses of all kinds."

"A strong body can hide many weaknesses within," Ragnar said, agreeing with the woman.

"I believe that you are strong, in more than one way,"

Grianna said.

"Yet I have come to your lands as a raider," Ragnar said. "To take my share of plunder and kill if I must. I would think you would see me as your enemy."

"Were it not for the plague of Macharriga now besetting these lands, and the afflictions she brings to all living things here, at her whim, I would," Grianna responded, her face solemn, and gaze boring into Ragnar's own. "Make no mistake of that."

In her eyes, Ragnar could see the look of a strong warrior who did not fear him. He respected her plain speech and manner, though he did not let his guard down. Life had long since taught him that deception could take an elaborate form.

"Let us call a truce for a time, and join as allies, to confront an enemy to us both," Grianna continued.

"Perhaps we will not remain enemies," Ragnar said.

"That will be a choice you and your comrades will have to make," Grianna said. "You are the ones trespassing in these lands."

Ragnar could not dispute her words. Little choice remained before him. He could take her aid against the things of sorcery, or reject it, and risk her being right about the Dark Host. If such a thing existed and was set loose to hunt Ragnar and his comrades, they would not see the next morning.

Every sense within Ragnar told him that Grianna did not seek to deceive him. If anything, he had a strong sense that she needed him.

"What of this trial? What would it ask of me?" he asked in a wary manner.

"You would be bound, and then given over to the judgment of the little ones, who dwell in these woods," Grianna replied. "You will experience tremendous pain, no matter what the judgement is. If you were found to be worthy, a measure of your blood would be taken to use in the ritual. If you were not found worthy, you would die. I cannot say how they would weigh you in judgment. Nor can I tell you what your chances are."

Ragnar took in her words with a brooding look upon his face. The notion of dying bound like a captive, without Raven Caller in his hands, was a phantom he looked upon with sheer anathema.

His decision rested upon whether he trusted himself to a deserved confidence, and not a reckless hubris. Ragnar would have to be deemed worthy by unknown judges for the purpose of giving blood to be used in a ritual. Any error in self-judgment could mean his death, that very day, in a manner he abhorred to the core of his being.

"Not an easy choice to make," Grianna said in a low voice, continuing to stare at him. "Nor is it an easy thing to look at oneself with an unforgiving eye. Even then, if you see yourself with clear eyes, and find that you possess strong blood, there will still be risk as the final judgment is not yours to make."

Continuing to think about the nature of strength and the path of his own life in a sober, exacting light, he made no response.

Grianna had already counseled him about the nature of strength. Without a splinter of doubt, he knew he had to base his choice on something more than the strength contained within muscle and limb.

"There is one thing more to keep in mind," Grianna said. "You can walk away right now, and it is likely you could survive the night. The Dark Host will be guided to the main body of the raiders. You could slip away, unnoticed, and live."

Ragnar's eyes flared with aversion. A threatening edge crept into his voice, and he did not care whether or not Grianna wielded tremendous powers of sorcery. "Do not give voice to such a disgrace. It is a suggestion for lesser men, the kind who would not deserve the life gained in such a craven way."

"One must know of every choice, before turning themselves

over to judgement and trial," Grianna replied in the same tone, looking unruffled by his response.

Ragnar turned his eyes away from her. He knew himself to be a man who did not abandon friends and comrades; an immutable truth he had demonstrated once more when fighting the massive sea creatures on the approach to the shores of Petranni lands.

His loyalty, once given, did not waver, even when it put his life at great risk. In that sense, he knew he had inner strengths that would be demonstrated in the mere act of accepting a trial, to gain a chance to help his comrades defend themselves against an otherworldly menace.

Yet he could not turn his eyes from other truths and claim hands devoid of bloodstains. If anything, Ragnar's past had been soaked in blood.

Multitudes had died at his hands, and he could not deny that many of those he had slain might not have deserved such a fate. While he did not kill in a spirit of cruelty or malice, Ragnar had spilled blood to assuage wounded pride, and gain profit, whether through raiding, bounty, or mercenary payment.

Not given to mercy, he had felled numerous warriors seeking to run away or capitulate on a field of battle. Little heated his anger more than the sight of a warrior he deemed to be craven. Raven Caller had ended numerous desperate pleas, the latter falling deaf upon his ears.

Carrying tidings of both strengths and weaknesses, other aspects of his life stepped to the fore.

Not one to shed an opportunity to indulge a burning lust, Ragnar had lain with a great many women over the past few years, but every last one of them had come into his arms of their own will. Though many women had sorrowed, and even raged, when he continued onward without them, Ragnar had never forced himself upon a single one.

Nor did he tolerate violence against them in his presence. The steadfast love that his mother and sister had shown to him while growing up amid a maelstrom of trial and struggle left him unable to stomach the things that other warriors accepted without a shred of guilt.

Many women had been spared untold horrors because of his intervention. A few of those freed from a lifetime of nightmares sought to reward him in ample fashion with their own bodies; and he had not hesitated to avail himself of the offered pleasures. A few comrades and others had disparaged him for doing so, but an act between two of an age to reason, born of mutual consent, was nothing he would ever see as wrongful.

Ragnar did not deceive women, or anyone else. Once his word had been given, his adherence to it could be expected to be unshakable, no matter what might transpire over a course of events. An oath-breaker, like a coward, provoked his temper to the fullest, and drew the greatest levels of disdain and ire from within him.

Ragnar's thoughts then returned back to the lives he had taken.

In a small number of years, Ragnar had left a torrent of death and destruction behind him. Many of those left in his wake, living in a broad range of lands, hungered for vengeance against him.

In a lot of those instances, Ragnar could not dispute that their desires came from a righteous anger and were justified in full. He had no doubt that a great volume of prayers for retribution existed; directed toward many different gods from the wives, sons, daughters, fathers, mothers, brothers, sisters, and friends of many he had slain.

Yet, at the same time, he had struck down tyrants, defended the people of many lands against invaders, hewn down numerous of the wicked and cruel, and saved a great number of lives, man, woman and child alike, through the wielding of his renowned war axe.

The conflict between the things justified and unjustified vexed Ragnar. He could not say which carried the greater weight in the balance, in terms of judgment.

In a world where there were so many ways a man's life could be measured, and where the things celebrated in one land were the things condemned in another, Ragnar found the task of looking at himself a much harder endeavor than he had ever thought.

Nevertheless, at the end of it all, Ragnar stood a man who lived his life the way he chose, without apologies or excuses. Everything that he had been through led to the man who now looked upon himself with eyes of self-judgment, in the face of a momentous choice.

Ragnar found it a sign of many kinds of strengths that he did not fear the coming of a new day, but rather faced every single one of them with his war axe gripped firm in his hands, and a fire blazing within his eyes. No matter what anyone thought, including the unknown entities who would be his judges in the trial spoken of by Grianna, Ragnar knew in his heart that it took blood of great strength to be able to live the kind of life that he had experienced.

Despite the solid conviction inside him, Ragnar knew he still had to put himself at the mercy of the trial's verdict. Given his fate if he was not deemed suitable to provide blood for the ritual, the thought of choosing to be rendered defenseless troubled him to the depths of his being.

Great courage would be needed to give himself over to the trial, become bound, and accept its uncertain outcome. But courage Ragnar had in abundance.

Undergoing the trial stood the only way to give his companions a fighting chance against a looming threat. As he had recognized during his introspection, Ragnar did not abandon friends and companions, no matter the danger they faced.

Taking a deep breath, Ragnar made the decision to give himself over to the trial.

Looking over to Grianna, he looked her in the eyes and said. "I will do this."

"You will accept their judgment, no matter what it is?" Grianna asked.

"I shall," Ragnar answered.

"Then we shall proceed to the trial," Grianna said. "The little ones must be summoned."

"The sooner this is over, the better," Ragnar said.

"I wish a different kind of magic was needed ... the strength and pleasure to be gained from lying with you," the woman said, her demeanor relaxing, eyeing Ragnar with a slight grin, and a clear trace of hunger in her tone. The rest of her words carried a hint of regret. "If only there were time for other pursuits, but night marches toward us and we must act now."

Grianna's multi-pupiled eyes echoed the yearning she had given voice to. Always suspicious of the ways of sorcery, Ragnar did not know what to make of her pronouncement, but the matter had no relevance to the hour at hand.

Nevertheless, a trace of a grin came to his lips at her expression of desire. It was the only response he could give, as no distractions could be invited.

Night drawing closer with every fleeting moment; Ragnar's life now depended on a mysterious trial's verdict. The time had come to meet his judges.

"Let us begin this trial, and get it over with," Ragnar told Grianna, taking a deep breath and girding himself for the binding.

***

After a short walk, Grianna led Ragnar into a grove of hazel trees ringing a small, circular pool, the water glittering in the rays scattered about by the canopy of branches sheltering it. A narrow stream trickled down into the pool from a rocky slope on the side opposite them.

Surrounding the open swathe of ground leading to the pool, an abundance of mushrooms rose up from the soil. Surmounting their short stalks were broad, colorful caps, exhibiting a wide range of hues, including yellow, red, deep blue, and black.

Ragnar had not encountered the like in any other part of the forest and wondered at their nature. Mushrooms could nourish or poison, and the beautiful appearance of the ones before his eyes told him nothing of their kind. A mushroom pleasing to the eyes could just as easily feed and replenish him, as it could leave him sick or dead, if he consumed them.

Ragnar saw no sign of the ones who would be judging him. Light winds whispering through the trees and the steady flow of water added to the serene atmosphere about the place. A part of him would have liked nothing more than to rest and take in the peaceable air of the woodland grove.

Before approaching the water, Grianna raised the hood of her cloak and covered her head. Walking forward, she came to a stop before the pool and gazed upon its surface for a few moments in silence.

Turning, she beckoned for Ragnar to approach her. Looking around the grove and pool once more, and still seeing no signs of anyone else, he strode forward, each step silent upon the pliant surface beneath his boots.

Grianna indicated for him to disrobe. He took off his belt, tunic, trousers, and boots, setting everything to the side alongside Raven Caller.

Guiding Ragnar down to the ground, Grianna had him lay on his back with his head resting at the edge of the pool. The soft ground and cool touch of the misty air did little to comfort him when she brought out several lengths of interwoven vines, and then set about tying them around his arms and legs.

With one end of each group of vines secure to a wrist or ankle, Ragnar began wondering where Grianna would tie the other ends to when she closed her eyes and started chanting words in a language unfamiliar to him. To his amazement, the other ends then took on a life of their own.

Moving in serpentine fashion out to the sides, the vines wrapped themselves around the trunks of trees close by. Pulling themselves taut, the vines left Ragnar's arms and legs spread far apart, rendering him immobile.

On instinct, Ragnar tested the bindings, putting his strength into the effort, and found that he could not move his limbs. Helpless, and at the total mercy of whatever Grianna intended to do, he awaited the trial with a growing sense of disconcertment.

Grianna stood over his right shoulder and looked down upon him. Ragnar gazed up into her mesmerizing eyes, but he could read nothing in her gaze or expression. The ambiguity did nothing to assuage his unease with the situation at hand.

Spreading her arms wide, Grianna began chanting again in the unknown tongue. The rhythm of her voice lulled him after a few moments. Ragnar's thoughts quieted down, and he found himself becoming entranced by the melodic incantation.

Movement out of the corners of his eyes snapped Ragnar out of the dreamy state. At first, it seemed to him that a host of butterflies had flown into the grove from the surrounding trees, until one of the newcomers flitted closer to his face.

Had his hands been free, Ragnar could have fit the tiny winged creature into his palm with ease.

No insect, the creature's body had a humanoid form. Eyes of a solid, golden hue peered back at Ragnar. Narrow of face, it had a human-like visage, but it wore no clothing on its lean, long-limbed body.

Delicate of form, the little entity's wings were quite large in proportion to its body. The appendages had a slight translucence to them, giving off a bright glow when they caught the sun's light.

Ragnar recognized the creature as being one of the fairy folk, the storied fae, who came in many forms and inhabited a great number of lands. Adept at concealment, and possessed of magical arts, they could not be underestimated.

No different than humans, some pursued wickedness and others light, and Ragnar could only hope for the ones he now saw to be the latter. Clever and persistent, the fae were not ones to make an enemy of.

Ragnar had survived their kind before, but then he had the use of his limbs and a weapon. Now, he could do nothing if they proved to be an adversary. The thought spiraled the discomfort within him further.

Descending toward him, the little entities began alighting all over his body.

Grianna then stepped back, out of his field of view, leaving him alone with the throng of fae. Ragnar braced himself, knowing the trial to be imminent, and who his judges would be.

All over, the diminutive creatures bit into his skin. Having endured the stings and bites of all manner of insects, including some larger ones, Ragnar found the bites of these fae a torment like no other he had experienced.

Turning his head, he watched one of the creatures gripped firm to his right shoulder. Ragnar could see the fairy drinking of his blood, using a set of elongated fangs on its upper and lower jaws to puncture the surface of his flesh.

A few heartbeats later, the creature raised its head and closed its eyes and mouth, swaying in place, as if savoring the crimson nectar that it had just taken from Ragnar. Then, it lowered its head, and sank its fangs into him once more. Ragnar continued to watch, keeping his mind off the pain riddling his body.

This time, the creature did not look to be drinking from his body.

A swelling heat began spreading from where the creature's fangs penetrated his skin. The sensation began occurring all across his body, as the other fae bit into him a second time.

Despite the pain wracking his body from a multitude of bites, Ragnar recognized what was now happening. The creatures were transferring something back into him, though he had no idea what the substance could be.

Whether poison, a means of paralysis, or something else entirely, he would know soon enough. Far too late to stop any of it, he had trust his instincts and endure. Deep down, he suspected the worst was coming, no matter how the trial culminated.

Clenching his teeth, Ragnar held a cry back. Flowing through his veins, a fiery agony engulfed his entire body,

Shaking all over, Ragnar strained hard against the vines holding him fast and gritted his teeth in the embrace of the inferno within him. Sweat beaded and ran down his skin. The creatures kept their fangs buried in him, sending even more of the pain-causing substance into his body.

Relentless and encompassing all of his body, the sensation proved more terrible and agonizing than anything he had suffered before in a physical sense.

The ordeal seemed to last forever, but at last, one by one, the creatures began withdrawing their fangs and releasing their grip upon Ragnar. Wings beating fast, they lifted up from his body and took to the air.

A few moments later, the grove became thick with the flying entities. After gathering into a dense flock, the fairies departed from the grove, vanishing into the trees. The atmosphere within the grove settled back into a tranquil state.

The torment subsided over the next few moments, leaving Ragnar sweating profusely and taking deep, heavy breaths into his lungs. The hold upon his limbs then went slack, the vines loosening their hold upon wrists, ankles and trees.

Closing his eyes for a moment, and grateful to be unbound, Ragnar let his freed arms and legs rest in place on the soft ground beneath.

"Your blood has been deemed worthy, and shall not fail in the ritual," Grianna announced, walking back into his view.

"A relief to hear ... after enduring all of that," Ragnar said, continuing to labor with his breathing. "I am not certain ... how much more I could bear."

"You will have to bear a little more pain," Grianna told him. "I must now take a little blood from you."

Grianna kneeled at Ragnar's side and took up his right hand. Using a small blade, she made a cut across the palm. Placing a bowl of hardened clay underneath, she collected the blood that trickled and fell from the incision.

After the bowl had become about half full, she set it down. Grianna then tended to Ragnar's cut to stop the bleeding, putting an unfamiliar kind of moss into the narrow wound.

"Some reward for enduring all of that," Ragnar told her with a gruff edge, watching her use a strip of cloth to wrap about his hand and hold the moss in place.

"Your comrades stand a chance to live because of you," Grianna responded, looking into his eyes. "Few in all the land are capable of surviving that trial."

"There were moments I wished I could have died," he replied, scowling. "The pain is beyond any words I could use to describe it."

Grianna let go of his hand. "You will have to gather yourself and seek out your friends. There is little time left in the day. The Dark Host will bear down upon your comrades after nightfall."

Ragnar eased himself up into a sitting position. The shadows had grown longer and the light in the grove looked to have dimmed a little more since the outset of the trial. Standing, he remained in place for a couple moments, letting a wave of dizziness pass over him.

Donning his clothing, and taking up Raven Caller, Ragnar looked around the grove once more. The winds rustled through the leaves and the water continued its steady flow down the rocks into the pool.

Ragnar found it hard to believe that he had experienced his greatest bout of suffering ever within such a beautiful, peaceable place. Now steady of breath, focused, and resolved, he looked over to Grianna.

"I will leave now, to find them," he said.

"And I will join you by nightfall, with others who will assist," she replied.

***

Finding his way back to Strala and the other warriors when twilight loomed nigh, Ragnar wasted no time, telling the gruff warrior of everything he had observed and experienced. Working to set up an encampment for the night, Thorsalla and many of the other warriors broke off from their tasks and gathered close around. Eyes widening at his tale of the grove and the mystical trial he had endured, they listened to his every word.

During their own march eastward, Strala and the others had seen the bizarre assemblage atop the great hill, but only Ragnar knew what the gathering represented. A pensive hush fell over all the warriors when Ragnar explained what would be coming for them that night.

"We will do as you have counseled us, Ragnar," Strala said, when he had concluded. "Let us await this sorceress, and hope that she does not take much longer to find us."

Looking up, Ragnar set his gaze on a couple of squirrels eyeing them from a branch above. Having taken notice of the animals about midway through his account of the trial, he knew what they represented.

"I do not think it will take much longer," he replied, staring at the small animals, who showed no hint of skittishness.

Close to the edge of night, Grianna arrived, as she had promised.

"Grianna," Ragnar greeted her. "You are a welcome sight here among the shadows."

"We are almost out of time, I must begin my task at once," she replied, with an air of insistence.

A small group accompanied her, consisting of four long-bearded men and three women, all of them clad in long tunics and cloaks. All wore silver torques about their necks, in addition to small egg-shaped amulets similar to that worn by Grianna.

Representing an array of ages, a few had gray hair while the full luster of youth graced the countenances of a couple of others. Looking among the new arrivals, Ragnar noticed that they did not have multi-pupiled eyes like Grianna.

Using a thick timber pole, the men carried a large cauldron along with them. Without uttering a word, they set it down among the throng of warriors.

Without delay, the men and women with Grianna set about making a clearing with the cauldron located at the center. From a nearby creek, and using small buckets of yew, they filled the cauldron with water.

When the cauldron had been filled, Grianna chanted over the water, her melodious voice ringing through the trees. After a few moments, she took a vial out from a pouch tied at her waist, and then poured the viscous contents into the cauldron.

Ragnar knew at once what liquid the vial contained. In silence, he watched his blood pouring into the large, bronze vessel. Memories of the ordeal in the grove still raw in his mind, the sight of the blood reminded him of the tremendous suffering he had withstood.

After returning the vial back to the pouch, and chanting for a little longer, Grianna closed her eyes and fell into silence.

Turning to Ragnar, she announced in a low voice, "It is done. Let your weapons be anointed now."

The conclusion had come just in time, as the last violet hues of twilight's gloaming had ebbed into the darkness of night.

Ragnar summoned the other warriors to approach the cauldron. Handing Raven Caller to Grianna, he watched as she dipped the blade into the cauldron's mixture of water and blood.

"Do not wipe this blade clean," she told him, giving the weapon back.

Ragnar stared at the glistening edge of the axe head for a moment. He began to turn, to step to the side, when her hand caught his arm. Before he could ask a question, she dipped her right thumb into the cauldron and raised it to his forehead, making a mark in the center.

"Your axe is a weapon, and so are you," she said in a firm tone. "Do not forget that. Now both weapons can strike them, when they come."

One after another, the other warriors gave their weapons over to Grianna and she repeated the process for each of them. Ragnar could see the unease permeating their faces, and he could not blame them for the reaction. Being asked to trust in sorcery, in the face of an unknown, otherworldly enemy, the warriors had little to be certain of. For their part, all of the warriors cooperated with Grianna, accepting the dipping of their blades and the marks upon their foreheads.

When all of the warriors and their weapons had been attended to, Grianna nodded to Ragnar and said, "It will not be long before they come."

Trees swayed and groaned as gusts of wind whipped through, bringing a deep chill to the air. Many of the other warriors turned about, eyeing the trees and keeping weapons at the ready.

"It is just some wind, and the cold of night," Grianna told them. "You will know when they are here. You will not be able to mistake it."

From the expressions on their faces, Ragnar could see that her words did little to ease their tension. Gripping Raven Caller, he stared into the night, awaiting the arrival of the Dark Host.

***

Night brought the raiders blood-craving horrors.

Howling, shrieks, and wails in the distance heralded the approach of the Dark Host. The noises chilled the blood in Ragnar's veins, but he girded himself for what Grianna said would come.

To his eyes, they appeared at first like a glowing, silvery mist, coming toward him from the depths of the forest. Drifting above the ground, each of the fell spirits gave off a low, spectral light.

Withered and skeletal, wisps of hair flowing in some unseen wind, the spirits had a ghastly appearance that embodied the nature of disease and decay.

Standing before his comrades, Ragnar had chosen to be the first to confront the entities and discover whether their anointed weapons could affect a creature of spirit. One of the entities angled toward him, showing no concern the axe in his hands. Reaching out with bony hands, it came within range, a look of malice upon its rotted face.

Ragnar swung his axe. Cleaved in two across its midsection, a guttural cry erupted from the entity.

Its form dissipated and scattered, accompanied by a fading, otherworldly scream that Ragnar found to be one of the purest cries of terror to ever reach his ears. For an instant, it seemed that the darkness deepened, to an impenetrable level, in the spot where the shrill cries had waned to silence.

In a moment, all traces of the wicked spirit were gone.

Buoyed at the sight of Ragnar's axe cutting the thing apart, the other warriors surged forward to meet the oncoming, ghostly throng. A moment later, the two sides clashed together.

All around Ragnar, a cacophony of screams and cries from humans and spirits alike broke out. Many raiders were taken to the ground, each of them pulled down by several spirits, the ghostly attackers digging their nails and long, jagged teeth into living flesh.

Several times Ragnar recoiled from the icy touch of a would-be assailant. Bringing his axe around to confront each new threat, he hacked at the specters with a livid fury. His blows cut through them with no trouble, condemning one after another to dissipation.

While the entities slew many warriors, Ragnar sensed a growing fear and hesitancy among the rogue spirits, the ghosts fast coming to realize that the weapons of the warriors, and strikes from fist, elbow, forehead, and foot, could harm them; and sever their ties to the physical world. Before long, the dark spirits began moving back from Ragnar, giving him a wide berth, and trying to evade him, but he gave them no quarter.

Charging them down, Ragnar continued slashing through their incorporeal bodies, sending more horrific, fading screams into the night as their forms disintegrated. Bashing one across its jaws with his left fist, Ragnar saw the entity's lower jaw shatter into bits that floated a short distance before vanishing. A blow from Raven Caller finished the maimed spirit off.

Everywhere Ragnar looked, his fellow warriors slashed, hacked, chopped, and stabbed at the ghosts, filling the air with their terror-laced cries and dissolving forms. The spectral horde had possessed a significant advantage of numbers at the outset of the fighting, but now had been whittled down until more raiders than spirits occupied the battleground.

Like a retreating mist, the remnants of the ghost horde fell back into the forest's depths, their swift departure showing they wanted nothing more of blades that could send them into the maw of an even worse existence than the one they abided.

Thorsalla, who had survived the battle unscathed, made her way out to Ragnar where he stood at the farthest edge of the defenders' position. Raven Caller in hand, he glowered in the direction the malignant spirits had retreated.

"I have never slain a ghost with a blade before this night," Thorsalla said, her eyes still blazing with the fires of battle. "Do you think they will return?"

Ragnar shook his head. "Those spirits want nothing more of us. And I do not think they were slain. I saw patches of a deeper darkness when they dissolved ... their final screams went into that darkness."

"The Abyss claimed those fiends?" Thorsalla asked.

"Yes, and the ones that fell back deemed going there a fate to avoid," Ragnar said.

"It must be a place of nightmares, if they prefer a tormented existence roving desolate haunts," Thorsalla commented.

Ragnar glanced at his axe blade. Though it had just hacked apart many enemies, no blood graced its honed edge other than his own, from the anointing conducted by Grianna. Setting his thoughts on enemies whose bodies could be split open without any rituals to enhance his weapon, he looked back to Thorsalla.

"When morning comes, I will deliver a greeting of blood and iron, to those who believe us dead now," Ragnar said, his tone low and brimming with anger. "You, and any of the others, are free to join me."

***

When daylight arrived, the servants of Macharriga found themselves caught by surprise. Having labored to the summit of the great hill from which they gazed out upon the surrounding land, the witches and warlocks cried out in alarm when a large number of warriors leaped out from the nearby rocks and trees.

Their faces filled with shock and dismay, Macharriga's servants looked upon warriors who should all have been dead after the summoning of the Dark Host the previous night.

Striking with unrestrained rage, Ragnar, Thorsalla, Strala and the others waded into the cluster of one-legged witches and warlocks. The price each of Macharriga's servants had paid to gain knowledge of mysteries and sorcery rendered them helpless against the sudden onslaught.

Because of their sorcery in conjuring the Dark Host, Ragnar had been subjected to a torturous ordeal. Many strong warriors had died in the night, their bodies ripped into by ghastly abominations called forth from barren haunts.

Furor boiled within Ragnar, and he saw to it that several of the mutilated servants of Macharriga did not die at once. Bringing Raven Caller into vicious, downward slashes that severed the lone leg of a witch or warlock at the knee, he sent their bodies thudding to the ground, blood gushing into the rocky soil.

With targeted swings of his axe, Ragnar cut off each of their single remaining arms. Storming onward, he left each of them to bleed their life out into the hill; unable to do anything to halt their dire predicament.

Consumed in pain and losing blood fast from two massive wounds, none of those who Ragnar left behind lasted for more than a handful of moments. Even so, Ragnar derived a little satisfaction knowing that they had been denied the mercy of a quick kill, and had ended their wicked lives in a bloody, helpless, ruin.

When the slaughter came to an end, the bodies of Macharriga's witches and warlocks littered the hill summit. Not a single one of them drew breath.

Melting back into the cover of larger rocks and trees, Ragnar and the other warriors waited. The slain witches and warlocks were not the only ones Ragnar sought vengeance against.

It did not take long before the remaining three Witches of Night, all that survived of Macharriga's nine greatest servants, came across the site of the massacre.

Screeching, the trio of crow-headed sorceresses descended from the heights and landed amid the carnage. Before they had a chance to look over the dismembered bodies of the witches and warlocks, the warriors emerged once more, shouting war cries and brandishing their weapons.

Rushing the nearest of the crow-headed trio, Ragnar swung his axe with all his might. The blade shredded through a membranous wing and cleaved deep into the thing's side, eliciting a high-pitched screech.

Tearing the blade free, Ragnar brought it overhead and chopped down with enormous force, splitting its body apart between the left shoulder and neck down to the middle of its torso. With a hard, forward shove, Ragnar sent the creature to the ground and wrenched his axe loose.

Stomping down hard on its chest and cracking bones, he pinned the thing against the ground. Reduced to a pitiful state, the creature gurgled and gasped, unable to muster any defense.

Ragnar brought the axe blade racing down once more, cutting the thing's head from its body. Around him, blood sprayed, and shrill cries pierced the air, and then all fell into silence.

Two warriors lay dead, but the remaining pair of crow-headed figures had been felled. Both of their headless bodies had been hacked up, leaving no shred of a chance that the shape shifting beings could reconstitute themselves.

"Now, it is over," Thorsalla said, looking over the blood-drenched scene. Leaning over, she picked up one of the crow heads. "I got this one. That makes four of the crow heads for me."

"And four for me as well," Ragnar said. "And I have not forgotten that I should share in one of the kills you have claimed."

"Maybe it is finally time for us to talk about that," Thorsalla replied with a grin.

"I am not done, just yet," Ragnar said, though he smirked at her.

Thorsalla raised her eyebrows. "All nine of the crow-heads are dead. All of their other scum are dead. What is there left to do?"

"Come with me, and you will find out," Ragnar said.

She rolled her eyes. "I expect a full night of you ... doing everything I want."

Ragnar grinned, but made no reply.

Thorsalla shook her head with an exasperated look on her face. "You are maddening, Ragnar Stormbringer!"

He shrugged. "I go where I go, and I do what I do ... and one more threat exists. We are not free from danger yet. You can choose to go with me ... or not. I must go to speak with Grianna now."

With a glint in his eye, he cast her another grin and winked, before walking over and taking up the other two crow heads.

***

Standing before the massive, dual hill fortress of the Petranni, Ragnar, Thorsalla and Strala flung nine large crow heads into the open stretch of ground spread in front of them. A short distance away stood the front gates of the stronghold's lowest line of defense, a timber palisade and earthen rampart.

Her hood pulled back, and eyes fixed upon the fortifications looming high above them, Grianna stood to the right of Ragnar. Hair flowing in the winds, she had a majestic and confident air about her. Grianna's face held a stern look; one that exuded strength and carried no inhibitions about her purpose.

Behind them stood one of the raiders, a veteran of many raids named Kalladan, who understood and could speak many Petranni words. Strala and Thorsalla had insisted upon his presence, as they did not have the trust in Grianna that Ragnar had.

Ragnar took in the sight of the ramparts warding the higher levels of the fortress, culminating in the stone walls atop the summits of the two hills. Lining all of the walls and peering downward, multitudes watched the five figures in a pensive, encompassing silence.

Only the bellowing of cattle and the whinnies of horses coming from deep inside the fortress broke the heavy stillness saturating the atmosphere.

Smoke wafted up from the numerous conical and rectangular thatch-roofed structures visible on several levels of the fortress complex. The stronghold teemed with inhabitants, and Ragnar could not understand what kept the Petranni back from the newcomers.

After a few heartbeats, and no response from those inside the fortress, Grianna called out in a loud voice, using the language of the Petranni. Her words reverberated through the stronghold, leaving no doubts of them being heard.

"I have announced to them that the nine Witches of Night have been slain, as well as Macharriga's witches and warlocks," Grianna told Ragnar and the others, when she had concluded addressing the Petranni. "Every last one."

Behind her, Kalladan nodded, acknowledging her translation.

"I would think they would take that as welcome tidings,"

Ragnar said a few moments later, when nothing stirred from within the stronghold. "Why do they remain huddled behind their walls? Surely it is not us they fear."

Grianna shook her head. "No, it is not us they fear. It is something more."

She looked up, peering toward the gray, overcast skies above. A grim look on her face, Grianna appeared to be searching for something particular.

Ragnar's brow furrowed. He could see the expectation in her gaze, though whatever it was, she had made no mention of it to him.

"What are you watching for?" Strala asked her.

"The heads of all nine will draw Her forth, it is only a matter of time," Grianna replied, continuing to look above.

"Her?" Thorsalla exclaimed, eyes widening. "You do not mean Macharriga?"

"You must trust me," Grianna said, casting Thorsalla a sharp look. "She has to be confronted here, in front of all these witnesses."

A look of exasperation clouded Thorsalla's face. "You did not say this was the purpose. We were to seek the aid of this king!"

Though irritated at the pronouncement, Ragnar had come to trust Grianna, and he knew the matter of the malevolent goddess had to be settled. When they had spoken after the massacre of the witches and warlocks, she had told him the next step was to present the heads of the Witches of Night to the Petranni, and nothing more.

At the time, Ragnar thought Grianna meant to gain the help of the Petranni, in some way, against Macharriga. The Petranni had many priests and priestesses, and there were other gods revered in their lands.

Now, he saw that Grianna meant to draw Macharriga forth,

in a direct confrontation.

"Trust her, Thorsalla," Ragnar said, fighting back his own frustration with the sudden development.

"This is reckless!" Strala said, looking fearful and incensed.

"It is the only way to bring Her forward, into the open," Grianna said. "You do not want her seeking revenge from the shadows."

Ragnar said nothing. Following her gaze, he waited.

Not long afterward, a great black crow descended out of the skies.

When the huge bird neared the ground, its form changed, becoming a dark, churning funnel that slowed and dissipated to reveal a stunning-looking woman clad in black, flowing robes.

A scowl upon her face, the woman's dark eyes cast a piercing glare in the direction of Grianna, before taking in the sight of Ragnar and his companions.

Proud of bearing, the woman had a strong chin and jaw line, higher-set cheeks, and an aquiline nose, all of her facial features holding a well-balanced symmetry. Thick, wavy masses of crimson hair draped about her shoulders.

"You have denied my harvest, and slain all of my servants," the woman said in a low, authoritative tone. "Who are you to deny me, Grianna?"

"You have plagued these lands for long enough, Macharriga," Grianna responded, showing no intimidation in the other's presence. "I could bear the groaning of the land no longer."

"You think that you are a match for me?" Macharriga replied, a mirthless smile coming to her face. She looked to the warriors with Grianna. "Or any of them?"

"None of us are, by ourselves," Grianna replied.

Far behind them, from the tree line, a lone horn sounded.

"What is this?" Macharriga asked, looking past Grianna toward the woodlands.

Out of the trees, another woman walked into the open ground. Striding barefoot with the limber, graceful step of a hunting cat, she wore a simple brown tunic and carried a long spear. Several long braids descended amid her disheveled locks of black hair.

When she drew closer, Ragnar saw that she had the same, multi-pupiled eyes as Grianna.

"Bodmana," Macharriga stated. "It has been a long while."

The spear-bearing woman glowered at Macharriga, and said nothing in reply.

"This changes nothing," Macharriga said. "The slaying of my servants will be answered for. If Bodmana wishes to join her sister in this, then that is her choice."

"We slew those who attacked us," Ragnar said, unable to hold silent any longer. "Nothing more. There is nothing in the world more natural than to defend oneself. The blame for their deaths lies only with them."

Macharriga turned to face Ragnar, a cold smile creeping onto her face. "A boastful mortal. You should be on your knees before me."

"I kneel to no one," Ragnar said.

"You, and all of those with you here, will die," Macharriga said with a tone of certainty. "Your deaths will be witnessed by all within the fortress. After this day, none will repeat your folly during my times of harvest."

"This plague must end, Macharriga," Bodmana said.

Macharriga did not reply to Bodmana or even look in her direction. She fixed her gaze upon Kalladan.

"What about you, mortal?" Macharriga told him. "Would you reject my embrace?"

She beckoned for him to come forward.

"Do not listen to her," Ragnar cautioned him.

Kalladan hesitated for a moment, but he did not heed

Ragnar's warning and took a stride toward Macharriga.

Stepping forward, Macharriga brought her right hand up and caressed Kalladan's cheek in a manner that any observer would deem affectionate. Every instinct within Ragnar tensed, knowing the goddess harbored no good will toward any of them.

The area of Kalladan's skin that Macharriga touched darkened fast. The change in hue then began radiating outward, in all directions. In addition to changing color, Kalladan's skin began turning leathery in texture, and tightened against his bones underneath until his face began reflecting a more skeletal countenance.

Kalladan gasped and wheezed, his breath becoming more labored until it rattled in his throat. His golden locks filled with gray, before falling out and blowing away in the cold breezes. In moments, Kalladan looked unrecognizable, like some long-decayed corpse found in the depths of an ancient tomb.

Finally, his skin flaked off and turned to dust, trails of the latter carried away in the air currents. His bones, still draped in his clothing, crumpled to the ground in a disarrayed heap.

"I wield the power of something none of you can run from, resist, or hide from," Macharriga said. "Yet you seek to destroy what is mine."

The display of power instilled great caution in Ragnar, but it did not temper his ire. "We defended what is ours ... the life within us, which belongs to each of us, as long as it may last."

"If you die thirty years from now, or today, what does it matter it matter in the end?" Macharriga replied in a chiding tone.

"All I know is that it matters to me now," Ragnar answered.

Macharriga stepped toward him. He remained in place.

Out of the corners of his eyes, he saw both Grianna and Bodmana begin to move. Whatever they had planned for Macharriga was about to be unveiled.

Before the two women could engage the goddess, Strala attacked. Drawing a single-edged knife out of the sheath at his waist, Strala flung himself onto the back of Macharriga. Bringing his arm around, he plunged the knife deep into her chest.

A sonorous, otherworldly howl erupted from Macharriga. Shock reflecting in her eyes, she clutched at the knife, but Strala held fast with all of his might.

A change came over Strala similar to what befell Kalladan. Aging before Ragnar's eyes, his skin grew mottled, leathery and wrinkled, and then became sunken and desiccated. Though his breaths became more strained, and every part of him weakened, Strala clung to the knife and somehow managed to keep his hold.

Macharriga's form swirled and dissipated into several black tendrils. Strala, now little more than a skeleton, fell to the ground at last. His bones shattered and broke apart, though somehow his right hand still remained wrapped about the hilt of the knife.

One last wail pierced the skies, as the last wisps of Macharriga vanished from sight.

Ragnar looked upon the knife lying on the ground, and realized what had happened. "It was still coated with the blood and water from the ritual. He must not have used that weapon during the night."

Sadness filled Grianna's expression. She knelt by Strala's remains. "He struck before Bodmana and I could assail Her. There was no time to stop him."

"Strala killed Her?" Thorsalla asked, a hesitant edge to her voice. "How can this be so, if She were a goddess?"

Grianna shook her head. "He did not kill Her, but she could no longer hold the physical form She manifested in this world. She has been made to retreat into darkness."

"Then She is not gone forever?" Thorsalla asked, a look of worry deepening on her face.

"No, she is not," Grianna said. "One day She will return and seek to bring darkness to this world, as do all such as her."

"I would rather not be here when that happens," Thorsalla said.

"It will not be for some time," Grianna said.

"When she returns I would be glad to send her right back into the abyss," Ragnar said, in a voice akin to a growl.

"Ever fiery of heart, Ragnar," Grianna told him, the hint of a grin on her lips.

"If it ever burns out, then I am no longer alive," Ragnar replied, meeting her unusual eyes.

"May the fire burn always then," Grianna said, the grin expanding into a smile. She stood up and looked toward the fortress. "As for now, a reward should be given. Do not expect them to roast a boar and fill your cups with heather ale, but I will see to it that you will not leave empty of hand. What you all have done is a great boon to these lands, no matter the purpose that brought you here. Stay here, and I shall return in a short time."

Grianna started toward the fortress. Ragnar and the others watched her in silence. When she reached the gates in the rampart on the lowest level, they swung open and allowed her passage inside.

Ragnar then turned his eyes back to Strala's bones.

For a man who loathed being reckless, Strala had cast aside all caution in attacking Macharigga. Giving his life for his comrades, in an act of will that defied his usual sensibilities, Strala had risen to become a hero like those in the tales he had so often enjoyed around campfires.

Leaning over, Ragnar took up the small silver pendant about Strala's neck. Closing his hand about the pendant, Ragnar made a quiet oath that he would never forget the old warrior and his courage.

***

Grianna emerged from the fortress a short while later, accompanied by a large contingent of armed warriors. A tall, broad-shouldered man walked at her right side. Just behind him, two stout-looking warriors carried a wooden chest along with them.

From their appearances, all looked to be Petranni warriors. Long-haired, with thick moustaches and beards, the warriors were clad in knee-length tunics. Most of red, brown, or pale, yellow hues, the tunics had been woven either of a solid color, or with patterns of stripes or squares. Several wore trousers, many covered in square patterns echoing those on some of the tunics, but a fair number of the warriors went bare of leg, and some wore no shoes at all.

The skin visible on their arms, legs, and necks displayed numerous designs, all of them a blue color. Some of the images depicted beasts or warriors, while others were in the form of intertwining patterns; several of various repeating shapes, and others of serpents.

The warriors carried long swords and spears, the latter ending in broad heads with sharp tips and sides. Several of them also carried small wooden shields of a square or round shape.

When they drew near, the large group slowed down a few paces from where Ragnar, Thorsalla, and Bodmana stood, and spread into a wide semi-circle facing them. Grianna and the tall, authoritative-looking warrior stepped to the forefront. Behind them, the men bearing the timber chest set it on the ground.

Ragnar kept wary at the presence of so many warriors, but he saw no hostile intent within their eyes and postures. He perceived a lot of suspicion and distaste directed toward himself and Thorsalla, but that came as no surprise. Ragnar and Thorsalla had come to the Petranni lands as raiders, with the intent to plunder and spill blood if necessary.

Toward Grianna and Bodmana, he could see nothing but reverence and respect within their gazes and expressions. Their deferential reactions deepened the mystery further about the two women, whose origins Ragnar grew ever more curious about.

More than a few troubled glances were cast toward the skeletal remains of Strala and Kalladan. Stark testaments to the power of Macharriga, the bones served as a reminder to the Petranni of what they had been liberated from, and the price that had been paid.

For a long time to come, the Petranni would all be able to live without fear of Macharriga and her malignant servants. A lot of death and suffering had been dispelled from their world due to the actions of Ragnar and the other raiders.

Ragnar did not expect affection from the Petranni, but he did not think they would be ungrateful to the raiders. The sight of the chest gave Ragnar a strong sign that they would acknowledge what he and the others had achieved, raising the likelihood that the Petranni would not get in the way of the raiders' departure.

"King Chethalcen of the Petranni has come in person to reward all of you, for bringing an end to Macharriga's servants, sending Her back to the abyss, and giving these lands a rest from the long nightmare She inflicted on them," Grianna announced in a raised voice.

She then spoke a few words in the Petranni tongue to the prominent-looking man at her right, who Ragnar understood to be the king just mentioned. The Petranni king nodded back to her, and then gestured to the men behind him.

The two brawny warriors who had carried the chest from the stronghold picked it up, walked several paces forward, and set it down on the ground before Ragnar and Thorsalla. Opening the chest up and backing away, they exposed a bounty in gold and silver to Ragnar and Thorsalla's eyes. Neck and arm torques, brooches, bowls, cups, and all manner of finely-crafted objects could be seen piled inside the chest.

Ragnar had no doubt that the contents of the chest represented an amount equivalent to, at the least, what could be plundered in a large raid on a rich target. Even better, not a single drop of blood would have to be spilled to take the ample bounty being given as a reward.

"The king asks that you return to the lands you came from, but extends his gratitude for what you have done here," Grianna stated in a formal air. "Accept this chest, a gift from the king and the Petranni, so that you, and all those with you, do not depart empty of hand."

"Tell the king that we thank him for this reward, and that we shall leave these lands without delay, as he asks," Ragnar replied, looking to the king as he spoke, and keeping his tone even.

Grianna translated for Ragnar. Upon hearing the response, a glimmer of relief passed through the king's somber gaze and expression. In that moment, Ragnar could see that the king had feared bloodshed in getting the raiders to leave Petranni lands.

Ragnar extended the king a short bow of his head. The king nodded back to Ragnar in acknowledgement of the gesture. Turning, the king started back for the stronghold, accompanied by his warriors, who fell in behind him.

"Their king is eager to see us go," Ragnar said, with a grin, watching the group of Petranni warriors striding away. "Did not waste a moment longer than necessary."

"Do not fool yourselves," Grianna said. "Despite giving you this chest, the king still sees you as an enemy. Had it not been for the timing of your raid, during one of Macharriga's cullings, you would have ravaged his people and lands. You can not blame him for thinking this way."

"It is nothing more than the truth," Ragnar admitted. "But there is nothing for you, or any in this land, to be concerned of. Know that we will honor our word and leave, as I told him. Rest assured of that."

"And I will see that you are given a chance for a safe voyage home," Grianna replied.

"If the king and his warriors do not get any foolish notions and try to get in our way, there will be peace," Ragnar said, an edge of threat rising into his voice. "It is up to him. I hope that he is a wise man and that he gives his word in the way that I do."

"I do not speak of the king, or any dangers on the land," Grianna said, looking into Ragnar's eyes with a solemn expression.

"There is no place in this world without danger," Ragnar said in a dismissive air, though her words caused him to recall memories of the ravenous monstrosities that had beset them on their approach to Petranni shores.

"Even so, I will do my part to help you, in gratitude for what you have done for these lands," Grianna said. "You risked everything in the sacred grove."

"It was the only way anything could be done," Ragnar said. "I did not have much choice."

"And your blood measured strong and true," Grianna replied, an undercurrent of commendation in her words and look.

Ragnar gave her a slight bow. "And it will remain so."

"It is my sincere wish for you that it does," she replied, with no trace of threat in her voice.

Instead, he sensed genuine affinity within her tone. Had circumstances been otherwise, Ragnar would have liked to remain in the woman's company for a little while longer.

She intrigued him, in many ways, and Ragnar knew there was much he did not know about her. He knew there stood a reason Macharriga did not attack Grianna or Bodmana outright. Ragnar also had a strong suspicion that her origins, like Bodmana's, were rooted in something very different from the world of human men and women.

Ragnar then looked toward the bones of Kalladan and Strala. "I do not wish to leave their remains out in the open, here."

"I will have those who dwell with me gather them up, and we shall give them a proper burial in a place where they will not be desecrated," Grianna told him.

"Thank you, Grianna," Ragnar said. Looking down one more time at Strala's bones, he reaffirmed his oath inside his mind. Then, he uttered in a whisper, "I will carry the memory of you for as long as I live, Strala. May we meet again in a better place."

Ragnar took in a long, slow breath, letting it out in the same manner. Leaning over, he shut the chest. Reaching around both sides, he picked the wooden container up by himself.

Looking over to Thorsalla, he remarked, "The others will be glad to see this."

"I am glad to see it," she responded, with a laugh.

"I have to say that I do not mind taking some gold and silver along with us,," Ragnar admitted. Looking over to Giranna and Bodmana, he started walking in the direction of the woods and said to them, "We will now begin our journey back."

The two enigmatic women looked to each other. A silent understanding passed between them, as they both nodded.

Grianna turned her attention back to Ragnar.

"We will both go with you, to do what we can to assist your return from these shores," she said.

***

Grianna and Bodmana stood together on a ridge top overlook, accompanied by more than twenty male and female acolytes clad in long white tunics. Watching in silence, they bore witness to the quartet of long, sleek vessels in the sea far below them.

Making their way from the shoreline, the vessels glided

through the rolling waves, propelled by the rowing of oars at a steady rhythm.

Ragnar eyed the group on the ridge from where he stood near the stern of a longship. He thought of the look in Grianna's eyes when they had parted, a short time after reaching the shore. A desire unfulfilled could be seen within her mesmerizing gaze, and Ragnar could not deny harboring a similar feeling.

He wondered if his path would ever bring him again to the lands of the Petranni. A large part of him held out hope that it would.

The march back to the shore had gone smooth enough. The chest given by the Petranni king bolstered the moods of all the raiders. They had all had quite enough of Petranni lands and were eager to return back to their homelands.

No harm had come to the vessels, or the small group assigned to warding them. It took little time to prepare the ships for departure and move them from the beach into the water. The crews manning each of the ships were thinner than when they had arrived, having suffered many losses in the fighting against the servants of Macharriga, but enough survivors remained to handle all four longships well in the open seas.

"Ragnar!" Thorsalla called to him from the bow, her voice urgent.

Hurrying to the other end of the longship, Ragnar saw at once what caused the look of fear and alarm on her face. Farther ahead, and heading in the direction of the longships, a tall black fin cut through the surface of the water, followed by several others.

Everything within Ragnar tensed at the dismaying sight. Too far from shore to have any hope of turning back before the creatures reached them, the raiders were caught out in the open.

A volcanic anger surged from within Ragnar. Glaring at the fins drawing nearer, he grasped the haft of Raven Caller, intending to take it out from the loop at his belt.

At that moment, a sudden burst of water to the right of Ragnar diverted his attention from the troubling view of approaching dark fins. Looking over, his eyes widened, taking in an unexpected new sight.

The creature Ragnar saw in the water, just off the bow of the longship, exhibited a man-like upper torso and arms, both brimming with a very pronounced muscularity. Its head also reflected that of a man, though several elements held a stark contrast with the appearances of humans.

The being had eyes of solid black, like those of a shark. Its mouth, large in proportion to the rest of its face, contained an array of sharp, triangular teeth. Slits resembling the gills on a fish ran down each side of its thick neck.

When its head was out of the water, its broad, flat nose had large, open nostrils, but Ragnar noticed membranes closing off both, just before the creature dipped its head to pass through a passing wave.

At the end of its arms, the creature possessed large, webbed hands, each of the fingers ending in sharp tines. In its right hand, and carried tight to its body, the creature gripped the haft of a long spear fitted with an extended, narrow head. Set a little way back from the sharp tip, a pair of hook-like barbs sprouted from the spearhead.

The lower half of its body, sleek and covered in silvery scales, ended in a single broad fin that it used to propel itself through the water with great power. The being had no difficulty keeping pace with the longship.

In full size, from head to tail fin, the creature extended at least one and a half times as long as Ragnar rose in height.

Others of its ilk began surfacing among the longships. Several of them had female-like torsos with round, prominent breasts. All carried spears similar in fashion to that of the one swimming near Ragnar, but they made no aggressive moves toward the ships.

Its voice deep and resonant, the creature near Ragnar made a pronouncement in a strange tongue. Bringing the spear higher, out of the water, it made a gesture that Ragnar took to be a salute of some kind. Directed toward the longships, the gesture was repeated by the others.

Submerging beneath the waves, the waterborne throng disappeared from sight.

"What is happening?" Thorsalla asked, her voice rife with concern.

Looking ahead, listening to the waves lapping against the strakes of the vessel, Ragnar eyed the cluster of tall, black fins drawing closer. It would not be long before they were among the longships.

"We are about to learn if Grianna's word holds true, or if she will make certain that we can never be a threat to Petranni lands again," Ragnar said. "We can not outrun the bastards, it is best to stop and fight as we can."

Using horn signals, Ragnar called for the vessels to take to arms and reduce their pace. Pulling most oars aboard, and grabbing up their bows, spears, axes, and swords, the warriors on the ships scrambled to ready themselves for defense.

The waters ahead began churning and frothing, and chaos broke out among the incoming threats. A few black fins disappeared from his view, before reemerging on the surface elsewhere. To Ragnar's eyes, the massive creatures beneath the waves were scattering fast, their course disrupted by some unseen cause.

The spear-carrying beings could be seen everywhere, raising their weapons out of the water and thrusting downward, or chasing after black fins in small groups. Those and a number of other movements told Ragnar that the sea beings were harrying and attacking the hulking black and white brutes.

Moving slow and in a tighter cluster, the longships proceeded through the midst of the spreading fracas.

Floating along the rolling waves, one of the beasts slain by the sea beings loomed ahead. The vessels adjusted course, navigating around the bobbing corpse and giving it a wide berth.

Drawing close enough to see its bulk in detail, Ragnar could see where the creature had been punctured many times. Driven deep, a couple of spears remained embedded in its flesh. The water around it had taken on a different hue from all of the blood ebbing from the wounds riddling the carcass.

"A feast for sharks," Ragnar commented as they passed by the dead creature.

"And good fortune for us," Thorsalla added.

"Looks like we have made it through," Ragnar said, looking back.

A few more black and white carcasses could be seen floating along the surface, and the frenzied activity had ebbed. Here and there, a few of the spear-bearing beings could be seen, lingering about one of the carcasses or moving along the surface.

After several moments passed, with no changes in what he observed, Ragnar issued the command for the others on the longship to put up their weapons and take to their oars. The time had come to focus once more on the journey east.

A powerful force jarred the longship near the bow, sending Thorsalla toppling over the side and splashing into the water. Ragnar came within a wisp of being pitched into the sea himself.

Twisting his body, he caught the top strakes of the ship at the last moment, leaving him hanging off the side of the longship. With a burst of exertion, he managed to haul himself back aboard.

Pulling Raven Caller out from his belt loop, he leaned out and extended the haft end toward Thorsalla, who had drifted a little further from the longship. Lurching forward and kicking, she reached for the haft, grabbing the end a moment later.

Ragnar pulled her in to the side, and yelled, "Do not let go! Hold on with everything you have in you!"

Urgency filled him, seeing a large form coming up from beneath her. Jaws opening wide to take human prey, the black and white mass ascended, growing larger by the moment.

Crying out with all the strength he could summon, Ragnar yanked Thorsalla free of the water and into the longship. Letting go of the axe haft, she rolled to a halt.

Ragnar turned around just as the hunter of the deep breached the surface, sending large plumes of water upward, before hitting the water again in a great splash that jostled the longship. Stepping to the side and raising his axe with a two-handed grip, he espied several arrow shafts sticking out of the brute's head.

"You bastard!" Ragnar shouted, as the creature raised its head out of the water. A crazed look came into his eyes. "You want more of me? Then have it!"

Shifting a step to his right, Ragnar brought the axe down on a diagonal plane, burying the head into the dark eye of the monstrous thing. A torrent of high-pitched cries erupted from the stricken creature.

"I may yet die today, but you pay a price!" Ragnar boomed, tearing his axe free and bracing for the creature to ram into the ship, or bring its bulk onto the side.

The creature did not have time to attack or retreat before it found itself swarmed by the spear-bearing beings that had intervened on behalf of the raiders. Ragnar looked on as spears sunk into flesh all over the brute.

Moments later, riddled with spear shafts, the large creature tilted in the water and ceased in its movements.

A large number of the sea beings bobbed in the water, some holding their spears aloft and saluting the occupants of the longship. Ragnar raised his bloodied axe in response, grinning, and giving them a salute in return.

"Well done, warriors of the sea!" he called to his benefactors.

He looked back to Thorsalla, who had a look of astonishment on her face.

"You attacked that thing, one on one," she said.

"It is all I could do," Ragnar said, giving a shrug. "I will not meet death begging for mercy."

Up and down the longship, the rest of the crew resumed setting oars to water. They spoke in low voices among each other, keeping a constant look upon the surrounding waters.

"I think that is the last of the brutes," Ragnar said. He gave a low chuckle a moment later. "Same bastard that tried to get to me before, too. Did not learn the first time, I guess."

"Grianna sent them to help us," Thorsalla said, eyeing the sea beings ripping their barbed spears free from the huge corpse, now farther behind them. Water dripped from her hair and soaked clothing, pooling on the timber planks beneath her feet.

"I have no doubt of that," Ragnar agreed.

The wind tousling his hair, Ragnar took in a deep, cleansing breath of the salt-tinged air. Clear skies and a bright, majestic sun reigned overhead, holding no sign of threats from the weather.

The dangers from beneath the waves had been eliminated through the unexpected intervention of the humanoid sea beings. All stood clear for Ragnar and his companions to resume their journey.

Looking back, Ragnar could no longer see Grianna, the shore now a distant, hazy, line spanning the horizon. In his heart, he thanked her for the aid of the sea beings, knowing their appearance to be some working of the mysterious woman.

Grianna held his life in her hands more than once, and had not betrayed him, despite the reality that Ragnar and his companions were foreign raiders in her lands. It would have been a simple, expedient act to allow the pack of massive, black-finned killers to put an end to any chance of the raiders coming back to her shores.

In allowing them to survive, Grianna placed Petranni lives in Ragnar's hands. While he could not stop others from raiding again, Ragnar swore another oath to himself; he would never enter her lands again, as anything other than an ally and friend.

Grianna had earned his respect and loyalty, both of which would remain unshakeable.

Ragnar turned his gaze back toward the east. Beyond the sea and far horizon, new lands offered the promise of adventure, growth, and discovery.

Where Macharriga possessed knowledge of death surpassing most anyone in the world, the goddess knew so very little about life. Each man or woman, drawing from every moment lived, created something unique and unrepeatable.

Hardships, struggles, and sorrows intertwined with triumphs, passions, and joys to forge the man Ragnar had become, at that very moment. If he were to die in the next instant, Ragnar knew that he had brought something into existence that Macharriga, with all of her tremendous power, could never take away; a life he called his own.

He had the distinct feeling that somewhere, far away, in a place Ragnar could not yet find or even see, Strala had come to know much more about the mysteries of life. The thought brought a smile to his face; of the kind that soothed pain in the heart.

For his own part, Ragnar did not wish to attain such knowledge just yet; and not for a long while to come, if he could help it.

"What are you grinning about, Ragnar, the renowned Stormbringer?" Thorsalla asked, coming over to his side.

She smiled at Ragnar, all traces of the harrowing experience that she had undergone absent from her face. Her wet strands of hair glistened in the sun's embrace.

"When we reach land, we must drink and feast, to celebrate Strala's life," Ragnar replied.

"I'll agree with that," Thorsalla said. Her smile took on a mischievous edge. A gleam danced within her eyes. "And we still have a matter to discuss ... regarding the number of crow-heads we each slew."

Ragnar grinned and his eyes sparked with amusement. "Yes, we do have something to resolve, and I'm sure it will take a full night."

"I intend it to," Thorsalla said, giving him a wink. "Maybe a full week."

"Good," Ragnar said, putting his arm around Thorsalla and drawing her close, eliciting a spirited laugh from the woman.

Ragnar laughed himself, and for a moment he did not have a single care in the world.

Others could choose to let the days drift by in a gray fog, and simply endure.

Ragnar would never become one of those tepid souls. A man who surmounted tremendous odds time and time again, Ragnar had come to learn that the real essence of life was not about mere survival.

Rather, the essence of being alive centered around making the choice to thrive.

WHEN THE COLD BREATHES

A RAGNAR STORMBRINGER TALE

STEPHEN ZIMMER

WHEN THE COLD BREATHES

Blotches of crimson mottled the brilliant white surface. An expanse of snow reflecting the rays of a bright, midday sun, the relentless glare pressed Ragnar Stormbringer's eyes into a tight squint. Frost tendrils riddled his thick beard and lengthy mass of dark hair, lending him the appearance of years far beyond his own.

A scowl deepening on his face, Ragnar eyed the broad paw prints adjacent to the spattered blood and staggered trail of human footprints. The bestial impressions in the snow showed evidence of great claws, the weapons of a predator well-suited to bringing down larger prey.

"These tracks were made by a great beast, a lone hunter, and it could well be cause of the vanishings," Ragnar announced, his pale blue gaze engulfing the smaller figure to his left. Looking back to the tracks they had just come across, he stared at the blood spots marking where the predator had engaged its prey. "These are not the paw marks of a snow tiger. What manner of creature leaves marks such as this? They are unfamiliar to me."

Though one of the larger men in the woodland settlement, Cnut's head did not reach Ragnar's shoulder. Looking up at Ragnar, the man's eyes glistened with fear.

"There has not been a Mayak sighted in this area for as long as anyone can remember, and not since the Jarl came to these lands," he told Ragnar, eyeing the wide impressions. "Yet these tracks belong to one. There is no mistake of that."

"What great fortune of ours, to come across the first Mayak tracks seen in ages," Ragnar said, with a sharp edge of sarcasm.

Though he had never encountered one, Ragnar knew enough about the rare, fearsome beasts that dwelled in the ice-cold wilderness of the far north. His mind remaining calm, the prospect of being hunted by one did not frighten him, but it did instill a heightened caution that he knew could not be relaxed for a single moment.

A heartbeat of time could be all the warning that he or Cnut might get in a Mayak attack.

Sweeping his gaze across the snow-blanketed terrain, he gripped the haft of his great war axe Raven Caller tighter. Several low, dark objects lying in the snow, far ahead and to the right, beckoned to him. The tracks in the snow, both human and beast, all headed straight toward them.

Saying nothing to Cnut, Ragnar strode toward the area, his long cloak flapping in a stout, icy gust of wind. Keeping his axe up, in a two-handed grip, he looked all about, remaining alert for any hint of the Mayak.

When Ragnar reached the scattered cluster of objects, his expression did not change. They were what he thought they would be.

What remained of the man who had made the human tracks littered the ground. Not a single limb remained attached to the eviscerated torso wreathed in a heap of blood. The shattered remnants of a skull had been strewn across the snow, a short distance away.

A spear lay just beyond a severed hand. The head of the weapon had no blood upon it, telling Ragnar that the hapless victim had not gotten so much as a single strike in upon the beast.

From the state of the remains, Ragnar gleaned that the kill had taken place not long ago, perhaps as recent as late that morning. Maintaining his caution, he knew it could well be that the Mayak stalked close by, though it looked from the scant flesh left on the bones that the creature had fed thoroughly.

Tendrils of wind whistling in his ears, Ragnar walked over to the edge of the shredded torso. A glint below the tattered stump of the corpse's neck caught his eyes.

Leaning over, he reached into the midst of the gore and took up a silver amulet, crafted in the image of the rune symbolizing the northern god Tireya. Wiping the blood off on the snow, Ragnar gazed upon the amulet, listening to the sounds growing louder from behind of heavy breaths and snow crunching under booted footsteps.

"Heimval, yes?" Ragnar asked, glancing toward Cnut, who came to a halt close to his right side. Holding up the amulet for the other man to see, he continued in a declarative tone, "The amulet you described to me earlier. You have found him ... or what is left of him."

"Why did he not listen to me?" Cnut lamented, staring at the amulet, a look of horror splayed on his face. "Had he just waited a little longer, many would have gone with him. Now he leaves behind a wife, and two healthy children."

Ragnar respected the courage of the dead man, who had acted when so many others, including Cnut, remained timid. Nevertheless, a part of Ragnar wished Heimval had heeded Cnut's plea for caution.

While rugged, none of the settlers Ragnar had encountered were the kind of warriors who could stand much of a chance alone braving the dangers of a hostile wilderness like that surrounding them. To undertake such a risk with a wife and children to care for made Heimval's choice a foolhardy one.

Even so, Ragnar determined to avenge Heimval and honor

the man's courage, while also aiding the settlers, whose leader had taken him in for the harshest stretch of winter afflicting the northernmost lands.

Not wanting to begin a southward trek in the depths of a northern winter, Ragnar had elected to stay for a time as a guest of the Jarl Thryggvi. Long ago, the old warrior had fallen into conflict with one of the northern kings. Driven from his lands, the jarl had traveled east with his family, servants, a number of loyal warriors, and their families; eventually finding a place to settle amid the remnants of a forest-dwelling tribe battered by war and hardship.

Eager to bring an end to their longstanding plight, the tribe had welcomed the jarl's arrival. Not long after, in a peaceable manner, at the tribe's acclimation, Jarl Thryggvi had come to rule over them.

During the ensuing years, the jarl's followers and the tribesmen formed several villages and homesteads. The area had now become a stopping point for northerners readying to enter the river-crossed, rolling seas of grassland to the south. Ragnar, like many others before him, hearkened to a route offering a chance for rest and sustenance within the midst of a harsh, frigid wilderness.

Having developed an affinity for a strong drink found in those lands made from rye grain, and possessing a growing taste for honey, pickled cabbage, and many other things common to the region, Ragnar had been more than content to pass the days and nights of mid-winter in relative calm. He found staying inside, drinking and eating by warm fires, and enjoying the sensual company of a couple eager, beautiful women far more preferable to enduring the bitter cold and dangers of the northern wilderness that pressing ahead with his journey would have demanded.

The worst of the winter was set to pass soon enough, and then he could head southward in a refreshed, hale state.

Then Cnut had arrived at the Jarl's homestead, asking to speak with Ragnar on an urgent matter. The aging Jarl had wanted to dismiss the man at once, but Ragnar agreed to listen to his tale.

Eight men had disappeared from area villages over the course of a few weeks. No trace of the cause had been found, and nor had there been any witnesses.

Cnut and others had been talking about putting together a large, armed party to search for them, but the rash of disappearances had unnerved many. A few more days had passed, and none had ventured forth.

Impatient, and unwilling to wait for the others' consensus, one of the settlers named Heimval had declared his intent to set out to find the others by himself. Early the next morning, he had acted upon his words.

Desiring to catch up to Heimval, but not wishing to venture after him alone, Cnut had tried to gather others, but to no avail. With no other options, he had then sought out Ragnar, whose tales of exploits and lands visited had captivated the hardy settlers on many nights.

Where many refused to join Cnut, Ragnar had been willing to accompany him alone. In his eyes, it would gain a chance to limber up and stretch his well-rested limbs. He had been idle more often than not in recent weeks. There was also the possibility that he could help the villagers discover the cause of the disappearances, and perhaps bring an end to them.

Whether the menace of a wild beast or an incursion from an enemy tribe, Ragnar had intended to get to the root of it soon enough, but he had not expected to find answers on the same day they had set out. Now, his wits and skill would be tested against a rare and formidable predator.

A part of him relished that challenge.

Surveying the grisly carnage, Cnut's fear-flecked eyes cast

all about the wintry landscape, as if expecting the thing that slew his unfortunate comrade to strike at any moment. Ragnar did not fail to see the white-knuckled grip the man had on the haft of his spear.

"If it watched from near, you would not see it," Ragnar told Cnut, his tone measured and unruffled. "But its belly has been filled, not that long ago. It has likely gone somewhere to slumber. I doubt it will undertake another hunt, just yet."

"A Mayak could bring down a hunting party of ten," Cnut replied in a low voice, brimming with anxiety.

"A hunting party that I was not counted among," Ragnar replied, an edge to his tone. "It will not find me such easy prey."

Though the words conveyed the immutable confidence dwelling within Ragnar's heart, he respected the power of the predator in plain evidence before him. His brief scrutiny of the bloodshed showed that the beast possessed bone-crushing jaws, and claws that could open a man's torso from neck to gut in one swipe.

From the broad paw marks, he estimated the creature to have a mass comparable to the great brown bears of his own homeland. Ragnar also had little doubt it could run down most anything out in the open.

"How long will this creature plague us, if it is not stopped?" Cnut remarked.

"For as long as it finds a good source of prey to satisfy its gullet," Ragnar said. "You will have to warn all the villages in this region. It is not wise for any in your villages to stray alone, when something like this stalks in the shadows."

"Such an ill-fated end for Heimval," Cnut bemoaned. "His eldest boy is only now coming of age, and the other is so young."

Squatting down, Ragnar untied a small pouch and a sheathed knife from the slain man's belt. Along with the amulet, he extended the items toward Cnut.

"See that the eldest boy and his mother get these," Ragnar told him.

Cnut nodded, taking the items from Ragnar.

A torrent of wind whipping Ragnar's long, dark locks all about, the great warrior rose up to his full height. Turning his eyes to the north, Ragnar looked to the edge of a forest in the distance, where white-barked trees and towering pines marked a sea of woodland that ran for leagues and leagues.

"What of the remains?" Cnut asked, after a few moments of silence.

"Burn them," Ragnar said. "It is all you can do. But gather many and come well-armed when you do."

Walking past the blood-stained area, Ragnar found the Mayak's tracks leading away from the kill. The tracks led toward the north and east, where some low hills rose above the flatter terrain he now trod.

"What are you thinking?" Cnut asked.

Ragnar looked back at the man and smirked. "It may have taken a liking to human flesh and intends to keep hunting us. But I am going to hunt it. Should bring us together much sooner."

Cnut's eyes widened at Ragnar's words. He looked as if he was about to say something in response, but no words came from his lips.

"From here, I go on alone," Ragnar announced. "Go back to the villages, see to this man's family, and gather a large party to get his remains."

"Should we not remain together?" Cnut said. "Who is to say where the Mayak will go?"

"It has fed, and headed for the forest, out there," Ragnar said, sensing the man's deep fear, and pointing in the direction indicated by the tracks. "If you return the way that we came here, you will be safe."

"May the gods look over you, Ragnar," Cnut said.

"I have Raven Caller with me," Ragnar replied, a sharp glint in his eyes. "That gives me a chance ... and a chance is all I ever need."

Cnut started back for the villages at a brisk stride. Ragnar imagined the other man found him to be foolish, in the grip of madness, or a combination of both. The thought brought a smile to his face.

Common men always saw the ways of the courageous and bold in such a light. It prevented them from recognizing their own weakness and craven leanings. Yet such men always sought those such as Ragnar in the worst of times, as Cnut just had done.

Gripping Raven Caller mid-shaft with his right hand, Ragnar smirked again, and began following the broad paw prints in the snow.

***

The Mayak's tracks took Ragnar deep into the woods, until the slopes of the hills he had espied from the kill site rose high, all around him. By then, the sun had crossed the skies and begun its western descent. Shadows lengthening from the trees and light dimming, the onset of twilight loomed.

Flurries and gusts of frigid wind, the latter eliciting creaks from the surrounding trees, were all that broke the deep silence pervading the forest. Trudging forward through the snow, Ragnar took great care with his steps, striving to keep them as quiet as possible.

A violet hue descended over the woodlands upon the arrival of dusk, heralding the imminence of night.

With the snow-covered ground and the light of a bright, full moon radiating from a star-filled sky above, visibility remained good for a fair distance despite the coming of darkness. Lashing into Ragnar's face, the bite of the winds increased with the deepening chill.

When the Cold Breathes

At last, the tracks of the Mayak turned and led up the side of a hill. A short distance up the slope, the black maw of a cave entrance beckoned within a cluster of jutting rocks. Eyeing the shadowy opening, Ragnar came to a halt.

Not wanting to confront a huge predator inside its lair, Ragnar backed away from the hill, using his own tracks to guide each step. After finding a place among some pines, and still within site of the cave, he concealed himself as best he could.

Pulling his cloak tighter about him, Ragnar began a vigil.

***

Movement caught his eyes. Becoming rigid at once, every sense within Ragnar heightened. All of his thoughts focused on the scene before him, his breath remained calm and steady.

Emerging from the depths of the cave, a massive beast padded out into the moonlight.

Long of body, the creature had a low, squat build, with four stout legs ending in wide sets of claws. Covered in white fur that matched the hue of the pristine snow around it, the beast would have no trouble blending into open terrain.

In some ways, the creature up the slope resembled a wolverine to Ragnar's eyes, but in others, the Mayak's form reflected elements of a great hunting cat.

Sniffing at the air with its short, broad snout, the creature's jaws spread apart just enough that the moonlight glinted off a huge set of fangs. Looking around, the beast prowled down from the cave, displaying smooth, nimble movements; showing that the creature carried its considerable size with a feline grace and ease.

Reaching the bottom of the hill, the Mayak started forward along the low ground. With all of his attention fixed upon his quarry, Ragnar watched the creature's approach in a patient, poised state.

The creature snapped to a halt where Ragnar's tracks had come to an end within sight of the cave entrance. Casting its gaze about, a rumbling snarl came from the depths of its throat. Though the wind blew in a favorable direction and did not betray his scent, Ragnar knew the creature was moments from seeing his position.

Reaching up slowly with his left hand, Ragnar unfastened the brooch at his neck, letting his cloak fall to the ground as he got up from where he crouched by the trunk of a towering pine.

Roaring at the top of his lungs, Ragnar gripped Raven Caller in both hands and charged headlong from the trees toward the Mayak. Startled, the creature whipped about to face him, and paused for an instant, as if in disbelief that a human would so fearlessly confront it.

Baring its great fangs and loosing a thunderous roar of its own, the beast lunged forward to meet Ragnar's rapid advance. Bounding through the snow, the beast covered the ground between them swiftly, springing at Ragnar when they drew close.

Raven Caller raised above his head, Ragnar swung the blade down with as much force as he could muster. Moving its head at the last instant, the Mayak avoided having its skull split.

Biting deep into sinew, muscle, and flesh, the sharp edge cleaved through the creature's thick white fur, between the neck and left shoulder. The Mayak loosed a horrendous cry, sounding like a blend of roar and screech.

Blood spraying outward, Ragnar slammed hard into the beast. Grunting at the impact, he tumbled over the top and right side of the creature, the latter's momentum carrying its bulk forward.

Holding tight to the shaft of his axe, Ragnar wrenched the blade free before hitting the snow. Feeling hard ground beneath his feet, Ragnar thrust out with his legs, propelling his body farther to the side.

Whirling about and gaining its footing, the wounded beast's right claws flashed, raking through the space where Ragnar had been a shred of an instant before. He found it difficult to believe a creature so big could move so fast, but a Mayak was a predator said to be from an ancient world; a time filled with monstrosities and giants.

Just after the claws missed shredding his legs by the span of a couple hands, Ragnar whipped his axe back through with urgent force. Using one hand at the far end of the haft to gain as much of a reach as possible, he caught the creature trying to rush in on him. Though the beast recoiled with quick reflexes, the Mayak suffered another wound, the blade slicing into its body once more.

Echoing off the hills and carrying far into the night, another grating cry erupted from the Mayak.

In the speed of the exchange, Ragnar could not tell for sure where the blow had landed. Pulling his weapon back at once, he regained his feet.

Backing away a couple more paces, Ragnar took up a battle stance and set his eyes upon his adversary.

Heavy breaths emerging like bursts of mist, the two combatants squared toward each other and locked eyes. Though maintaining composure and focus, Ragnar's mind absorbed his raw surprise at the beast's gaze.

A strange quality about the beast's pale eyes troubled the tall warrior. Recognizing the presence of something far more than a feral predator in the other's look, Ragnar's instincts told him that if the creature were to survive the fight a terrible fate would befall the villages.

In that moment, Ragnar knew he was all that stood between the creature and the slaughter of a great many men, women, and children.

Lengthy fangs gleaming and a rasping snarl sounding from

the depths of its throat, the creature continued glaring at him. In a steady cascade, blood dripped from the wounds Ragnar had inflicted, spattering the white surface beneath the creature. From what he could now tell, his second strike had opened a gash in the Mayak's neck.

Ragnar held his stance and readied his axe. The beast appeared hesitant to press an attack, and it could not be denied that the Mayak's breathing had become more labored. Ragnar sensed a weakening in the creature; and an opportunity to seize the initiative.

Bolstered at the recognition, Ragnar emitted an animalistic snarl of his own, before adding the words, "Come, you coward, and let me finish you!"

His words appeared to enrage the creature. Roaring, the Mayak barreled toward him once more. Ragnar dodged fast to the left, at the last instant, slashing hard with his axe and opening a third wound in the creature's side.

A pain-filled cry soaring into the heights, the Mayak turned to face him. Blood dripping from all its wounds, the creature kept up a sustained, menacing growl, but did not follow up on its attack.

Taking up a balanced stance once more, Ragnar saw that he now stood between the beast and its cave lair.

"If you want to run back to your hole in the ground, you will have to go through me!" Ragnar declared in a booming voice. Shaking his axe toward the creature, he continued to shout, taunting the Mayak, "You grow weaker every moment! The ground now drinks your blood! You will die this very night! Come at me, and be finished!"

Gnashing its teeth, and continuing to bleed out from three deep wounds, the beast snarled and growled in response to Ragnar's verbal barrage. Keeping its ground, and breathing becoming more ragged, a change then took place within the

Mayak's gaze.

Fear infiltrated the malice and rage holding dominion just moments before. Struggling more and more with its breath, the Mayak's fury ebbed. A few moments later, the creature's posture began to sag.

Seeing the Mayak's strength wavering, Ragnar braced, expecting the beast to muster a final, desperate attack.

Turning, the Mayak leaped into motion and bounded away, fleeing from Ragnar and abandoning the fight. Its powerful strides kicking up bursts of snow, the creature increased its speed swiftly.

"You craven bastard!" Ragnar bellowed in rage at the unexpected development.

Gripping his axe in his right hand, Ragnar broke into a run in the wake of the beast.

Strength remained in the Mayak's limbs and, despite the blood streaming from its multiple wounds, the beast widened the distance between itself and Ragnar. Lungs raw from rapid breaths of the icy air, Ragnar exerted himself as hard as he could to keep the creature within his eyesight.

Legs churning, Ragnar propelled himself across the snowy terrain, watching the Mayak's form continue to grow smaller and smaller ahead.

Without warning, the Mayak collapsed, falling to the ground in a heap and spurring Ragnar's spirits. Maintaining his pace, he closed the distance fast, ignoring the burn in his lungs and muscles.

Slowing down several paces from where the beast had fallen, Ragnar took a few moments to steady himself and regain some of his breath. With slow, careful steps, he approached the still form of the beast with great wariness, wondering whether its seeming collapse could be a ruse, intended to draw him close for a sudden ambush.

The Mayak's sides heaved, its breaths coming in rattling gasps. Then, its entire body began to tremble.

Blinking his eyes, Ragnar stopped, questioning his own vision for a moment. At first, it seemed like the creature's body was sinking into the ground. Then, Ragnar came to realize that its form was shrinking and drawing inward, condensing upon itself.

Filling Ragnar with caution, the recognition kept him rooted in place. He had witnessed such transformations before, and he deemed it best to let the process run its course, to reveal the beast's true nature.

The bizarre metamorphosis continued until a naked man covered in strange symbols lay within the bloodied snow. Ragnar took another couple of steps forward. Looking closer, he saw that the angular symbols were branded into the man's pale skin.

Standing, the man would have been about as tall as Ragnar. Round of face, thick of neck, and broad of shoulder, he had long locks of mixed black and silver-gray strands. An extensive beard, of a similar blend of hues, reached down to just past the middle of his big chest.

Beneath him was a large pelt of thick, white fur, long and broad enough to wrap around his entire body in the manner of a cloak. Ragnar did not have to examine the pelt to know that it had come from a Mayak.

Coughing up gouts of blood, the man fixed his pale eyes upon Ragnar. His lips spread in a semblance of a grin, though the look carried no hint of goodwill. Rather, the expression and gaze exuded hatred. His grin spreading wider, the light gray pupils and whites of the man's eyes then faded into a solid, coal black.

Arching his back, the figure loosed a piercing, otherworldly screech, sounding as if many voices conspired together to create the hellish cry. The air appeared to shimmer, and for a moment Ragnar swayed, overcome with a wave of dizziness.

Clenching onto the haft of Raven Caller, he recognized the presence of sorcery and knew that he had to do all that he could to overcome the fog clouding his mind. It took all of Ragnar's focus to keep hold of his thoughts and prevent them from melting into a paralyzing stupor.

Gritting his teeth, Ragnar concentrated on regaining command of his body and axe. Thinking of movements, ways to swing and strike with his weapon, and stances, he invoked a path of order within the miasma threatening to take hold. The feel of Raven Caller's haft in his hands reinforced the order gaining purchase in his mind, until he reached a point where the power working against him broke.

The instant clarity returned to his mind, Ragnar brought his axe up. A crazed look on his face, and staring back at Ragnar, the man on the ground began laughing, spittle and blood erupting onto his beard.

Whipping the axe downward, Ragnar cut the shrill laughter off, driving the blade of Raven Caller into the maniacal figure's face, splitting it apart into almost perfect halves. The man's body shuddered for a moment and went still.

"Laugh about that, you bastard," Ragnar declared, glaring at the corpse.

It was then that Ragnar took note of the undulating terrain spreading far beyond the dead figure; a sprawling mass of low, distinctive mounds upon which no trees grew. A light tremor rippled though the ground, the vibrations underfoot running up his legs and torso.

Another tremor followed just after, stronger and more sustained. A third ensued, of an even longer duration, and powerful enough to shake Ragnar. Keeping to his feet, he remained in place, wondering at the sudden upheaval.

A fair distance away from Ragnar, the ground caved in, layers of snow and earth falling away to reveal a large, gaping hole that swallowed up at least three of the mounds.

"What devilry is this?" Ragnar muttered into the uneasy silence about him.

Deciding to risk nothing with the shape-shifting man lying at his feet, Ragnar tore his axe free and swung it in a great arc. The blow sliced clean through the corpse's neck, severing the split halves of the man's head from his body.

With a couple of hard kicks, Ragnar put a fair distance between the two halves, the pieces tumbling to a stop at the end of shallow, blood-streaked furrows of snow.

A few solid hacks dismembered the body to a point where Ragnar deemed it almost impossible for the man to reconstitute any kind of form. Nevertheless, he took up the man's limbs and scattered them in several directions.

When finished, Ragnar took his axe and wiped the gore-coated blade off on a small, unsullied part of the white pelt beneath the corpse. Then, he eyed the hole.

With the corpse attended to, Ragnar could take a closer look. Stalking forward, wary and on his guard, Ragnar made his way toward the edge.

Peering down, Ragnar gazed into the depths of a large cavern. Unlike his surroundings on the surface, the interior of the cavern was anything but still and silent. Everywhere Ragnar looked, the cavern teemed with activity.

Movements within the shadows, and a cacophony of hissing, rattling, breathing sounds, warned Ragnar of a manifesting danger. Pairs of luminous eyes riddled the darkness of the cavern, though what creature they belonged to remained shrouded in the darkness.

All of the little, glowing orbs began orienting upon Ragnar, and the noises grew louder. A cold chill penetrated his veins, deepening with every moment.

Scrabbling, scratching sounds reached his ears. Around the

perimeter of the opening, Ragnar noted that some of the eyes were growing a little larger in size.

Something was climbing toward him, in large numbers. It would not be much longer before whatever lurked within the cavern emerged onto the surface.

Understanding the nature of what was happening in the cavern, Ragnar thought back on the shape-shifter's look of madness and laughter. He could now see that both contained a defiant air of triumph. In his final breaths, the man had lashed out, unleashing a dark power far more daunting and menacing than a Mayak.

"Dung-eating sorcerers!" Ragnar exclaimed, with the air of a curse, spitting into the maw of the cavern.

Sweeping his gaze across the low mounds, he estimated there to be hundreds.

Though part of him wanted to greet the first of the unknown things climbing up from the pit with Raven Caller, Ragnar chose to depart the area at haste.

He knew that he would be facing the occupants of the pit soon enough. Before then, he had to get back to Cnut and the others.

With no time to retrieve his cloak, Ragnar headed out, depending on body heat from exertion to make up for the loss of his outermost covering. Alternating between a light jog and a brisk march, he kept up a brisk pace.

While he could not exhaust himself too soon, Ragnar had no choice but to press hard. Faint on the winds, coming from behind, blood-curdling shrieks and cries carried through the night.

The unknown denizens of the cavern had reached the surface; and would soon be following in Ragnar's wake. Breathing a little harder, he continued forward with long strides that took him farther and farther from the cavern and barrows.

Striking out in the final moments of life, the shape-shifting sorcerer had set a horrific revenge in motion. A warning had to be spread to all of the villages and homesteads of the area.

Even then, a tide of death would be closing in, without respite. When that wave crashed upon the Jarl's people, their chances to survive the coming nightmare looked grim.

*∗∗

Raspy, guttural cries pierced through the winds and cascading snowfall. Coming from behind, the unnatural sounds carrying along with the night gusts chilled Ragnar's bones to the marrow. He knew them to be from something that had no place in the world he lived in.

Legs churning, continuing to put distance between himself and the things from the cavern, Ragnar pressed on through the forest without pause. At last, the trees gave way to open ground.

A fire in the distance drew his attention. Suspecting its nature, Ragnar hastened toward it without delay.

Ragnar found Cnut with a large group of armed men, gathered around a makeshift pyre. Flames still burned, though they had already consumed whatever had been left of Heimval.

Gathering around when he reached them, the men looked elated to see Ragnar. Quieting their hails and greetings, he wasted no time in telling them of the events in the woods and the threat now heading their way.

While still distant, unmistakable cries and shrieks slithered through the winds.

"Oh gods ... oh gods ... we are doomed!" stammered one of the men, eyes gleaming in fright at the sounds. He clutched at Ragnar in a frenzy born of desperation. "We will die this night!"

Using an open palm, Ragnar smacked him hard across the face, toppling him to the ground. "Get your senses! You may die, but do not include me or any others in that!"

In awkward fashion, the man got up to his feet. "I ... am frightened."

"It is not wrong to be frightened, but take command of yourself," Ragnar said, with a little less ire. "We have to stand together."

"Against what?" another man asked. "You did not see these things above the ground, Ragnar."

"I have no doubts it has something to do with the barrows I found," Ragnar said.

"Could they be Draugr?" a man asked. "They haunt barrows."

"Not in numbers like that," Cnut said.

"These things had to climb to the surface," Ragnar added. "A draugr could take shape above the ground."

"Then wights or ghouls," Cnut said to Ragnar. "Though the light from their eyes, from your description, make me think they are wights."

The explanation as good as any he could think of, Ragnar nodded.

"Wights! A horde of them?" one of the men cried out. "Coming this way? Are you certain of this?"

"They are headed this way, and there is little mistaking their purpose," Ragnar confirmed.

"How can we stop them? We would shun any place with even a few of them," the man said.

"You have to fight them, or they will kill you," Ragnar said.

The inhuman cries continued along the winds, the latter whipping through a thick, falling snow that obscured sight of the forest's edge.

"We are shedding time here ... let us go to the villages now and warn them!" Ragnar said.

"And lead them right into the villages?" one of the men asked.

"They will sweep through the villages, whether we go or not," Ragnar said, an idea forming. "Let us take a stand together. Gather all you can and take them to the Jarl's fortress."

"How long do you think we have?" Cnut asked, glancing in the direction of the woods.

"Not long, as these things have been called from the ground by sorcery. They will not tire, and they require no food or drink, so let us not tarry," Ragnar said, looking around at their anxious faces. "We go to warn the villages, now!"

Leaving the pyre and its dying flames behind, the men gathered up the things they had brought with them, and then followed after Ragnar. He led them at a brisk stride; the wails, howls, and cries chasing after them on the night winds.

***

Terrified men, women and children, roused from slumber in the dead of night, trundled through the snow. Growing louder as the night crept onward, the ghastly cries filling the darkness doused all arguments and spurred limbs into motion.

Streaming in from all the villages and homesteads, everyone that could be warned made their way to the jarl's hill-fort, an edifice built in a place central to the area under his rule. Carrying along whatever they could snatch up at a moment's notice, using baskets, sacks, pouches and other vessels, the people did whatever they could to scrounge up foodstuffs and other items before leaving their homes with little else than the clothes on their backs.

Featuring a ditch and high earthen rampart, the latter crowned with a stout wooden palisade, the circular fort topped the broad summit of a large hill. Inside the rampart, slanted roofs and entryways dug beneath ground level marked the locations of storage pits. A number of small timber huts and a couple of pens for animals rounded out the fortress' cramped interior.

When the Cold Breathes

Built as a refuge for the area's villages and homesteads during times of war, the fortress now offered the only chance the people had to defend against an enemy whose only desire was to slaughter them.

After a little while, the influx of villagers tapered off, reducing to a trickle before no more family groups arrived at the gates. The eerie cries beyond the ramparts continued growing in volume, though nothing could be seen through the dense snowfall.

More than once, men warding the ramparts shouted false warnings, as jittery nerves began giving rise to seeing things that were not there. Every flicker of a shadow sent fear rippling through the villagers on the watch.

Listening to the swelling cries, moans and wails, Ragnar stood at the fortress gate with Raven Caller in hand, ready to wield the great axe should something emerge out of the snowstorm that was not a living human being. Whispering of approaching death, the icy winds whipped through his hair.

A few more stragglers managed to reach the fortress during that time, stumbling out of the gray and white torrent engulfing the area. Each of them arriving to the hill-fort alone, and staggered well-apart, the last to reach the gates came from the outermost dwellings within the jarl's dominion.

Ragnar confronted each of them, determining their human nature before letting them pass. He had demanded that the others warding the gateway stay back and allow him to greet newcomers when the larger family groups had stopped arriving.

With the villagers growing ever more nervous, a lone figure emerging from the snow stood far too great a chance of getting skewered with a spear or hacked apart with an axe.

Nearly all of the solitary arrivals were men, save for one older woman, covered in furs and carrying a number of pouches. Ragnar took her to be a healer, or a practitioner of magic arts, of a type he had seen more than once before living on the outskirts of a village.

Looking over their shoulders and casting fearful glances back into the woods, the latecomers hastened through the gates.

When no more villagers had arrived for a little while, the men gathered about the gate began casting nervous glances toward Ragnar. More than one flinched at each sepulchral wail or howl from within the snowstorm.

All knew that the horde from the pit neared.

At last, Ragnar turned to the men with him and commanded, "It is time to shut the gates!"

From their reactions, his order came as a great relief. The others hurried inside, leaving Ragnar by himself.

Ragnar cast one more glance into the snowy miasma. A couple of dim shadows that were not tricks of light moved among the trees.

Turning away from the forest, he trudged back through the entryway. Behind him, the thick timber gateway was pulled shut and barred.

Ragnar then looked toward a large mass of armed men milling about the gateway. "A watch on the wall-walk in every direction. They are here."

***

Standing at the top of the rampart, Ragnar eyed a host of movements among the trees a short distance beyond the ditch. Gaunt, long-limbed figures with extended heads prowled through the forest, making their way toward the base of the rampart.

More and more of the things came into view, spreading apart in such a manner that the fortress would soon become encircled.

Bright, spectral lights shone from within the things' eye sockets, a look both unsettling and unnatural. The incoming figures made no attempt at silence, filling the air with hisses, screeches, shrieks, and other noises.

Before long, the area around the fortress teemed with the entities.

"All those who can hold a weapon, to the ramparts!" Ragnar called, trusting to his instincts.

Every man or woman who could wield a weapon hurried to the wall-walk. Looking around, Ragnar saw that a solid ring of humans defended the ramparts.

Far below him, the ranks of the entities thickened, with more gathering every moment. Outnumbering the villagers by a great margin, the mass of entities would have overwhelmed the humans with ease had it not been for the hill-fortress.

Ragnar and the others could do little more than wait for the inevitable. No signal or distinct call rang out when a surge of motion took place all around the hill-fort.

Swarming the ditch, the malefic horde began their assault.

Scrabbling and grasping, the things began ascending the long slope of the rampart. The entities climbed with ease, exhibiting dexterity and strength as they dug holds and pulled themselves up the steep incline.

Before long, the first of them would reach the palisade.

Looking down from a closer vantage, Ragnar could see their forms with more clarity. Tattered remnants of clothing still clung to their bodies, the pale skin of which resembled something long mummified in texture and tautness. The desiccated state of their corporeal forms gave the creatures a skeletal appearance.

If their bodies had once been of the world of humankind, some power had since altered them into something far different in proportion. Elongated of limbs and neck, the entities possessed jutting, oversized jaws. Many of the things climbing toward Ragnar had their thin lips pulled back, baring a jagged array of sharp teeth that included prominent upper and lower canines.

More monstrous than human, and echoing death more than

life, the forms of the creatures reflected the malignant sorcery that had called from forth.

When the entities reached the top of the rampart, they scratched and clawed at the wood of the palisade, a few gaining purchase and seeking to climb over the barrier.

Wherever their heads or dirt-encrusted, clawed hands breached the palisade, the villagers hacked, stabbed, and fought back with a fear-induced desperation. Stymied in their advance, and with more continuing to reach the top of the rampart, the area around the palisade clogged up in moments, forcing the entities lower on the slopes to halt in their ascent. The entities could not bring their great advantage in numbers to bear upon the human defenders.

With a hard swing of his axe, Ragnar lopped the head off one of the things trying to heave itself over the edge of the palisade. The body and head tumbled back down the length of the rampart. Knocking a couple more entities off the slope, the falling remains thudded into the ditch below, the dislodged creatures piling on top an instant later.

Ragnar could only hope that the headless corpse remained there. He could see all around him that the things could incur wounds that would have killed a living man or woman. Axes buried in skulls, throats gashed open, and midsections gutted did not stop the creatures.

Several of the macabre beings within Ragnar's view had been maimed in a severe way, losing an eye, hand, or arm, yet the mutilated showed no signs of pain or slowing their attack. All of them continued trying to surmount the palisade and get at the villagers defending it.

Casualties remained light among the defenders, though a few villagers met with horrid demises.

To his right, and not far from where he stood, Ragnar witnessed a throat being ripped open by raking claws that cut through flesh like honed blades. Several paces to his left, another villager's eyes snapped wide open in shock, as an entity drove its arm deep into the ill-fated man's belly, tearing his guts out a heartbeat later.

Not long after, one of the things lurched over the top of the palisade and clutched onto a man near Ragnar. Without a moment's hesitation, the entity clamped its wide jaws down on the man's face, engulfing it from his forehead to under the chin. Blood spattering everywhere, the creature bit down hard and jerked its head back.

Leaving a grisly countenance in its wake, the savage bite tore the nose and most of the skin off the victim's face.

While he could not save the dying man, who slumped down to the wall-walk, Ragnar hoisted his axe and fixed his eyes on the hideous assailant. Enraged, he tromped forward and beheaded the thing in one blow.

The head fell and rolled along the wall walk for a few paces, while the rest of the creature's body draped over the palisade.

Reaching out with his left hand, Ragnar grabbed the headless corpse at the shoulder. Frigid to the touch, the thing's skin had a clammy feel to it, and Ragnar did not want to remain in contact for an instant longer. With a quick, powerful heave, he sent the body hurtling down the slope, jarring a few more entities loose of their holds on the face of the rampart.

A grating snarl to Ragnar's left warned him of another assailant. Pulling itself up on the palisade's edge, the creature hissed at him and spread its jaws wide.

Turning, raising his axe, and chopping down hard, Ragnar cleaved the skull of the thing in two, down to the neck. Before toppling backward, the spectral light within the thing's eyes gave way to solid black.

"Fight them with all you have!" Ragnar shouted to the others defending the wall-walk, before looking out over the entities ringing the fortress.

For each one slain, another stepped forward to begin an upward climb. Those knocked down the slope by a falling body clambered out of the ditch and started to scale the incline once more.

Brandishing his axe at the relentless creatures, Ragnar unleashed a defiant, thunderous war cry, heard by friend and foe alike.

"Come to your ruin! We will not break!" he roared.

Responding to his morale-bolstering display, all along the wall-walk, many defenders cried out at the top of their lungs. Swinging their weapons with renewed vigor, and thwarting most of the attackers from crossing over the palisade, the humans continued to hold the ramparts.

A few of the entities made it onto the wall-walk, but none got any farther. The ditch at the base of the rampart collected more and more of the attackers' corpses, most of them headless and some with extensive wounds to the skull.

A few more villagers fell, but the massed attack on the palisade proved too difficult for the creatures. The ditch continued to fill with their bodies, and more and more of the entities lost fingers, hands, or entire limbs, crippling their ability to attack or climb the rampart.

Ragnar chopped, hacked, and slashed, killing and dismembering as many of the vile things that he could. After a little while longer, the numbers reaching the top began to ebb, until none of the things were able to climb over the palisade and reach the wall-walk.

Without any kind of signal, the assault ceased, and the entities began retreating down the rampart. Those around the ditch moved back into the trees.

Some cheering, and others hurling curses and insults, the defenders watched the entities fall back. Holding their places along the wall-walk, the villagers kept their weapons at hand.

After resting for a few moments, Ragnar took a slow walk around the perimeter of the wall-walk, making an assessment. While the creatures had incurred many casualties, enough of them remained to keep the fortress surrounded.

On open ground, the villagers still would not stand a chance against their hellish adversaries.

At Ragnar's command, after setting a watch along the ramparts, the villagers began gathering up their dead and any remains of the attackers that could be found. Building one pyre for human bodies and another for the creatures, they burned the remains.

Every last remnant of a wight that could be found, no matter how small the piece, was put to the flames. No chances could be taken when confronting an enemy of the kind they faced.

Soon after, the air began filling with the sounds of crying, sobs, and wails. The tension of battle giving way to a flood of emotion, the families and friends of those who had fallen mourned,

Weary, and having no desire for company, Ragnar strode away from the fires. Walking among a group of huts, he found a place where he could be left to himself for a little while.

Looking up and around, Ragnar satisfied himself once more that the wall had an ample watch set upon it. With eyes positioned at all points of the perimeter, nothing could approach the hill-fort without being seen well in advance.

Without the exertion of battle to warm his blood, the cold was becoming more of a nuisance. Inside the hut where Ragnar had claimed a place to sleep, he retrieved a cloak that he had been given upon arrival to the fortress.

Using a large brooch crafted in the shape of a wolf's head, he fastened the cloak at his neck. A replacement for the one he had left behind in the wilderness, the furred cloak was not quite as long as Ragnar would have preferred, but anything would help in warding against the penetrating cold of a northern winter.

Making his way back outside, he leaned against the wall of the hut, savoring the relative quiet and isolation. The respite would not last for much longer. The people of the village would be settling down soon enough for the rest of the night.

Using the lower border of his main tunic, Ragnar then set about cleaning the blade of Raven Caller. Taking a whetstone out from a pouch at his belt, he tended to the edge until he deemed the blade sharp enough for the next battle. When finished, he slid the weapon back into the loop at his belt and returned the whetstone to the pouch.

A few villagers began returning to the huts. Those who saw Ragnar acknowledged him with a brief greeting or nod. Sensing the increasing nervousness that the men and women bore toward him, he had no doubt that their tales of his fighting on the wall-walk had already been imbued with exaggeration.

He had seen it happen many times before. If Ragnar slew ten adversaries in battle, using all of his martial abilities, it would be said later that he smote fifty, wielding his axe single-handed.

In some instances, the loftier tales increased trouble for Ragnar, as those seeking quick fame sought to bring down a living legend. Now, such tales would serve a good purpose, in lifting morale and inspiring the villagers to fight back against the entities keeping them trapped in the hill-fort.

With villagers returning to the huts for the night, Ragnar decided to take a walk. Straightening up and pulling his cloak snug, he strode away from the hut, his boots crunching on the snow.

Strolling about the interior of the fortress, Ragnar turned his thoughts toward the situation at hand. A siege now underway, their enemy did not have the needs or limits of living beings.

In the urgency of the moment, far too little food had been

carried into the fortress to sustain the occupants for an extended period of time. The creatures outside the ramparts would not have long to wait until starvation began taking root and spread among their intended prey.

Periodic howls, wails, and screeches carried over the wall, the noises stark reminders of the entities outside the fortress. Hungering for the death of every living being inside the hill-fort, the things could not be negotiated with or bribed.

A means of overcoming the horde would have to be found.

Ragnar did not know where to begin in finding a way. The people could not outlast their enemy, nor could they survive a battle outside the walls. Even if a message could be sent out, no force existed within feasible range of the hill-fort strong enough to break the siege.

Swirling the thick snowfall about the huts and storage buildings, powerful gusts of wind whipped about the fortress. Howling and whistling, the brisk flows of air lashed and battered the villagers patrolling the wall-walk above. Ragnar watched his breaths emerge in light gray puffs.

Without deep stocks of wood, or the ability to go outside the walls to cut more, the cold would also become a problem that increased with time.

No matter which way Ragnar looked at it, the inhabitants of the fortress faced a daunting plight; one that looked nearly insurmountable.

Nevertheless, Ragnar refused to give in to despair. Walking onward in the cold night air, he kept searching his thoughts.

**

The night passed without incident, though the following day's pale light greeted the besieged villagers with more snowfall and overcast skies. Eerie cries persisted from beyond the ramparts, dashing the hopes of many who had voiced hopes that sunrise would get rid of the unnatural creatures.

Having gained an uninterrupted period of slumber running from late night until just after dawn, Ragnar arose in a renewed state, energetic and sharp in thought. Donning his full attire, he staved off the rumbling in his stomach through consuming a modest fare of berries in honey and a little salted fish.

Outside the hut, Ragnar took in a deep, cleansing breath of the crisp morning air. Stretching his limbs, neck, and back, he worked out a few areas with lingering soreness and aches from the previous day.

Ragnar then headed to the wall-walk. Finding that the watch had been kept well, he complimented the villagers now warding the palisade. Given the circumstances, all appeared to be in as good of spirits as he could have hoped for. Though still exhibiting signs of fear and anxiousness, they appeared far more composed than the rattled mob that had first arrived through the gates.

From the high outlook, the forms of several entities could be seen moving among the trees, not far from the ditch and base of the rampart. Milling about, the creatures looked to be doing nothing in particular, other than making their presence known to their intended quarry, trapped in the fortress.

Making his way back down to the ground level of the fortress interior, Ragnar thought of seeking out Jarl Thryggvi. Walking toward the center, where the largest of the huts had been built, he sought the old warrior to discuss the overall dilemma facing the people. Perhaps the jarl had some insights that Ragnar could add to his thinking in a search for a way to defeat the pit-spawned fiends.

"From the old burial grounds to the east, was it? A large number of barrows, deep in the hills? That is where these abominations came from, yes?"

Ragnar looked to his right, seeing an old man standing

outside the entrance to one of the larger huts. From his rougher attire and accent, Ragnar figured him to be one of the tribesmen who had accepted the rule of Jarl Thryggvi.

Peering toward Ragnar from beneath a bushy, silver-gray set of eyebrows that flared upward, the man's dark eyes shone with alertness. Scraggly ends reaching far down his chest, a dense beard cradled his round face. A furred cap rested upon his head, beneath which a rabble of disheveled locks staggered down over his shoulders and back.

"A work of dark sorcery called them forth," Ragnar replied, coming to a halt. "A vile magic brought these things out from a pit, beneath a place like you describe. You know of this place?"

"I know not what wickedness had been done by those who the mounds belonged to," the old man replied. "They were already here, and deemed to be ancient, when the first of my tribe came to these lands. Whatever that those who raised the barrows did is lost to the faded mists of time. But over the years that our tribe has dwelled in these lands, those grounds have drawn witches and sorcerers of the dark arts ... some from very distant lands. The people here have always driven them away, or slain them,"

"I caught one such, at the edge of those grounds, a shape shifter no less," Ragnar said. "The bastard got off a loud cry, before his final breath. I felt the power of the magic he invoked running through my body and the ground itself. Three times the ground rumbled, each time stronger."

"Must have been powerful magic indeed," the old man replied, frowning at Ragnar's words. "What then?"

"The pit formed after that, taking more than one of those barrows into it," Ragnar told him, recalling the experience. "I looked in and saw a host of shining eyes, spread throughout a great cavern. Many began to make their way to the surface up slopes of debris. I did not wait around for all of those cold-skinned louts to come up from the ground."

"You saved the people of five villages and many homesteads by coming to warn us," the man said. "Those things would have swept over our homes and killed every one of us, in little time. From the words of those who saw and fought the things on the wall, I would guess them to be a kind of wight ... and such abominations seek only to kill the living."

"Most seem to think them to be a kind of wight, and from what I know of such creatures I would agree," Ragnar stated. "I am doing all I can to see that as few villagers as possible die here. I would kill them all if I could fight them a few at a time, though it would take a while to lop the heads off that many of the cursed things.

"A great number of these scum still remain outside, and they do not appear eager to attack the wall again. I am thinking they will seek to outlast us. With dwindling food and wood, the people here are not in a good position and it will only worsen with time. I have thought upon..."

Interrupting the conversation, a shout came from the wall-walk, near to the front gates. "Riders! Approaching the forest!"

After a glance in the direction of the voice, Ragnar looked back to the old man. Needing some answers, and intrigued by what the man knew, he hated to break off their conversation.

"We must speak later," Ragnar said, his tone insistent.

"We will, as soon as you are able," the man replied. "Go on ... and see what is happening."

Ragnar then broke into a loping run, heading for the main gate. When he reached it, he wasted no time in climbing the wide flight of steps leading up to the wall-walk.

The commotion had drawn many of the villagers to the gate area, with a rising number of them gathering on the wall-walk. Jostling each other to get a good vantage, they murmured amongst each other in apprehensive tones.

None impeded Ragnar, who pushed through them to stand

above the middle of the gates. The spot afforded him a clear, unobstructed view of the approach to the fortress.

"We do not know who they are, or where they are from," one of the men atop the wall-walk informed Ragnar.

Bracing his hands on the edge of the palisade, Ragnar looked out toward a pair of riders heading at a slow pace toward the front gates of the fortress. From their rugged clothing and a fair number of pelts secured to the rear of their mounts, both of the figures appeared to be hunters.

Men along the wall-walk shouted to the incoming riders, urging them to turn back. The distance and wind hampered the dire warnings, but the tone of their shouts was enough to bring the two riders to a halt.

Keeping a rein on their mounts, the men looked toward the fortress. Ragnar could sense the confusion in them.

Those watching from along the wall-walk could do nothing but look on as tall, gaunt things that had no rightful place in the world of the living swarmed out of the trees. Surrounding the riders and blocking all paths of escape, the wights fell upon them in a savage, blood-letting frenzy.

Clawing, gouging, and biting into flesh, the wights took both horses to the ground in moments, dragging the riders down with them. The screams of beast and man blended with the screeches of the wights in a hellish chorus that shook the spirits of all in the fortress; save for Ragnar.

The slaughter enraged him. A part of him wanted to lay into the wights with Raven Caller right at that moment, hacking and cleaving the vile things apart one by one.

Cursing, and taking his eyes away from the grisly scene, he shouldered his way through the villagers and descended to the ground.

"Ragnar!"

The voice of Cnut sounded from his right. Turning his

head, Ragnar saw the man walking toward him at a fast pace, a worried expression spread across his face.

"What is it?" Ragnar asked him in a terse manner.

"Come with me," Cnut replied, sounding insistent. "There is something you need to see, and it cannot wait."

Ragnar followed Cnut to one of the huts on the outskirts of the fortress interior, not far from the wall-walk. A terrible smell permeated the air within the vicinity of the small edifice.

Recognizing the rank odor of death and decay at once, Ragnar looked to Cnut. "Tell me, what has happened."

"Inside," Cnut said, standing to the side of the hut entrance. "You must see it first."

Stooping over to enter, Ragnar proceeded into the hut. Adjusting to the dim interior, he set his eyes upon the forms of several villagers, four men and two women, lying atop a few skins. All looked to be in the grip of an advanced sickness, one that had reduced them to an emaciated state.

Standing against a wall, a spear-bearing man stood watch over the sickly group in the cramped environs. Looking distressed, he cast a nervous glance toward Ragnar.

Gasping and wheezing, the men and women on the skins stared upward with dull looks to their eyes and listless expressions. One issued a low moan, and another coughed up a mixture of phlegm and blood.

Ragnar frowned, recognizing a couple of the unfortunates. Walking back to the huts after the burning of the corpses on the previous night, the two had been in far different states the last time Ragnar had seen them.

Both villagers had appeared hale to his eyes, and none the worse for wear. Now, in less than a day, they teetered upon the edge of death.

"Let us go outside and we can speak further," Cnut said.

Ragnar nodded, and the two men went back outside. Glad

to be free of the air within the hut, if not the stench, Ragnar took a deep breath of the winter air.

"What happened to them?" Ragnar said. "They were not like that at all before I turned in for sleep."

"Every one of them was bitten by one of those things during the fighting yesterday," Cnut said, looking pensive. "Their wounds turned worse during the night, like they were rotting, and this sickness came over them fast. Those among us with knowledge of healing say nothing can be done. We do not think they will last much longer. Several others who had also been bitten have already died. We had these few moved here, not knowing if they could become threats to the others, in the way that an illness can spread ... but no one else has fallen sick."

"A wise choice," Ragnar said. "Have you burned the bodies of those who died?"

"It is being done now," Cnut replied, nodding.

'Sometimes the dead come back," Ragnar said. "Though never in the way they were before."

"I have heard such tales," Cnut replied, a hint of fear in his voice.

"There is truth to those tales," Ragnar said. "Evil arises in the shells of the living. I think we are facing such a thing now, gathered out there in the woods."

"I do not think there is anything inside the fortress for the rest of us to be worried of," Cnut said. "Those who have died will be ash soon ... and only the six you have seen remain of those who were bitten."

"So there are no others who were bitten, who have not fallen ill?" Ragnar asked.

Cnut shook his head. "Not one."

"Then we know one thing," Ragnar said, his countenance grim. "The bite of the vermin outside this fortress brings death."

"All need to be warned of this," Cnut said, his eyes betraying a growing fright within him.

Ragnar looked him in the eyes. "See to it that all are told. As soon as possible."

"I shall," Cnut responded.

"Do not waver in spirit," Ragnar said. "No matter what the bite of those things can do."

"It is no easy thing to keep the spirit strong when we are surrounded and trapped in here," Cnut said.

"Are you still alive?" Ragnar asked.

"Yes," Cnut answered.

"Then you must not waver in spirit, if you wish to remain alive," Ragnar told him, holding the other's gaze for a moment longer. Looking away from Cnut, Ragnar turned his gaze toward the larger huts at the center of the fortress. "I must take leave of you now ... I have a matter of importance to look into."

***

Ragnar found the old man where he had left him, standing alone, outside the entrance to one of the larger huts.

"If there were a way to get past the damnable things, to seek some aid, I would take it," Ragnar said, lamenting his predicament. "But even for me, there are too many. I would go to certain death. That would gain nothing for anyone, and I am not about to toss my life away in a foolish act. You seem to know something of what we are facing. If you know of any way, no matter how impossible it may seem, then tell me."

The old man looked to Ragnar with a peculiar expression, as if he were making some sort of determination. After a few moments, he replied in a solemn tone. "I would like to show you something about this place that you may not know of. Follow me, and I will tell you more."

The old man stepped away from the hut and headed in the direction of the outer wall. Shortening his stride, Ragnar kept pace with him, walking along at the man's side.

When they had proceeded beyond the huts, the old man guided Ragnar toward the base of the rampart.

"This is an old fortress site ... very old," the old man said as they walked, glancing over to Ragnar. "The jarl made good use of this place, and he centered his land about it. He has improved it greatly, but it goes far back, to when the people of my tribe first dug an outer ditch and formed an earthen rampart.

"I explored here often as a child, and I made some discoveries. Few know of it, but a concealed tunnel runs from within the fortress to a place deep within the trees. I do not know if it is far enough to take you beyond the ring of creatures surrounding us, but it is a way out of here."

"And a way into here, should those fiends come across it," Ragnar said, both intrigued and concerned at the revelation.

The old man nodded. "I doubt they will. The place where it emerges is overgrown and well hidden by now."

Slowing down, the man eyed the wall for several moments, and then looked toward the ground. To Ragnar's eyes, the man appeared to be searching for something specific in nature.

"The place where it begins is well hidden too," the old man remarked, continuing his inspection. He peered at the inner facing of the wall, and then looked to the ground again.

"That should be the spot," he muttered, speaking to himself.

Where the man had been looking Ragnar noticed a distinct, bowl-shaped cavity in the surface of the wall.

"Did you think I would not have made a mark where I discovered it?" the old man asked, having taken notice of Ragnar's gaze. "Looks like a gouge in the wall's surface. No one else would take notice of it."

Taking a few steps forward, the old man came to a stop at the base of the wall, just beneath the depression in the wall. Using his right foot, the old man cleared a patch of ground, brushing away the snow on top of it.

With an air of triumph, he exclaimed, "There! My memory is not yet faded! It is as I remember it."

Bending over, the old man reached downward. Clutching with both hands onto a rust-covered ring set within a square made of rough, wooden planks, he grunted with exertion, a strained look coming to his face.

Pausing, he took a few deep breaths, and tried again. Nothing budged or came loose.

"This may be a better task for you," the old man said, stepping back, and breathing harder. "It has likely been many years since this was opened, and I do not have the strength for this."

Walking over, Ragnar crouched down and gripped the ring. Using his legs, in addition to his arms, back, and shoulders, he worked to open the tunnel.

With a sudden release of tension, the timber covering popped free of the frozen ground. Ragnar swayed back, holding onto the covering and keeping his feet in place.

A dark passage beckoning from within, the tunnel entrance lay open.

The old man smiled, looking into the tunnel opening. Falling snowflakes drifted into the dusky maw.

"As tall as you are, you will not be able to walk upright down there," he said. "But it will get you a good distance beyond the walls, in a way the things outside cannot see."

Staring at the hole in the ground, Ragnar boiled up with frustration. Scowling, he shook his head.

"But what does it matter?" Ragnar asked. "Even if I could get past the wights, where could I seek help for the people here? Any other settlements or villages are many days ride on horse away from the jarl's land. There is no horse to take through the tunnel, and the people here could not hold out that long."

The old man looked straight into Ragnar's eyes. Speaking

in a solemn timbre, he said, "I told you I would tell you more. The tunnel is only part of this. There are other things I did when younger, that may be of help now."

"If you know of anything that might be tried, do not delay in telling me," Ragnar said, growing impatient.

The old man reached inside his fur cloak and pulled out a small bronze amulet hanging from a leather cord about his neck. Taking the amulet off, he handed it over to Ragnar.

The circular piece had been crudely fashioned, containing some markings that Ragnar did not recognize. He suspected them to be some manner of runic symbols, though they resembled nothing he had ever seen among the northern people.

"What of this?" Ragnar asked, continuing to examine the amulet.

"A gift, given to me by someone I helped long ago ... someone who dwells by himself in the depths of the woods to the east," the old man replied. "I am sure he is still there, as the years do not take much of a toll upon him. I believe that he can help us."

"A sorcerer?" Ragnar asked, glancing back to the old man.

The old man nodded. "Yes, but not one who would call abominations from the ground. He stays to himself, and he has never had a quarrel with the people of this land."

"That does little to ease my concerns," Ragnar said, frowning. "Sorcerers can wield many kinds of powers, and, like any man or woman, they can choose to follow a different path from the one they took before."

"This one cares only for the things of the natural world, and would find these wights to be abominations, a violation of life itself," the old man responded. "Find him ... and give him this amulet. Tell him of everything that has happened here, and I assure you that he will help, if he can."

A chance, no matter how fraught with uncertainties, sounded far better than doing nothing. The relentless march of time would spare no one. Eroding the fortress' meager stocks of wood and food, the passage of a single day hastened an inevitable doom.

"How would I find this sorcerer?" Ragnar asked, resolving to undertake the attempt to find him.

"A broad stream leads to the cave where he lives," the old man said. "If you go east, from here, you will find the stream. Turn north and follow it. To reach the cave, it would not take you more than a day, at a modest walk. "

"If I found this sorcerer, who should I say sent me?" Ragnar queried, realizing he had not yet gotten the old man's name.

"I am Dvar," the old man replied. "He will remember me."

"And by what name is the sorcerer called?" Ragnar asked.

"Belshezan", the old man answered.

Ragnar nodded to the old man. "Then I will set out to find this Belshezan.".

***

Parting from Dvar, Ragnar took a little time to let Jarl Thryggvi and a few others know of what he had chosen to do. After filling a couple of small pouches with foodstuffs and tying them to his belt, he made his way back to the wall-walk.

Walking the full circumference, Ragnar admonished those involved with warding the ramparts to remain vigilant in their watch.

At last, he made his way to the ground and headed toward the tunnel entrance, finding Dvar still there when he arrived.

"It is time for me to see how far this tunnel goes, and then I will find a sorcerer," Ragnar announced.

"Return soon, Ragnar," Dvar said in a low voice, extending him a slight bow. A look of concern on his face, Dvar brought his eyes up to meet Ragnar's. "I shall pray to the gods until you have come back."

In the old man's eyes, Ragnar could see that Dvar feared for him. Knowing that he shouldered the fates of all within the fortress, including the old man, Ragnar sought to allay Dvar's worries.

"I do not intend to stay out there a moment longer than I need to," Ragnar replied. Setting his right hand down on the old man's shoulder, he continued, "Thank you for letting me know of the tunnel, and the sorcerer."

"I am defending myself, my tribe, and all who are in this fortress by doing so ... it is nothing to thank me for," Dvar replied, giving Ragnar another bow. "I have merely given what I know to a brave warrior, who can make good use of the knowledge."

"And I shall, Dvar ... and I will not say farewell, because I will see you again," Ragnar declared, before turning his full attention to the tunnel.

Lowering himself down into the hole, he readied to traverse the passageway. To his relief, the tunnel had been cut just wide enough to accommodate his broad shoulders without the need to turn sideways.

Needing to hunch far over to make his way through the tunnel, Ragnar pressed ahead in the dark. Keeping a hand in front of his face, he swiped away any cobwebs or detritus that he came into contact with.

The tunnel continued onward for a long while. Despite being slowed down from having to walk at a crouch, Ragnar knew the channel would take him a considerable distance from the rampart. Whether or not it was far enough to get past the wights encircling the fortress he had no way of telling until he emerged.

Ignoring the mounting discomfort, Ragnar made steady progress. Nothing disturbed the silence other than his breaths and the sounds of his boots, scraping and shuffling upon the dirt underfoot.

Coming to the end of the passageway, Ragnar found a square of timber planks above his head, similar to the hole covering at the other end. Setting his ear against it, he listened for a few moments, hearing nothing from the other side.

Placing his palms against the wood, he pushed upward. At first, the covering did not budge. It took a few powerful shoves to move the covering and break through the piled snow beyond it.

Able to stand up to his full height once more, Ragnar took in a long breath of the surface air, finding himself relieved to be free of the cramped, stagnant confines of the passageway. Grabbing onto the edges of the hole, Ragnar hoisted himself upward and climbed out of the tunnel.

Once outside, Ragnar looked around, ready to take up his axe in an instant. Alone and surrounded by trees, he could hear the cries of wights farther away.

Before moving onward, he took a few moments to put the covering back in place, laying brush and snow over it until he deemed the entryway well-concealed. After finding the faint form of the sun above, through a thinner patch of the drifting, gray cloud masses blanketing the skies, he set out to the east.

Light flurries of snow descended through the trees. Sharp tendrils of wind, carrying a deeper, biting chill, beat against Ragnar's face. Keeping his eyes out for any signs of movement, he marched through the woods, listening to the otherworldly cries growing more distant behind him.

Ragnar had begun to think that he had made it past all of the loathsome wights when a hideous shriek erupted from close by, resembling the grating of two pieces of metal. Taking up Raven Caller and holding the weapon in a two-handed grip, he looked about.

A short distance spread between them, two wights loped toward Ragnar through the trees, their gangly, long strides giving them an even more surreal appearance. Both had their teeth bared at him, lending their skeletal faces the appearance of morbid smiles.

Ragnar knew that he could not outrun them. Axe held firm, he conserved his energy and waited for the creatures to reach him. The gap between the two gave him a small boon, affording Ragnar the chance to engage the things one at a time.

The closest of the wights covered the remaining distance and bore down upon Ragnar. While imbued with unnatural strength and speed, the creature attacked in the manner of a feral beast, rather than a trained warrior, and rushed right at him.

Ducking low at the last moment and swinging his axe, Ragnar severed the right leg of the charging wight at the knee. The creature raked its claws through the right side of his cloak as it passed by. Toppling down fast, the wight slid a few paces on the snow-covered ground.

Ragnar took a few strides forward, putting some distance between him and the wounded creature. Readying to face the second incoming wight, he set his feet in a balanced stance.

Almost upon him, the wight barreled toward Ragnar in the same direct manner as the first. Jaws spreading wide, the creature bounded across the fast-dwindling ground remaining between them.

Behind Ragnar, the wounded one flopped about, making futile efforts to stand up.

With an ear-piercing screech, the second wight vaulted at him with its claws extended. Ragnar struck at the wight's head with his axe.

The blade rushed in over the outstretched claws, splitting the thing's skull between the jaws from the side. The upper part of the creature's head lolled at a bizarre angle, but the creature's momentum carried its body into Ragnar.

Knocked backward, but keeping to his feet, Ragnar grimaced as the tips of the thing's claws stabbed into his chest.

The countering force of his axe blow, in addition to the layers of his clothing, helped stymie the impact of the claws and prevent them from driving deeper, but the shallow wounds sent a sharp wave of pain throughout him.

Ragnar grabbed the creature with his left hand and threw it off him. Coming within a wisp of shouting curses at the thing, he held back at the last instant, not wanting the sound of a human voice to alert the wight's ilk to his presence.

Eyes blazing with furor, Ragnar advanced and stomped his right boot down, again and again, on the top and bottom of the creature's skull. Smashing and pulping its head to bits, Ragnar made sure there remained no viable chance the thing could reform.

Pulling itself along the ground in a scrabbling manner, using its remaining leg and arms, the first wight neared from behind. The cold light of its eyes fixed upon Ragnar.

Hearing the wight's movements, Ragnar turned around to face it. A crazed grin spreading across his face, he gripped his axe in both hands and leaped forward to meet the wight's approach.

Rearing up, the creature set loose a guttural screech. Taking one clumsy swipe at Ragnar, its claws raked through nothing but air before the wight fell under a torrent of heavy axe blows. Hacking and chopping the thing apart, Ragnar reduced the wight to pieces in a handful of moments.

Ceasing the mutilating barrage, Ragnar straightened up. Holding Raven Caller in his right hand, he lowered the weapon rest at his side.

The area fell back into silence as he paused to regain his breath. Eyeing the carnage about him, the trace of a smile remained on his lips.

Looking around, he saw no signs of any other wights through the trees. With his chest throbbing from the light wounds that he had incurred, Ragnar resumed his eastward march.

When the Cold Breathes

Ragnar continued east for several more leagues, stopping only now and then for a brief rest. He consumed a little of the food in his pouch, and for water melted snow in his hands.

The winds eased into a periodic flow of light breezes. Though thickening to where Ragnar could no longer make out the sun, the gray cloud masses above sprinkled thin flurries across the wooded landscape.

Trudging through a sea of birch and evergreen, Ragnar found the pervasive silence about him soothing. His chest still ached, but the pain had ebbed.

Only a few animal tracks marred the pristine snow blanketing the forest floor. The distant howling of a few wolves broke the stillness for a moment, but nothing other than Ragnar's breath, and his footsteps breaking through the snow, could be heard as he made his way farther east.

With the dense, overcast sky concealing the sun, Ragnar could not be certain about the time of the day, but he guessed it to be late in the afternoon when he finally came upon a broad stream. Now frozen and covered in snow, the winding channel had fashioned distinct embankments over the years on its southward flow.

Relieved to see the stream, Ragnar decided to take a short rest and consume a little more of the food he had brought with him. Making his way down to the edge of the stream, he took Raven Caller out and sat down, leaning his back against the embankment. He set the axe down at his right side.

Having kept a solid pace, Ragnar doubted he had much farther to go. His legs remained strong, and he judged that he could press harder if he needed to.

Reaching into one of the pouches at his belt, he scooped a few hazelnuts into his palm. Putting one into his mouth, he crunched it to bits and swallowed.

A light scraping noise and a puff of snow was all the warning Ragnar had when a large form hurtled down from above. Slammed to the ground, he rolled to the side, grappling with his assailant as his ears filled with a sound now all too familiar; a raspy, rattling hiss.

Grabbing both of the creature's narrow arms, he pinned the wight against the ground.

Jaws spread wide, the wight's head shot forward, set on a course to engulf Ragnar's face within its maw. The creature's elongated neck giving it enough range to reach him, Ragnar had no choice but to release his hold on the creature.

Letting go of one of the wight's arms, he brought his forearm up fast. Just before the wight's jaws covered his face, Ragnar jammed his forearm deep into the creature's mouth.

Pain raced through his arm. Crying out, Ragnar pressed down hard, knocking the wight's head against the ground. Lodged deep between its jaws, Ragnar's arm kept the thing's mouth wide open.

Shifting up on the wight's body, Ragnar brought his weight to bear upon the force applied through his forearm, pushing down harder and harder. The movement allowing him to bring his left leg high up, Ragnar drove his knee into the shoulder of the wight's free arm, immobilizing it once more.

Growling with exertion, Ragnar put every bit of strength he could muster into the downward press of his left arm.

A sharp crack accompanied the sudden release of pressure on his left arm. The upper and lower jaws of the wight slackened and shifted askew of each other. Rendered useless, the jaws no longer remained a threat.

Ragnar shouted in rage and yanked his left arm free of the wight's jaws. Ignoring the stabbing pain, he balled his hand into a fist and smashed it over and over into the wight's eyes. He continued the furious pummeling until the creature's skull fractured and the light in its eye sockets went dark.

Cursing and wincing in agony, Ragnar got up from the creature and retrieved his axe from where it lay on the ground. After dismembering the wight's body, he turned his attention to the burning pain afflicting his left arm.

Blood gleamed amid a shredded area of his tunic. Pulling the sleeve of the woolen garment up, Ragnar exposed a sight that stilled the breath in his lungs.

The wight's teeth had torn through the tunic and ripped into his flesh.

Using snow, Ragnar did his best to clean the wound. With the edge of his axe, he cut a strip from his cloak and bound the area of the bite.

Making his way up the embankment, he looked back on his tracks, seeing a second, distinctive set running alongside them. The wight had followed him all the way to the stream.

Ragnar could not ignore the stark truth facing him. All of those bitten by a wight had died, after less than half a day.

Time would now work against him fast. He had to find the sorcerer very soon, or death would claim him.

Cursing his predicament, Ragnar set out for the north, following the course of the stream.

After awhile, his entire body started to heat up, and a lightheaded sensation came over him. Ragnar knew the changes in his condition did not come from fatigue. The doom inflicted by the bite had begun to advance and take hold.

Setting his mind on the one imperative task looming before him, Ragnar pushed doubts and fears to the periphery of his mind.

When the light began dimming, Ragnar picked up his pace, hoping to find the cave before nightfall permeated the forest. Sweat trickled down his face and a slight dizziness came over him, though not yet enough to affect his balance.

Ragnar concentrated on his breathing and putting one foot in front of the other. Looking about, he tried to keep alert for any threats, but knew that he was growing less and less wary with the disease rising inside him.

Lungs beginning to strain from sustained exertion in the frigid air and the mounting effects of the sickness, Ragnar finally espied a cave ahead. The sight came as a tremendous relief, but he knew his task was far from complete.

Slowing down, he approached the gaping opening with caution, doing his best to keep an eye out for any movements. Not wanting to present any signs of hostility, Ragnar chose to keep Raven Caller in the loop at his belt.

A lone figure then walked out of the cave entrance and came to a stop a few paces beyond. Ragnar slowed further, but he did not stop.

Covered in furs, and thick of hair and beard, the figure before Ragnar looked to be something other than a man at a distance. In some lands, Ragnar had heard tales of beings who had characteristics of both beasts and humans, and he wondered if he was about to meet such a creature.

Ragnar kept walking forward. The figure remained in place, eyeing him, but making no movements.

A closer proximity dispelled any notions of an encounter with a non-human being. Ragnar knew that he looked upon a man, or at least something in a human guise covered in fur-skins.

Ragnar was the first to break the silence.

Though weary and increasingly ill, he called out in a steady voice, "I am Ragnar, son of Eirik ... sent to find one named Belshezan, in an hour of need. A man named Dvar told me of Belshezan."

Several heartbeats passed, and Ragnar began to doubt whether the figure understood him.

Finally, the figure replied in a deep voice, having an accent similar to that of the old man, "You have found Belshezan. Come near, and tell me of everything, Ragnar, son of Eirik."

Ragnar stepped forward, maintaining his caution. He drew to a halt a few paces way from Belshezan.

Ragnar spoke of all that he had experienced and witnessed, beginning with the pursuit of the shape-shifter and subsequent fight. He then told Belshezan of the pit and coming of the wights, and the urgent situation facing all within the fortress. Next, he related his encounter with Dvar and the revelation of the tunnel. He ended his account describing the trek eastward and the bite wound he had suffered while fighting the last wight.

Standing in silence and listening to all of it with an intent expression, Belshezan did not interrupt him.

When finished, Ragnar held out the amulet given to him by Dvar.

"Dvar told me to show this to you," Ragnar said.

The fur-clad figure gazed upon the amulet for a few moments, and then brought his eyes to meet those of Ragnar.

Within the other's gaze, Ragnar sensed no inkling of hostility, but he recognized the confident look of a fellow warrior.

"Dvar would not have given the amulet to you, if the situation was not perilous," Belshezan said, in an even tone. "We have no time to waste. Your wound must be tended. Then, before we go to bring aid to the others, a ritual must be performed. Remain here, I will be back in a moment."

Belshezan went back into the cave, returning several moments later with a small basket made of birch bark cradled in his left arm, and a little clay jar in his right hand. To Ragnar's eyes, the basket contained what looked to be a type of dried moss common to the area.

"Show me where the abomination bit you," Belshezan told Ragnar

Ragnar pulled the sleeve of his tunic up and unwrapped

the binding on the wound. A pungent aroma wafted up from the site, which now exhibited a greenish pus that oozed with the removal of the binding.

The skin around the wound had turned a reddish color. Like the strands of a spider's web, streaks of a similar hue radiated out from the site; the ones running up Ragnar's arm disappearing beneath the edge of his pulled-up tunic sleeve.

Ragnar had no desire to see how far the invasive, narrow streaks extended. The stench and pus dismayed him, telling him that the sickness had advance far.

After taking a close look at Ragnar's arm, Belzeshan set the basket down. Taking up a little of the moss in his left palm, he tilted the clay jar over it, sprinkling a fine powder atop.

After setting the clay jar down, he wetted the powder and moss with a handful of snow, mixing the two in the cup of his palm.

"Gird yourself," Belshezan said, looking to Ragnar with a firm expression.

Sending a searing pain throughout Ragnar's body, Belshezan pressed the wetted moss and powder mixture into the wound. Holding it firm in place, Belshezan closed his eyes and muttered words in a tongue Ragnar did not recognize.

Ragnar clenched his teeth and endured the fiery pain. At last, Belshezan released his hold.

"Keep your arm up, I will need to make a new binding," he said. "You must allow me to cut a piece of your cloak or tunic."

"The cloak," Ragnar muttered, the wound throbbing. With his free hand, he reached up and unclasped the cloak, letting it fall to the ground.

Belshezan took up the cloak. Producing a small bone-handled knife from a hide sheath at his waist, he took a few moments to cut another long strip.

When finished, he wrapped it snug about the wound.

"You will heal," Belshezan said. "And it will speed the healing where the abomination's claws stabbed into your chest."

"You have my gratitude," Ragnar said.

"You may not feel gratitude when I tell you that there is no time for rest," Belshezan said. "You must come with me now."

Ragnar leaned over and picked up his cloak, fastening it again at his neck. "I did not think we would tarry."

Belshezan collected up the basket and jar, and then took them back into the cave. When he returned, the sorcerer led Ragnar into the forest, continuing until they reached the edge of a small clearing, not far away from the cave entrance.

A broad array of objects, some of bone and others crafted of wood, hung down from the branches of surrounding trees. Facing inward, into the clearing, a large number of symbols had been carved into the trunks of several trees.

"Remain here, and do not fear what you see," Belshezan said. "I must take another form before I can summon the aid that is needed."

Leaving Ragnar at the perimeter, Belshezar walked slowly to the center of the clearing. Raising his arms, Belshezar leaned his head back and looked skyward, speaking a few words in a strange language before closing his eyes and appearing to fall into some kind of trance.

Though uneasy in the presence of a sorcerer, Ragnar watched the ritual unfold in a state of fascination. Though his breathing had improved somewhat, and sweat no longer beaded and trickled down his face, lingering dizziness from the effects of his arm wound added to the surreal atmosphere.

Belshezan then lowered himself to the ground. Remaining silent and keeping his eyes closed, he appeared to be waiting for something.

Skin tingling all over, the air distorted more than once before Ragnar's eyes, blurring his vision in successive waves. He sensed a gathering energy around him; though for what purpose he did not know, until Belshezan began to twist and convulse.

Though Belshezan appeared to be enveloped in the throes of a terrible pain, Ragnar heeded the sorcerer's admonition and stayed in place. His eyes widened when Belshezan's skin began pulsing and contorting, accompanied by a series of cracking and popping sounds.

On instinct, Ragnar's hand lowered and grabbed the haft of his axe. Seeing that Belshezan was changing form, a deeper unease spread through him in moments. Leaving the axe in the loop at his belt, he kept his hand in place. He had to trust Belshezan, who had forewarned him that he would take another form, but Ragnar was not about to abandon caution.

The fur-skins that Belshezan wore appeared to be merging with his body. His nose and jaws protruding to form a broad snout, the sorcerer's form expanded further in bulk and height.

Higher on Belshezan's head, a pair of large, rounded ears rose into view and pushed upward. Limbs repositioned and thickened, with hands and feet enlarging and widening, becoming huge paws.

When the transformation finished, a massive brown bear stood in the center of the clearing before Ragnar's eyes. The creature was much larger than any bear that roamed Ragnar's homelands.

The great bear then turned his gaze toward Ragnar.

In the bear's eyes, Ragnar saw the same quality he had recognized in the eyes of the other sorcerer that had taken the form of the Mayak. He had to remind himself that he still looked upon Belshezan, and not a wild beast.

The bear then reared up on its back two legs, reaching a towering height. Angling his head toward the sky, Belshezan loosed a roar that shook the forest.

Instead of ebbing, the roar took on a deeper tone and

persisted, a sound unlike any made by a bear of the natural world.

After sustaining the unusual roar for several moments, the bear fell into silence. Dropping down, the bear returned his bulk upon all four of his legs. Belshezan remained in place, and he looked to be waiting for something.

Far in the distance, a group of howls broke out in the night. Then, coming from afar, in the opposite direction, another cluster of howls erupted.

The wolfish chorus was then followed by a staggered cascade of lone roars; a few of them sounding akin to bears, and others unfamiliar to Ragnar's ears.

Captivated at the extraordinary development, Ragnar could only wonder at what was taking place. More howls and roars broke out all over the woodlands, several of them sounding faint, coming from even farther away.

Belshezan then looked to Ragnar again and gave a low growl. Ambling forward, the bear started for the side of the clearing opposite from where Ragnar stood. After a few strides, the bear looked back and growled at Ragnar once more.

Understanding what Belshezan wanted, Ragnar followed after as the bear resumed walking. He kept a little distance between himself and the bear, but had no trouble keeping up with the massive creature.

The sorcerer's treatment worked fast upon Ragnar's bite wound. The dizziness and increased body heat that had been plaguing him faded in a gradual manner. The area of the wound ceased throbbing, and then settled into a dull ache.

Heading west, Ragnar set his mind to a long night march that he knew would culminate in the besieged fortress.

**

Night had long since fallen and weariness tugged with insistence at Ragnar's limbs when the bear departed from their course along the lower ground running through a series of hills. The telltale shrieks and cries of wights had been carrying along the night winds for some while, and Ragnar knew they had drawn close to the fortress.

Holding his axe in hand as a precaution, Ragnar could only hope that the bear did not lead them right into a mass of the vile things.

Following the great bear and trudging up the slope of a small hill, Ragnar soon found himself looking out over the fortress from the north. Standing a few paces to his right, Belshezan gazed downward.

Sparse flurries enabled Ragnar to see everything well enough.

Sentries patrolled the wall-walk, all around the perimeter, and several fires burned in the open among the huts and roofed storage pits within the fortress interior. Ragnar took a little relief from the sight of the fortress still being warded and in good order.

Ragnar could see the shadowy forms of wights moving among the trees all around the stronghold. A cursory appraisal of their numbers told him that far more of the things were out there than he had first thought, or else more had come since he had left to find Belshezan.

Doubting the latter, Ragnar found it most likely that the cavern under the barrows had emptied out when the wights had been set free. The presence of so many more than he had first estimated reinforced the absolute necessity of Ragnar's mission to find the sorcerer.

Belshezan then padded forward. Taking his axe out, Ragnar took a step and began to follow after him, when the bear turned and stomped his front paws hard upon the ground. A rumbling growl coming from the depths of his throat, the bear fixed his gaze upon Ragnar.

Glaring at Belshezan, Ragnar said in a firm voice, "I do not avoid battles. Do not stop me from going."

Even harder than before, the huge bear hammered his front paws against the ground. Locking eyes with Ragnar, Belshezan roared, swinging his great head back and forth.

Comprehending the bear's gesture, and deciding to trust the sorcerer, Ragnar nodded. Sliding Raven Caller back into the loop at his belt, he took a step back. The bear grunted, and made an exaggerated nod in response, before turning away from Ragnar.

Keeping to the top of the rise, Ragnar watched as the bear trundled down the slope, heading toward the fortress.

About midway down, the bear slowed to a halt. Rearing up, Belshezan loosed another sustained roar of the type Ragnar had heard much earlier that night, back in the clearing near to the sorcerer's cave. The sonorous call reverberated off the hills and carried into the far reaches of the night.

When finished with the extended roar, the bear took to four legs again and resumed his downward path.

Ragnar could see an outburst of movement within the fortress in reaction to the thunderous outcry. Sentries on the wall-walk looked in the direction of the hill Ragnar stood upon, while others from within flocked to the wall along the northern side.

The wights outside the rampart also responded to the bear's roar, with many of the things starting at once for the base of the hill. Striding fast through the trees, they converged from all over into a broad mass flowing north.

Their shrill cries, shrieks and wails carrying up the slope to Ragnar, he readied to take up his axe when they got past Belshezan..

The bear continued lumbering downhill, showing no sign of concern at the approach of so many wights. Ragnar knew the bear could see the pale-skinned fiends. Seeing no possible way that Belshezan could face such large numbers of the fell creatures, he wondered at the sorcerer's purpose.

Ragnar did not have long to wait.

Another cacophony broke out and filled the night. Entirely different from the ghastly chorus heralding the oncoming horde of wights, nothing unnatural dwelled within the sounds erupting all around Ragnar; howls in abundance, accompanied by a rising number of roars.

From all directions, sleek forms raced through the trees in great numbers, many of them with coats of a tawny hue, others more gray in appearance, and a few either black or white. Their emergence preceded a substantial number of much bigger, dark shapes, whose powerful bounds threw up tufts of snow.

Here and there, large, more elongated white shapes propelled fast across the snow upon massive paws. Outpacing the others, a couple of them reached the forefront of the newcomers by the time they closed in upon the wights ringing the fortress.

Ragnar found it hard to believe what he was seeing, but he could not deny the astonishing sight before his eyes; a host of wolves, bears, and snow tigers, running together as a single, combined force.

Ragnar's eyes widened moments later, recognizing a few brawny creatures with a unique appearance that he identified at once. Exhibiting pronounced, sabre-like fangs, the huge, muscular cats charged across the ground, adding their number to the incoming throngs of predators,

A fair number of smaller shapes then joined with the burgeoning multitude. Ragnar realized from their distinctive gait that they were wolverines. Though not as large as the others, the creatures possessed great ferocity rivaling the most formidable of the other predators.

The last to arrive in the attacking horde surprised Ragnar the most. Broad of body and set lower to the ground, displaying elements of both wolverines and large hunting cats, at least two

Mayaks could be seen among the growing multitude of predators.

Hastening from all over, the rightful denizens of the forest had the wights encircled, trapped against the ditch and rampart of the stronghold. The mass of wights striding toward Belshezan came to a halt, just before the two sides collided.

A battle like no other Ragnar had ever witnessed commenced.

Fangs and claws tore into the bodies of the wights.

Wolves worked in tandem to bring many entities to the ground, where groups of them ripped the things apart in a savage frenzy.

Using their huge claws, bears mauled several of the ghoulish figures. Ragnar witnessed more than one wight's head go flying, batted off its body by a single, powerful swipe. The ursine assailants wielded their massive jaws to devastating effect, tearing limbs off some wights and decapitating others.

Adding to the growing carnage, Mayaks, snow tigers, wolverines, and sabre-toothed cats leaped onto wights everywhere Ragnar looked, clawing and sinking their fangs deep.

Using their own lengthy talons and crushing bites, the wights fought back against their attackers. Whether eviscerated, mutilated, or having their throats ripped open, many of the forest predators fell during the ferocious struggle.

The sprawling melee around the fortress soon reached a crescendo, the cries of beasts and wights swelling to a peak.

Ragnar could then see the fighting tilting fast in the favor of the forest and mountain predators. Their numbers diminishing with every passing moment, more and more of the wights succumbed to the relentless onslaught.

The woodland beasts rushed to the assistance of each other, wherever one of them found themselves in peril from wights.

Ragnar observed a Mayak come to the aid of a hard-pressed wolf, the latter snapping its jaws at a pair of wights poised to attack it from two sides. Slamming into one of the wights from the side, the Mayak engulfed the thing and tore into it, while the wolf lunged at the other, clamping its jaws about the wight's extended neck. Moments later, the Mayak and wolf bounded away to seek out other opponents, leaving two headless corpses lying in the snow behind.

Not long after, Ragnar witnessed a snow tiger race in to help a brown bear under assault from three wights at once. Barreling into two of the wights, the snow tiger broke the entrapment of the bear. The snow tiger and bear then assailed the wights, shredding the things apart in quick fashion.

The cooperation astounded Ragnar. It seemed as if all enmity between the wild predators had been put aside for a common cause; to rid their lands of wicked entities that belonged in the realms of death.

Ragnar then understood why Belshezan had reacted so forcibly when he had tried to follow the bear down the slope. Everything on two legs among the trees stood as an enemy in the eyes of the bestial attackers. In the speed and confusion of a swirling, frenzied battle, the sorcerer did not wish for Ragnar to find himself beset by both animal and wight.

Whittling down in number, the wights made no effort to flee the battle. Fighting against their attackers to the last, they continued lashing out with their bites and claws until the air no longer carried even one of their otherworldly cries.

A deep hush fell across the fortress and woodlands.

Corpses of those that had fallen littered the forest all around the human stronghold. Ragnar remained in place for a little while, watching the beasts congregating in a great mass a short distance beyond the gates of the fortress.

A lone figure stood before the predators, a great bear Ragnar suspected to be Belshezan, the one who had summoned all of them to come together in defense of the lands they hunted.

When all of the surviving predators had gathered into a single, sprawling multitude, the bear walked forward, the others parting to allow him passage through their midst. Once through, Belshezan led the beasts onward in one great horde, heading eastward.

Wolves walked alongside bears, wolverine and Mayak padded forth side by side, and sabre-tooth cats strode shoulder to shoulder with snow tigers.

Like the battle, the massive procession was like nothing Ragnar had ever seen. In silence from atop the hill, the northern warrior gazed upon their departure, until the last of them was lost from sight.

Ragnar then took his axe up and started forward, heading down the slope. Reaching the base of the hill, he made his way around to the front gates of the fortress. His path took him through a vast swathe of carnage from the brutal conflict.

Keeping his axe in hand, he remained guarded, eyeing the corpses around him. Nothing moved, and the only interruption in the stillness came when Ragnar drew within sight of the ramparts. Many of the sentries atop the wall-walk called down to him in a jubilant spirit, breaking the heaviness clinging to the air.

From atop the wall-walk, Cnut shouted to Ragnar when he finally neared the front gates. "Ragnar! It gladdens my heart to see you! Praise all the gods and goddesses!"

"Open these gates and let me in," Ragnar replied, smirking. "I am beyond hungry and thirsty, and there are no longer any threats out here. You better have a little meat, honey, and drink in there, or I will ransack this fortress by myself!"

"We still have all three, and none would dare prohibit you from having as much as you want!" Cnut said, his words cheered by many of those around him.

"Keep that thought in mind when I am filling my belly and going through cups," Ragnar called back, chuckling.

"We owe our lives to you," Cnut shouted back.

"You owe your lives to yourselves," Ragnar said. "You kept your discipline and held this fortress."

"The beasts? Was that of your making?" Cnut asked, as Ragnar reached the gates, now creaking open.

"Yes, they were, and there is much to tell," Ragnar answered, evoking looks of amazement on Cnut and all those standing on the wall-walk, watching him pass through the entrance.

Just inside the gates, among the throng milling about, a familiar figure smiled in greeting at him. Ragnar paused before the old man.

"You have returned," Dvar stated. "And you found him."

Ragnar grinned. "Not what I expected him to be."

Reaching inside his cloak, Ragnar took out the amulet Dvar had given him. He handed it over to the old man.

"I am alive enough to say I am able to return this to you," Ragnar said. "I have no need of it."

The old man cradled the amulet in his wrinkled hands, looking upon it with a fond expression. He looked back to Ragnar.

"Thank you, this brings good memories to me in the winter of my life," Dvar said with a genuine air of gratitude.

"Perhaps a story to tell me over many cups of that drink made of rye so loved around here," Ragnar said, giving the old man a wink.

"Ah yes ... *kvas* is good ... very good," Dvar replied, smiling and laughing.

Extending his right arm, Ragnar patted the old man on the shoulder and continued past him. "We will speak later. It is time for me to indulge in a little food, drink, and rest."

"Food, drink, and rest that is more than earned, Ragnar," Dvar replied, lowering his head in a bow to the striding warrior.

When the Cold Breathes

***

Before taking to rest inside one of the huts, Ragnar met with Jarl Thryggvi and told him of everything that had happened. The old jarl listened to the tale with a spellbound expression.

A couple of women hurried to fashion a meal for Ragnar, consisting of salted fish, a rather filling mushroom soup, honey, and a large quantity of berries and hazelnuts. Famished, Ragnar ate to his fill, drinking the fare down with several cups of *kvas*

Adding weight to the fatigue bearing down upon him, the drink relaxed him further.

When finished eating, Ragnar returned to the hut where he had been sleeping. Piling up a few skins in the corner of the rectangular hut, Ragnar shed his cloak, boots, and main tunic. Setting Raven Caller by his side, he then lay down.

Little time passed before Ragnar eased into the refuge of a much-needed sleep.

***

When Ragnar awoke, daylight reigned.

After donning his clothes, boots, and cloak, he proceeded outside, filing his lungs with the fresh winter air. A late-afternoon sun peeked out now and then between large, gray swathes of clouds. A few snowflakes drifted down here and there, but for the most part everything stood clear.

Ragnar found that most all of the villagers had gone outside the fortress. Walking through the gates and looking around, he saw that a gruesome task was well underway. Every able-bodied man, woman and child worked together in the ongoing effort, helping to gather all the pieces of the wights that could be found into a great pile that was put to flame soon after.

Nothing was left uncollected. The smallest chunk of flesh, ear, or other body part from the wicked entities was picked up

141

from the forest floor and added to the fire. Sending thick coils of smoke skyward and emitting a flurry of hisses, sizzles and pops, the flames consumed every last bit of the corrupted flesh.

The bodies of the villagers' four-legged benefactors were brought to another, more formal pyre. The second pyre stood as a gesture of respect to the sorcerer who had called them, and an expression of gratitude and reverence to the wilderness creatures themselves.

A brief inquiry of a passing villager informed Ragnar that there had been no signs of the beasts that had survived the battle, since the mass of them had headed east with Belshezan. The tidings left him with a gnawing uncertainty, and concern for the fate of the sorcerer.

Seeing Ragnar after heaving another body of a wight into the fire, Cnut strode over to him.

"I hope you have gained some rest," he said.

"Enough for now," Ragnar replied. "What you do here is wise. And it is good that you show regard to those who saved the people here."

"We would deserve to have the fiends overrun us if we did not," Cnut replied. He shook his head. "It is still hard for me to believe everything that happened last night, even if I saw it with my own eyes, from the wall-walk."

"There are many things in this world I find hard to believe," Ragnar said, with a rueful chuckle. "And a great number of those things do not involve wights, sorcerers, or an army of forest beasts. We can choose to ignore our instincts, what we see with our own eyes, or what others see with theirs, but a great many things still happen, whether we believe in them or not."

"I understand," Cnut said, looking back to Ragnar with a somber expression. "And I do know what I saw last night."

"Has it been decided how long everyone will remain in the fortress?" Ragnar asked. "The villages are no longer under threat."

"We will stay one more night in the fortress, just to be careful," Cnut said. "Then we will return to our villages and homes. Everyone is filled with relief. The food here would not have lasted for much longer."

"The forests are yours to hunt and fish again," Ragnar said.

"We have sent some groups of hunters out, and some others lower lines through the ice, not far from here," Cnut said. "There is a chance we shall all eat better tonight."

Ragnar smiled. "Let us hope their hunts and fishing meet with great success."

"Thank you again, Ragnar, for what you did," Cnut said. "You have the gratitude of all of us. I promise you, the tales of Ragnar Storrmbinger shall be told in these lands for ages to come."

Ragnar nodded, though in his heart he derived no particular thrill from the promise of tales told in future ages. When he no longer drew breath in the world, Ragnar could derive no joy from anything spoken about him in future ages.

His actions had made certain that his own life and path would proceed, into an unknowable future. Once again, Ragnar had been measured, and been judged up to the task, but that did not mean he could become lax or overconfident. An even greater challenge could loom on the near horizon.

The only thing Ragnar could be certain of was that he was determined to meet any challenge with a raging fire in his heart and Raven Caller in his hands.

***

When the winter drew toward an end at last, and the promise of spring loomed near, Ragnar set out from Jarl Thryggvi's settlement. Resuming his journey to lands far to the south, he carried only the most essential of items in the pouches at his belt.

Taking a different path at first, Ragnar headed west. After coming across a familiar stream, now flowing with sparkling, clear waters, he turned north, finding his way once more to the cave dwelling of the woodland sorcerer who had aided the villagers.

An answer awaited him, to a question that had lingered ever since the villagers had returned to their homes.

As had occurred upon their first meeting, a man covered in thick furs emerged from the cave opening at Ragnar's approach. This time, a welcoming smile rested upon Belshezan's face.

The sight flooded Ragnar with relief. The last time that he had seen Belshezan, he had been in the form of a bear leading a teeming horde of feral predators farther east. Predators had returned to hunt in the forests, but there had been no sign of the sorcerer.

Ragnar had undertaken two jaunts to the cave, finding no one there, and the visit he now made stood as his last chance to learn whether Belshezan had survived the ordeal with the wights.

"You look relieved to see me alive," Belshezan greeted him.

"I cannot deny that," Ragnar said, grinning back at the sorcerer. "I made two journeys here since we last parted, and I did not find you here."

"I have had to attend to many things," Belshezan replied, offering no more in the way of explanation.

"I never got the chance to thank you, Belshezan," Ragnar said. "You left before I could get down the hill."

"We could not spare a moment. I had to make certain nothing was left under the barrows," Belshezan said. "I looked into other matters and then returned here, after all had been done. I have little interest in the affairs of villages and settlements. I am content to live here, the way I wish."

"I can understand that," Ragnar said, chuckling. "One day I may seek such a place to live myself."

"What else brings you here?" Belshezan asked, a curious

look to his eyes.

"Perhaps it is just to set my eyes on you, and see that you came to no harm, before I leave these lands behind," Ragnar said. Though a smile remained on his face, the words held no exaggeration.

A glint of amusement reflected in the sorcerer's eyes.

"I must say, a lot of time has passed since anyone had concern over my well-being," Belshezan replied, rumbling with laughter.

"Call it honoring a fellow warrior and ally, who came to my aid in a great hour of need," Ragnar said.

"I could say that you came to my aid," Belshezan replied, the levity fading from his tone and face.

"How would that be so?" Ragnar asked, puzzled at the response.

"The sorcerer you killed ... the shape shifting one who summoned the wights ... was my brother," Belshezan stated.

"Your brother?" Ragnar asked.

Taking the revelation in, Ragnar found that he was not as surprised as he thought he would have been.

Memories of eyes looking back at him, one involving the gaze of a Mayak, and the other the gaze of a great, brown bear, passed through his mind. He recalled the strange, distinct nature of the two creatures' eyes.

Neither human nor bestial, but rather a blending of both, the eyes testified to a bond shared between the two creatures. Both sorcerers able to shift their shapes, the words of Belshezan made perfect sense.

"A brother who chose another path and vanished long ago ... to pursue that darker path in the frigid haunts of the far, far north, where powers ancient and wicked thrive in wastelands devoid of living beings," Belshezan continued, with an air of regret. "Those barrows west of the fortress contained a great concentration of dark energies that many others have sought to harness.

"Not long ago, I sensed my brother had returned, and now all is clear to me. The barrows offered a source of dark power irresistible to him ... and behind them something got its tendrils into him ... to manipulate him for another purpose. Such is the path when one turns to darkness. Seeking to become a master, one becomes a slave.

"I knew he would seek to invoke the things that can be drawn from the depths of the world ... things that should never walk in the light of day or under the stars at night. It is good that you reached me when you did. Though my brother died, he had unleashed a terrible power that would have grown fast if it had not been stopped."

"Is there still any threat from the barrows?" Ragnar queried, his curiosity piqued further.

"The grounds where the barrows are found have been searched," the sorcerer replied. "What had been in them was emptied out, when the wights came forth, and any darkness lingering there has been cleansed."

"Is it certain that this darkness cannot return?" Ragnar asked.

"Who truly knows what will happen today, or much less tomorrow?" Belshezan responded. "Why worry about what might come? Decide to act, when something happens. It is all we can do in this world."

In full agreement with the sorcerer's perspective, Ragnar grinned. "It would seem you and I hold a few things in common."

"I see that as well," Belshezan said, with another smile. "And if you are ever in these lands again, know that you will always have an ally in me."

Giving a short bow of his head, Ragnar replied, "Know that you will always have an ally in me, as well."

Ragnar looked up to the sun, still climbing from its morning rise. A full day's march remained, and he could not delay his journey any longer.

"The day waits for no one and I must go onward," Ragnar said, looking back to the sorcerer. "But I will leave with more ease of mind, after coming here."

"May your travels bring you to a place where your spirit shines brightest, warrior" Belshezan declared.

"May your journey bring you to such a place as well," Ragnar replied, his grin growing broader.

Turning, Ragnar strode away from the sorcerer and the cave entrance, heading for the south and even greater challenges on the horizon.

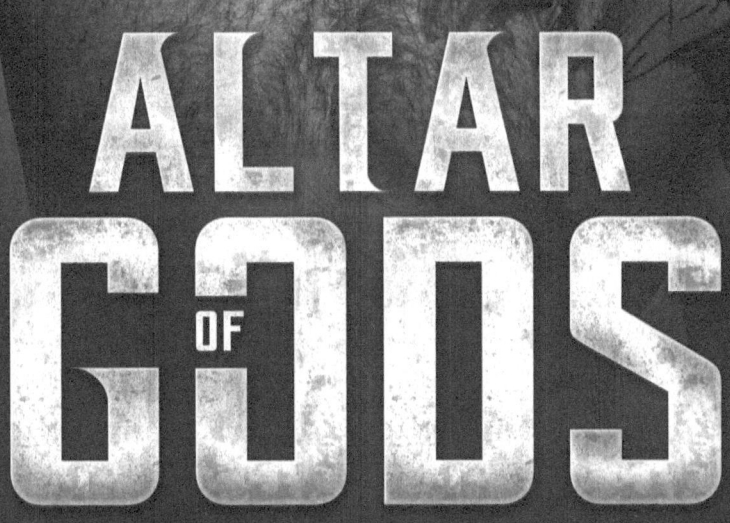

ALTAR
OF GODS

A RAGNAR STORMBRINGER TALE

STEPHEN ZIMMER

ALTAR OF GODS

"Give me the worst of a northern winter over this oppressive, hell-spawned heat," Freyyar muttered. Soaked in sweat, the brawny warrior breathed heavily, leaning against a tree.

"Watch where you rest yourself," Ragnar warned him. "These forests are full of unwelcome things."

"You cannot guess at anything in this infernal place," another warrior named Magnolf said, an exasperated look upon his face.

Ragnar shook his head. "To guess wrong is death."

Images of one of his fellow warriors clutching at his stomach in agony passed through Ragnar mind. Dead before night had fallen, the man had eaten just a little of what looked to all eyes to be a luscious fruit. In his hunger, the man had gotten careless, and he had paid a terrible price.

To Ragnar's eyes, it seemed as if death lurked beneath every leaf, within every hole or crevice, and under the surface of every body of water within the strange land. From bizarre, lethal plants to giant insects, the land the stranded warriors traveled through held a multitude of threats.

Pursued by tribal war parties, lost in a hostile wilderness with less than seventy-five fellow survivors from the north, Ragnar did not dwell on their chances for survival. To do so would be to burden his spirit; right when he needed every last bit of inner strength.

Yet he could not evade the truth. Even if they somehow escaped their pursuers and made it out of the dense forests, a return to their homelands looked impossible.

Their well-built northern vessels had held together during the storm that had carried them so far off course. Another storm, following a seemingly endless trial on the open seas, had been far too much for the fleet of long ships.

Dashing them against rocks in shallows, the last storm had shattered the sleek vessels apart. Many warriors were lost to sea and drowned in the aftermath, save for a small number hardy enough to reach the shore.

Everything that could be salvaged along the shoreline the following day had been gathered up, and every significant portion of ship wreckage was searched through for weapons, foodstuffs, and other materials.

Ragnar had been counted among those who emerged from the seas with their lives. Somehow, during the chaotic tumult he had also managed to retain his great war axe, Raven Caller.

The weapon had since demonstrated a thirst for the blood of the area's native inhabitants, who had shown nothing but hostility to the shipwrecked northerners. No less than two small war bands had skirmished with the band of survivors so far.

The attacking warriors' unfamiliar weapons and attire, painted faces, pierced lips and noses, distended ear lobes, and distinctive hair arrangements made it clear that the northerners faced an enemy unlike any they had before. Even stranger, the fighting showed that the enemy warriors were more interested in taking prisoners than killing the foreigners outright.

The realization left a great mystery in its wake as to what the native warriors did with a captive. Ragnar imagined the discovery of the answer would prove to be an extremely unpleasant experience, and he intended to take the life of any warrior seeking to make him a prisoner.

A faint rustling drew Ragnar's attention toward the ground. Emerging from some foliage, a huge, thick-bodied spider covered in vivid blue hairs stalked across the forest floor. Passing right in front of Ragnar, the creature paid him no heed and disappeared back into the damp undergrowth.

"I thought you might have stomped that ugly thing into the ground," remarked Magnolf.

"We are not its prey, and it is far more accepting of our presence here than the humans who dwell in this miserable land," Ragnar told the tall, dark-haired warrior.

"Those I would like to stomp into the ground," Magnolf replied. Whether conscious of the action or not, he ran his right hand over a torn strip of cloth wrapped about a section of his arm, where he had suffered an extended gash at the hands of enemy warriors.

The sight reminded him of the different nature of their enemy's weapons. They did not use honed iron, or any other metal, in the making of them. Instead, they made extensive use of a black type of stone that could be fashioned into edges having a hellish sharpness to them.

Before Ragnar could respond to the warrior, an urgent cry rang out through the trees.

On his feet in an instant, Ragnar kept a firm grip on his axe and bounded in the direction of the outcry. After hurdling over a fallen tree trunk, he set his eyes upon a couple of his comrades, kneeling on the ground ahead.

Leaning over, they looked to be pulling hard at something beneath them.

A muffled cry sounded, and Ragnar realized that it had come from underneath whatever the two men were yanking at.

"Grenna is in there!" the warrior on the right shouted, his words tumbling out fast in an air of panic. "This has shut tight over him! It is a plant, but of a tough substance! I cannot get it open!"

"Not too tough for this," Ragnar declared, with a growling edge to his voice. Shortening his grip on Raven Caller, he told the men before him, "Back away! Now! Give me space!"

At once the other two ceased in their feverish efforts and made way for their huge comrade.

Using his right hand, Ragnar swung the axe and cleaved through the back edge of the oblong shape. Well-honed iron sliced through the plant growth, cutting the top free in an instant.

Reaching down with his left hand, Ragnar took hold of the near edge and pulled the top away, exposing a big cavity beneath. Within the pit, Grenna reached upward, treading some kind of liquid.

"It burns!" Grenna called out, his face brimming with terror. "The sides! They are slick! There is nothing to grab onto! Get me out of here, Ragnar!"

True to Grenna's word, the sides of the bulbous space had a smooth, glistening surface all throughout. A trap for prey of flesh and blood, the carnivorous growth had rendered Grenna helpless.

"Grab onto the haft," Ragnar instructed Grenna while changing the grip on his axe. He extended the lower part of the haft toward the trapped man.

Reaching upward, Grenna grabbed tight onto the lower end of the haft. Using both of his arms and stepping back, making use of his powerful legs, Ragnar hauled Grenna out of the pit.

Once free of the cavity, Grenna loosed his grip on the haft and collapsed in a heap to the forest floor.

Looking closer at Grenna, Ragnar eyed the reddish hue that covered the warrior's skin. He glanced back to the opening in the ground, large enough to swallow up a man or large animal.

"Today, you are a fortunate man, Grenna," Ragnar stated.

"How?" Grenna asked, looking up to Ragnar with a confused look on his face. He winced. "I am burning all over. My head, my neck, my arms!"

"Find water, get it off," Ragnar said.

"Get what off?" Grenna asked. "What is happening to me?"

"You were being eaten by that plant," Ragnar told him, coming to a full understanding of what had just happened. "You would not have been able to climb out with the smooth, slick sides. You would have tired and sank into the plant's juices. In time they would have consumed you, like food in our bellies."

"I thought it was water. It smelled so sweet too. I did not realize how deep that plant went!" Grenna said, his eyes still wide with fear. "I leaned over to get a drink, and that top closed fast, knocking me inside."

"It is good that we learned of this kind of plant," Ragnar said.

"What other horrors lurk in this accursed forest?" Grenna said.

"We must be wary, at all times," Ragnar told him. "Now go … and get those juices off you."

Ragnar looked up at the two men who had been trying to save him.

"Go with Grenna to the stream near us, and keep a watch over him," Ragnar said. "As you have seen, this place is full of dangers."

The two helped Grenna to his feet and led him off to find the stream near to their place that served as a temporary encampment. A host of thoughts weighing upon his mind, Ragnar turned and strode back in the direction he had come from.

***

Night had fallen and a variety of unfamiliar sounds swelled from within the forest depths surrounding them. The strange noises served as a constant reminder to Ragnar of their ultimate predicament; being stranded in an unknown land with no solid idea of a route of return to their homeland.

"What we have seen is much like Gardar described," Ragnar said, eyeing Ursalka and Magnolf. Both sat to his right, near the crackling flames of a small fire they had used to cook the meat of some kind of wild pig that one of the warriors had taken down with a well-thrown spear a little earlier. "A strange and dangerous land, with promise of an abundance of gold and silver."

"Do you think were are now in the lands Gardar spoke of?" Ursalka asked. A distinct lilt in her voice betrayed her keen interest in the matter to Ragnar.

"Many thought his tales to be the fanciful ravings of an old man wishing to be remembered," Magnolf stated, staring into the fire. He looked over to Ragnar. "Also, do not forget that many tales grow with the telling of them."

"And sometimes they are ravings, with other men," Ragnar said. "But my father's father spoke of how Gardar had a rare courage and restless spirit. If anyone braved lands reached by no northerner before, it would be him."

"We sought to find the lands spoken of by Larthros," Magnolf said. "But at least he brought back many objects of proof. There are no doubts of his claims."

"Gardar was said to go much farther than Larthros, and then somehow he found his way back toward the end of his days," Ragnar said. "I believe we were almost at the lands spoken of by Larthros, when the first great storm took us far to the south. It is possible the next storm pushed us to the coast of the lands Gardar roamed."

"Then, if Gardar spoke true, maybe it is true that lands filled with gold and silver exist," Ursalka said, a grin forming on her lips. "And maybe it is true that we are in those lands."

"My father always told me to be very cautious of what you

desire," Ragnar said.

"We have over sixty warriors here," Ursalka replied. "We have seen little of the people in these lands, and what few we have seen have been in small bands of warriors. We have battled them off twice now, with little trouble."

"A wilderness with a few small tribes, nothing more," Magnolf added, with a dismissive air.

"We have barely scratched the surface of these lands," Ragnar said, glancing to each of them. "Who knows what is hidden within the depths of these accursed forests? Plants that form traps that can swallow a warrior like Grenna ... spiders with bodies as big as my hand ... long, fast creatures that possess a host of legs. No, these are not our forests. We must go forward with caution."

Ursalka laughed. "Maybe there are threats to one of us, here or there. But nothing that can be deemed a threat to a war band of northerners."

Ragnar looked at her and said nothing. She reflected the overconfidence that he saw building in many of the warriors after the second skirmish with the native warriors.

He knew that they had just begun working their way deeper inland. In his view, new discoveries could be forthcoming that presented graver threats than what they had encountered on the outskirts of the land.

"What concerns you, Stormbringer?" Magnolf asked, in a low voice.

"I will fight anything that comes against us," Ragnar said, a flare in his eyes. "But it is like we are adrift at sea. We have nothing to guide our course."

"The gods will look over us," Ursalka said.

"What about the gods who hold dominion here?" Ragnar asked her. "We do not even know what gods are followed here."

"Then we will have to trust to our gods," Magnolf said.

***

Delving deeper into the hot, damp forest, heading further west, Ragnar and the others set out to explore the land and discover what they could. The morning passed without any signs of human habitation.

Sustenance did not prove difficult to find. Arrows brought down another wild pig like the one from the previous day, and several fish were pulled from a deep stream they came across.

All of the warriors took a few moments to gaze in wonder at a snake track that one of them had come across a short distance from where the fishing had taken place. From the scale of the furrow left in the moist soil, the creature that made the impression had to be monstrous in size.

The track led into the water, prompting all of the warriors to eye the broad stream with great wariness.

Many were tempted to partake of a patch of dark mushrooms, but hesitated due to the uncertainty surrounding its nature. Their reticence proved to be prescient when one of the warriors did consume a couple of the mushrooms and fell into a bout of madness not long after.

Wide-eyed and inconsolable, he started babbling about towering monsters coming to tear all of their hearts out. Overpowering the feverish warrior, before he threw himself into the stream, Ragnar got to hear all of the man's ranting.

"Like a giant corpse! Rotting! It is half-skeleton, but it lives!" the man told Ragnar with great urgency. "It wants our hearts! You must believe me!"

"You fool, you do not take chances with the things that grow here," Ragnar admonished the man, holding him down.

He knew that his words fell upon deaf ears. The man reacted to things that no one else could see.

"It hates us! It wants to rip our hearts out! A demon!" the man continued with his tirade. His eyes spread even wider. "A giant beast of a cat! Fangs like knives! It wants our hearts! A waterfall of blood!"

A crazed laughter burst from the man.

"Blood flowing like rivers! A waterfall!" he continued. "Our hearts torn out!"

"Your wits have fled you!" Ragnar shouted into the man's face.

Though tempting, striking the man would do no good. The mushrooms had cast a spell over him and would have to run their course.

Looking back at Ragnar for a brief moment, the man laughed. "Waterfalls of blood! Tumbling down the rocks! Flowing down the rocks! Pouring down the rocks!"

Freyyar and a couple of other warriors came up with lengths of vine that they had cut from the trees around them. While Ragnar continued to hold the hallucinating warrior in place, they bound him tight. Using a thin strip of cloth cut from one of the warrior's tunics, they gagged the man to suppress unnecessary noise.

"How long until the power of the mushroom wears off?" Freyyar asked Ragnar.

"Who knows?" Ragnar responded, with a shrug.

"Imbecile!" Freyyar said to the man, whose eyes continued to shift all over, focusing upon things invisible to all the others.

The hysterics of the man cast a pall of unease across the war band when they resumed their westward march. Visions of monsters and waterfalls of blood rekindled the tension that most of the warriors had carried prior to their two skirmishes with the native inhabitants.

Steeped in a brooding silence, even Ursalka showed the effects of the bound warrior's mushroom-spurred diatribe.

Unchanged in his demeanor and outlook, Ragnar strode at the head of the long column. Sweat beading all over, an oppressive heat encompassed him. The humid air rendered each breath thick, and he knew it would take some time to acclimate to the hotter atmosphere.

Several times, following a sharp sting or bite, Ragnar smacked an insect against his flesh. Yet no matter how many of the little aggressors he crushed, another took its place.

The flurry of tiny assaults added to the misery of the prevailing conditions. Ragnar blocked most of it out of his mind, though he could not deny that he longed for the crisp, scented air of a northern pine forest, or the salt-tinged, fresh breezes of the open seas.

A few times, if only for a fleeting moment in each instance, Ragnar sensed eyes upon him. He did not doubt that the native warriors kept a watch over them, and could keep themselves well-concealed, but they had shown no inclinations to engage in another melee with the northerners.

Their restraint disappointed Ragnar. He would have welcomed a distraction from the monotonous trek, with its rash of insects, heat, and humidity.

Sooner or later, they would find out whether or not they had come across the lands spoken of by Gardar. In the tales of his travels, Gardar had gone inland from the coast to discover a population awash in gold and silver.

Ragnar and his comrades had not come across any signs of such a place. No gold or silver adorned the native warriors they had fought with.

If anything, there had been a real paucity of metal visible among the enemy warriors. A couple had small axe heads of copper, but the bulk of the material used in their weapons and adornments had been of stone, leather, and wood,

***

Moving out of the forest, Ragnar and the others started across a broad meadow. The high grasses rippled in the breezes coming in from the east.

The serenity within the scene before him did not lull Ragnar into lowering his guard. Slowing to a halt and caked in sweat, Ragnar wiped his brow while peering across the meadow, toward the line of trees marking the boundary on the opposite side.

Freyyar came to stand by Ragnar, on his right side, while Ursalka and Magnolf took up positions on his left. The other warriors, coming up from behind, massed around them.

"I do not like it," Ragnar announced to the others, eyeing the swaying grasses.

"If we head west, we will find them," Freyyar remarked. "When we do, we will find out whether they have the abundance of gold and silver that Gardar claimed."

"I am more concerned about living than gold or silver," Ragnar responded in a dour timbre, shifting the grip on his axe. "Gold and silver avail you nothing if you are dead."

"Let us cross this open ground and be done with it," Freyyar replied, with a hint of impatience.

Taking a step forward, Ragnar told the others, "Keep your weapons at the ready."

The tall grasses brushing across his trousers, Ragnar walked forward. The others fell in behind him, reforming the staggered column they had maintained since setting out just after dawn.

Keeping to silence, the warriors directed their gazes all about. Taking step after step in caution, Ragnar's eyes took in nothing to cause alarm, but every instinct within him remained heightened.

Reaching the center of the meadow without incident, he could not shake the sense of unease clinging to him. Looking down to the right, and then to the left, he could see only stalks of grass all the way to the edge of the treeless expanse.

Continuing forward, he took his axe in a two-handed

grip. Something deep within, honed by a multitude of deadly encounters, told him that he would not reach the trees without disruption.

He had taken only five more steps when a cry broke out behind him.

"Ragnar!" Ursalka exclaimed. "An attack!"

The warning unnecessary, Ragnar had already set his feet and taken up a battle stance at the first flicker of movement that did not involve the surrounding grasses.

All around them, dark figures rose up from places of concealment. Shallow pits and grass carefully affixed to backs veiled a large force that had been lying in wait for the passage of the northerners.

Weapons in hand and filling the air with their war cries, the native warriors surged from both sides, falling upon Ragnar and his companions up and down the length of the column.

Carrying a long, sword-like weapon, with an elongated wooden blade lined with sharp pieces of obsidian, the warrior charging at Ragnar had his hair shaved on the sides to form a crest down the middle. Black streaks of paint on his face and large, circular ear spools, the latter creating pronounced, capacious ear lobes, bestowed the warrior with a harsh-looking countenance that reflected the frenzy within his eyes.

Clad in a tawny, tight-fighting cotton garment that covered his body from the neck down to the leather sandals on his feet, the warrior held a circular shield, the facing of which had a colorful, painted image of a serpent upon it. Several narrow strips of leather descended from the bottom of the shield.

Bellowing his own war cry, Ragnar swept his axe from right to left, batting aside the first slash from the oncoming warrior. Leveling the axe, he took immediate advantage of the opening he had just made.

Jabbing the end of the weapon into the other's prominent,

hawk-like nose, he struck hard. Crushing and bloodying the warrior's nose upon impact, the blow stunned Ragnar's attacker, leaving him vulnerable for the short, backward strike that cut through the flesh of his throat with ease.

Blood pouring down his chest, the shocked warrior dropped his weapon and shield, wavered for a moment, and then slumped to the ground.

Ragnar tromped past the fallen warrior and slew another, this one holding a longer, spear-like weapon edged with the sharp, obsidian pieces so prevalent among the native combatants.

Another warrior rushed at him, swinging one of the distinctive, sword-like weapons. A golden ornament, with sides fashioned like the wings of an eagle, pierced his nose and covered his mouth. Blocking the warrior's slashing attack, Ragnar reached out fast. Grabbing onto the ornament and tearing it free, flinging bits of blood and flesh about, he elicited a howl of extreme anguish from his stricken opponent.

Slinging the gold ornament down, Ragnar closed his fist, and sent a heavy, straight punch barreling into the warrior's face. The blow knocked his enemy from his feet and onto his back, spreading his arms wide apart.

The unceremonious landing left the warrior wide open for a finishing, overhead chop from Raven Caller. Ragnar then braced his left foot on the chest of his dead opponent and yanked the axe free, from where it had lodged deep into the man's skull.

Wading into a mass of enemy fighters, and swinging his axe to the left and right, Ragnar brought two more of the native warriors down in swift succession.

Another fearsome, two-handed swing of his axe widened the eyes of a fighter wearing a wooden headpiece representing a dog or wolf, before head and headpiece both tumbled to the ground, free of the body.

Leaping forward, Ragnar hooked the lower, extended part

of his axe onto the top portion of a warrior's shield. Pulling the man toward him, and ripping the shield free in the process, he thrust his left hand out.

Catching the man's right wrist, Ragnar squeezed with all his might, forcing his opponent to drop his sword-like weapon. A short, hard chop to the neck followed, killing the enemy fighter instantly.

Looking about, Ragnar noticed at once the different nature of the men surrounding him. Hair bunched into distinctive tufts atop their heads, and wearing little more than breech cloths, the native warriors before him looked younger and far less resolute than the ones he had just fought.

Expressions of fear and panic filled many of their faces, and a number of them began to fall back, giving Ragnar a wide berth. A few stood their ground or came at him, uttering shrill cries.

Like a raging bear among dogs, Ragnar tore into them, leaving a swathe of bloody carnage in his wake.

Not wanting to advance so far that he found himself surrounded and trapped, Ragnar paused to see where his comrades were.

With blood-spattered bodies and faces, Ursalka, Freyyar, Magnolf, and several others fought close by. Striking with fury in their eyes and bringing more and more of the native warriors to a bloody doom, Ragnar's comrades carved a larger swathe out of the enemy ranks.

Accompanied by the pounding of drums, waves of extended, braying signals sounding from large conch shells broke across the blood-drenched meadow.

At once, enemy warriors began disengaging from the fighting and pulling back in haste. After putting many strides of distance between themselves and the northerners, they came to a stop and turned about.

Blood dripping from the blade of his axe, Ragnar caught his

breath and looked around, assessing the battlefield.

He saw that the northerners were surrounded. A multitude of newly-arrived warriors poured into the meadow from the trees ahead.

A large number of brightly-colored, feathered standards, attached to harnesses worn by armed warriors, rose above the heads of the newcomers. A few looked elaborate, with an abundance of varied plumage or rounded forms that extended over the head of the one wearing the standard.

Several of the enemy warriors had elevated displays of colorful feathers and fabric rising up from their shoulders and backs, where they were attached to body harnesses. The ornate battle standards served to mark the position of enemy units.

Charging in and thickening the ranks holding Ragnar and his companions encircled, the warriors brandished their weapons. Shouting and jeering at the northerners, a few of them made particularly lewd gestures, baring naked rears or genitals toward the trapped foreigners,

Ringed around by enemy warriors, Ragnar glared and waited, like a great beast held at bay. Raven Caller in his hands, he kept watch for the first one foolish enough to step forth from the dense mass of warriors and come within his range.

Many of the warriors clad in battle attire unlike any he had seen in other lands, Ragnar set his eyes upon representations of birds of prey, hunting cats, serpents, and other creatures. These formed the innermost part of the ring, positioned closest to him, and Ragnar guessed them to be the best of their fighters.

"Come at me, you craven scum!" Ragnar shouted at the enemy warriors, shaking his great war axe at them. "Have you lost your mettle to fight?"

Ursalka, Freyyar, Grenna and many other northerners stood near him, hurling insults of their own at the attackers.

"Come a little closer and I will hack your little stub off!"

Ursalka yelled at one of the enemy warriors showing his groin. "I may have to find a small knife to do the task ... with a tiny thing like that!"

The enemy warriors maintained their distance. Persisting with their taunts, they ignored the countering ridicule and gibes of the northerners.

Ragnar's heated ire rose fast when his eyes fell upon a few of his comrades grouped together at the rear of the enemy ranks. Under the guard of many enemy fighters, the northerners now had their heads in wooden collars, the latter each having a long rod secured to them, behind the neck.

Surging forward at the sight, Ragnar cried out at the top of his lungs and made for the enemy warriors assembled in front of him.

He had taken only three strides when a sharp, stinging pain in his right side brought his advance to an abrupt halt.

Wincing, Ragnar glanced down to where the pain had erupted. A long, dark, needle-like object protruded from his skin. Clenching his teeth, he reacted to another sting, this one on coming from the right side of his chest.

A third sting broke out from high on Ragnar's back, toward the base of his neck.

His vision began wavering in mere moments, blurring the forms about him. Becoming groggy and heavy of limb, he raged against the mutiny taking place within his body.

A sensation of falling then enveloped Ragnar, and darkness took dominion within his eyes.

***

Light filtered into Ragnar's eyes.

Staving off a wave of nausea, while blinking and seeking to clear his vision, Ragnar groaned at the aches riddling his body.

Muttering a curse, he discovered that his hands were bound

tight behind his back. Dismayed, he looked down and saw that stout vines had been secured between his legs.

After exerting for a few moments, he found that not even his great strength could break the bindings upon his arms and legs. The wooden bars of a cage surrounded him, along with four of his fellow northerners, including Grenna. All had been bound in the same manner.

The cage's ceiling had been set low, forcing Ragnar into a hunched position. Unable to sit upright, he leaned his shoulder against the timber bars.

A bustling commotion sounded from outside the cage.

While cramped and unable to get a full view of what lay beyond the cage, Ragnar could see a multitude outside one side. Men, women, and children, in an array of attire ranging from simple to ornate, milled about.

Other cages like the one confining him stood on two of the other sides. They contained more of his comrades. He identified Ursalka and Freyyar, but he could not see Magnolf.

The last side opened on a stretch of ground that ran to the base of what looked to be broad, stone steps. The edge of some kind of circular, stone platform with an intricately-carved outer facing depicting a wide ranger of figures engaged in battle could be seen just to the right.

"What is this place, Ragnar?" Grenna asked him.

"I ... do not know, Ragnar said, turning his attention to the throngs of people visible on the side to his left.

A darker-skinned people, they all had straight, black hair.

The men tended to wear it to the base of the neck, with a fringe cut along the upper forehead. Most of the women wore it long and free, though some had worked colorful ribbons of cloth into their locks. A few women had a unique kind of hairstyle involving plaits wrapped about the head with the ends turned upward at the front.

From their attire, Ragnar could delineate with ease the ones holding higher status within their society.

A large majority of the men in view wore little more than plain white loincloths. Some of them wore similarly hued cloaks, knotted at the right shoulder and wrapped around their body under the left arm.

Women in the company of these men were clad in long, skirt-like garments that flowed down near the ankles. On many of them, depictions of flowers, plants, and animals had been embroidered into the white fabric.

Both men and women alike within the larger group went barefoot. Wearing necklaces displaying pendants crafted of seashells or stones, a large number wore some additional ornamentation.

A much smaller portion of the crowd included men who wore loincloths woven in many colors, with some of them trimmed using fur or bright feathers. These individuals exhibited more elaborate cloaks, rich and vibrant in color, varied in designs, and a few looking quite exotic, featuring extensive uses of fur or feather. A larger fraction of the men in this group wore multiple cloaks, with a few bearing several of them on their bodies.

The women in the company of the better-dressed were clad in both a long skirt and a looser-fitting garment on the upper body, made of a single length of cloth fashioned with holes open on the sides for the arms. Like the men they accompanied, the women exhibited a variety of designs and colors in the material used for their attire.

Necklaces holding stones, or pendants of silver and gold, hair-and chest ornaments, and golden armbands decorated the more richly-attired individuals. All of them wore sandals upon their feet, the footwear coming in styles ranging from a type with a leather heel guard to others with criss-crossing lacing traveling up the lower leg. The men displayed further adornment in the form of ear spools, lip plugs, and nose ornaments.

No matter their attire or ornamentation, all of the people showed a keen interest in the foreigners held within the cages.

Fanning themselves with long feathers, a cluster of the upper status women talked amongst each other while eyeing Ragnar with great interest. He could sense more than curiosity in their gazes.

Children tried again and again to edge close to the cages, only to be called back by their parents or blocked by the guards warding the captives.

Ragnar found his clarity returning. Squeezing his eyes tight, he cleared a little sweat that had trickled down into them.

"Are you okay?" Grenna asked. "It looked like they used some kind of poison dart on you."

Ragnar looked to Grenna and nodded. "It is wearing off now. Did they do the same to you?"

"Not me, but to a few others, yes," Grenna answered. "Ursalka would not surrender. Freyyar would not. And some others. Darts brought all of them down too."

"What of the others? How many survived?" Ragnar asked.

"We lost about ten in the fighting," Grenna said, a look of anguish coming over him. "They could not be given to the flames or be given proper burial. Left for scavengers, wherever they fell."

A sorrowful pang running through him at the tidings, Ragnar shook his head and looked away. Despite looking straight at the crowd milling about the cages, his vision reached for something much farther away. "They all deserved more than that. Not a single warrior who set out with us could be said to be a coward."

"Nothing could be done for them," Grenna said. "We could choose to die, or we could take our chances as captives. For my part, I did not wish to abandon you either."

"I cannot fault you and others for the decisions you made,"

Ragnar said, glancing toward him. "Though I would have fought until they struck me down or I killed them all, after I saw a few of our warriors taken captive."

"We stood no chance," Grenna said. "Maybe there is a chance here for all of us. I do not know what they wish to do with us."

A rueful grin crossed Ragnar's face. "I would not wager that it is going to be anything pleasant."

"I do not think it will be long until we find out," Grenna said. "A crowd has been gathering for a long while out there."

"I do not like the sound of that," Ragnar said. "Crowds gather for spectacles ... and often they crave to see blood spilled."

"You do not think they will kill us, do you?" Grenna said. "If they wanted to kill us, they could have done so when they had us surrounded."

"They seek captives, but I do not know why," Ragnar said.

"Maybe they will seek to make us thralls," Grenna said. "I know they have them, or something like it. Earlier, I saw a few of their people wearing collars like the ones they put on us. It was clear to me that they served the ones they were with."

"Then they will regret trying to do so," Ragnar replied, his words carrying a simmering threat within them. "I serve no one."

"I just wish I could sit up, or stand up, for a few moments!" Grenna commented, reflecting great discomfort in his face. "These bindings and this low cage will become our tormenters after much longer."

"You will find no argument from me on that," Ragnar stated, grimacing as he shifted his body to loosen up some pressure on his lower back.

Staring back out at the crowds, Ragnar took notice of a few well-dressed women whose faces had been covered in a yellowish makeup. Their hair held a luxuriant shine.

The booming of drums then rang out, bringing a great hush

over the people outside the cages. A single blast from a conch shell followed.

A contingent of warriors approached the cages. Anyone near to them backed away, showing no inclination to impede the stern-looking, armed men.

Heavy stones were removed from the top of a few cages. Several moments later, more warriors moved in to assist the others. Lifting the enclosures up, and carrying them away, the native warriors exposed the captives within to the direct rays of the sun; and all eyes within the vast crowd encompassing them.

A number of cages remained in place with stones weighting them down, confining the rest of the foreign captives.

Using obsidian blades, native warriors cut through the bindings on the legs of the captives. In a rough manner, they began hauling the northerners up to their feet, leaving their hands tied.

Ragnar glared at the warrior who attended to him. Getting his feet beneath him, he pushed himself into a standing position before the warrior could lay a hand on him. Seeing him upright, the warriors cast him a hardened stare and moved onward.

Able to stretch out, Ragnar worked to limber up his body as best he could. Beginning to turn about, he took in the multitude of sights flooding his eyes

A horrific abomination stood on the other side of the cages, in an area that he had not been able to see while confined.

A host of human skulls gazed through empty eye-sockets upon Ragnar and the others. Lining extensive timber racks, set one above the other to form a wall-like display, the mass of sun-bleached skulls appeared to be leering at him.

A monument to death, the grotesque array held his gaze for several moments.

At last, he turned farther to his left.

Beyond the skulls rose the circular platform of stone with

the carved outer facing. Now, he could appreciate its size to a full extent. Rising to a level about as high as his knees, the surface had room for a throng of people. At the moment, it stood bare and Ragnar wondered as to its purpose.

Continuing onward, Ragnar drew to a halt at the next view.

A broad, towering structure built of stone loomed before him. The four sides of the massive edifice took an inward slant, converging from the widest part at the base to the square surface at the far peak.

Thick columns of dark smoke twisted skyward, ascending from huge braziers set at each corner of the side facing the crowd. A wide flight of steps, flanked at the base by two stone-carved jaguars seated on their haunches, reached all the way from the ground level to the summit.

Perched in the center, at the top of the steps, a huge stone jaguar peered outward. Crouched low, with jaws open wide and fangs displayed, the muscular creature looked to be on the verge of springing outward.

To the right of the jaguar, the edge of a raised stone surface could be seen.

Set farther back from the steps, a pair of rectangular shrines, each one constructed with its own entrance, adorned the summit of the massive temple structure.

Ragnar continued to turn in place, setting his eyes upon a labyrinth of stone buildings in a variety of sizes spread along the ground level. His back to the great temple, he also gained a broader perspective of the crowd that he had viewed from within the cage. What he had seen through the timber bars represented only a tiny fraction of the masses that he now beheld.

Drums shook the air. An eruption of wooden rattles broke out moments later, followed by a chorus of low, resonant blasts upon conch shells.

The sonorous onslaught drew a feverish reaction from

the multitudes gathered before the temple. Chanting, crying out, singing, and shouting, the crowd gave birth to a deafening cacophony.

Rapturous looks upon their faces, a number of men and women broke out into spontaneous dancing. The crowd's fervor escalating, the dancers found themselves joined in swift succession by many more individuals.

Heads raised all over, looking toward the temple heights. Seeing the mass shift in attention, he followed their gazes and turned back around to face the temple. Lifting his head upward, he looked toward the summit.

A lone figure then came into view to the left side of the jaguar sculpture.

The figure looked to be wearing some sort of outfit, perhaps echoing the form of a creature like others Ragnar had seen, though the distance remained too great for him to make out much in the way of detail. A batch of colorful, feather plumes decorated the figure's garb.

Holding a feather-decorated staff in the right hand, the figure raised its arms and a pensive quiet fell over the vast crowds.

With a deep, resonant voice, the figure cried out and gestured in the direction of Ragnar and his companions.

Several warriors headed in from the sides and moved to seize Grenna. Ragnar and the others standing with him tried to get in their way, but with their arms bound tight behind their backs they could do little to impede the will of their captors.

After shoving a couple of them aside, Ragnar found himself caught in a swarm. Many hands grabbing onto him, the enemy's tight clenches dug into the flesh of his arms.

Shouting his fury at the native warriors, Ragnar got pushed and shoved back from Grenna. He could do nothing to stop them and he cursed his predicament.

Pulling him toward the temple, the guards overpowered

Grenna's attempts to resist. Lifting, jostling, and dragging him, the burly warriors took him to the base of the temple and started forcing him up the long flight of steps.

Ragnar and his comrades could do nothing more than watch Grenna's laborious climb up the temple. Grenna lost his balance a couple of times and almost tumbled, but the guards escorting him proved to be quick in response, catching and bracing him before he could fall.

Augmented by rattle and shell blasts, the torrent of drumbeats resumed, rolling across the great plaza in a steady pattern. Undulating in place to the rhythms, men and women alike raised their arms high, with palms facing the sky.

Fighting to keep his wits, Ragnar fought against the mesmerizing effects of the thumping beats and grandiosity of the unfolding scene. He could not afford to be lulled into any degree of complacency.

After reaching the top at last, the guards accompanying Grenna herded him toward the stone table by the jaguar stature. Once there, they seized Grenna and hoisted him up, forcing him onto his back atop the stone surface. The guards held him in place, lying sideways to the staircase that he had just climbed.

Four other figures came into view. Garbed in colorful mantles and plumed headdresses, the newcomers took up positions at the table. Ragnar could not see everything that they were doing, but he could tell that the two in front were tying Grenna down, securing a wrist at one corner and an ankle at the other. He had little doubt that the same process was taking place on the part of the table out of his view.

Looking skyward and holding a dark, short blade, the priest who had called out to the crowd began chanting at the top of his lungs. The drums thundered and the cries from the masses gathered before the base of the temple rose louder.

Plunging the dagger down, the priest drove the blade deep

into the Grenna's chest. The ill-fated man screamed, but he could do nothing to stop the priest from reaching down into the open wound.

A moment later, the priest yanked his arm back, with an object gripped in his hand.

Walking over to the top of the stairs, the priest held up the object for all to see. A tenor of jubilation and celebration filling the air, the crowd roared their approval.

A cold chill ran through Ragnar.

His eyes remained locked on the priest's upraised hand, watching the dark drips falling to the temple surface. Ragnar had no illusions about what the priest held, or the nature of the drops; blood raining down from a severed heart.

Body trembling in a fast-growing fury, Ragnar closed his eyes and did the best that he could to form a prayer within his heart to the gods that Grenna had so much confidence in. Part of him wondered why such gods would allow the followers of another god to claim the blood of a man who had shown a fierce loyalty to the northern deities his entire life.

Opening his eyes once more, Ragnar eyed the priest who had torn Grenna's heart from his chest.

His eyes narrowing, Ragnar swore to himself that the blade-holding priest would be made to answer for the brutal killing.

Blood from Grenna's grisly wound pooled on the table and gathered in narrow channels carved into the surface. The furrows converged into a single duct that ran from the base of the table to an area beneath the statue of the jaguar. A few moments later, thin rivulets of blood began emerging from the maw of the stone jaguar, trickling from its tongue to fall upon the steps below.

With a ceremonious air, the priest walked over and deposited the heart into some kind of cavity or receptacle in the back of the jaguar.

The headdress-wearing individuals who had tied Grenna

down on the stone table then freed the wrists and ankles from their bindings. Taking up his body, each of them holding onto a limb, they marched over to the stop of the steps.

With an unceremonious heave, they sent Grenna's lifeless body tumbling down the long flight of stairs.

Ragnar watched his comrade's body bounce, slide, and skip downward, until the corpse landed in a heap at the bottom.

The slaying of Grenna proved to be just the beginning of a horrific trial.

Forced to bear witness to three more of his companions being sacrificed in the brutal manner that Grenna had suffered, Ragnar seethed and raged. Each kill appeared to spur the crowd's frenzy to even higher levels, until the view of the people began to sicken him.

More blood ran down the tongue of the jaguar statue, until the flow began to work its way down the stone stairs.

"*Waterfalls of blood!*" echoed the voice of Ragnar's mushroom-eating companion, from during their march through the forest.

The drums then began pounding in a different cadence. The rattles took on another timbre, and the waves of shell blasts fell lower in pitch.

The priest-figure that had cut open the chests of the four northerners came back into sight at the side of the jaguar statue. The crowd's fervor ebbed, along with the drums, rattles, and shell blasts, until a reverent silence remained.

Spreading his arms wide, the priest-figure shouted a number of words. Ragnar could not understand a single one of them, but he did not miss the commanding tone in which they had been delivered.

A large group of warriors approached the surviving captives at the calls from the figure above.

A few grabbed Ragnar and held onto him, while the

remaining captives standing near to him found themselves forced to climb the staircase. Confused and angered at being separated from all the others, he struggled against those holding him.

Gaining a little space after thrashing about in a wild burst of motion, Ragnar managed to drop one of the warriors with a knee to the groin. Turning, he downed another with a head butt, and then kicked a third in the knee, the latter strike eliciting an audible crack before the man collapsed to the ground.

Yet for every warrior that Ragnar could land a blow on, ten more remained at hand to replace them. Once more he found himself swarmed and subdued, forced to bear witness to the impending doom facing his comrades.

Once all of the captives reached the top of the stairs, the figure cried out. Gazing down at Ragnar, the figure then spoke several more words in the authoritative tone he had used before.

The warriors holding Ragnar in place shoved and prodded him toward the low, circular platform of stone set near to the racks of skulls. On his approach, Ragnar stared at the outer facing of the stone circle and its continuous relief portraying figures of gods, war, combat, and sacrifice.

The warriors paused at the edge of the platform. A couple of them leaped upward and landed upon its surface, exhibiting a keen balance.

Turning, they worked to help the other warriors pull Ragnar onto the platform, where they tethered one of his legs to a thick post set close to the edge.

Then, they freed his arms.

His first inclination to launch an attack, Ragnar summoned all the will that he could muster and held back from laying into the warriors nearest to him.

They had separated him from the others and put him on the platform for a reason. Though the prospects of survival appeared slim, perhaps the new development represented a chance to aid his fellow northerners; those now atop the temple and the ones still held within the other cages.

Across from Ragnar, a stout warrior armed with a shield and one of the obsidian-edged, sword-like weapons jumped onto the platform. Displaying dark streaks of paint on his face, the warrior eyed him from within headgear fashioned into the image of a serpent's head with mouth open wide. Elongated fangs framed each side of the man's head.

A couple of other warriors, their hair cut to form crests down the middle of their heads, with pronounced tufts to either side, stepped onto the platform from behind the armed warrior. Crossing the surface without delay, they approached Ragnar. One held a circular wooden shield, and the other carried one of the extended sword-like weapons that he had seen so many of their warriors using.

Ragnar saw at once that the weapon did not have the sharp, rectangular pieces of obsidian that were embedded on the similar weapons carried by the native warriors.

Drawing to a halt about a pace from Ragnar, the warrior with the sword-like weapon extended it toward him. Seeing that he was meant to take it, Ragnar accepted.

He ran his hand through the wrist-loop affixed to a ring at the base. Holding onto the lower end with a firm grip, Ragnar began gaining a sense of the weight and balance in the weapon.

The second warrior extended the shield toward him.

Taking it from the other warrior, everything became clear to him.

They expected him to fight the warrior standing across from him in single combat.

The weapons being given to him were conceived to be lesser versions of those used by the native warriors, including his opponent.

The disadvantage that Ragnar faced was intended. Not

meant to survive the looming combat, Ragnar stood an offered sacrifice, not unlike his doomed companions.

A scowl deepening across his face, the thought enraged him.

Ragnar could see that the armed warrior he would be fighting had some manner of quilted cotton tunic lurking beneath the fabric of his outer attire; a snug-fitting garment decorated to look like a covering of scales worn over both the upper body and legs. The presence of a form of body armor represented another intended disadvantage to be confronted by the one sacrificed.

Blood beginning to boil with the wrath coursing through him, Ragnar glared at his well-equipped opponent.

"You have no advantage here, you fool!" Ragnar said to the warrior in a low, growling tone. "It is you who have the disadvantage in facing me!"

Though the other man had not understood a single word spoken by Ragnar, his tone resonated clear enough. A frown darkened the other man's face and he started forward, weapon and shield raised into combat positions.

Calculating the right moment, Ragnar waited

Stepping forward with a level of quickness that his opponent never anticipated, Ragnar barreled the end of his weapon straight into the man's mouth. Shattering teeth into bits and leaving the warrior's maw bloodied, the severe blow staggered Ragnar's opponent. Arms slackening, the man looked dazed from the impact.

Continuing his assault, Ragnar dropped his shield and wrapped his freed hand around the back of the man's head. Rearing back with his right arm, he punched the end of his weapon into the warrior's mouth once more; although this time he pulled with great force using his left hand, such that the long piece of wood drove deep down the man's throat.

Hearing his opponent's weapon and shield clatter to the

stone, Ragnar held tight and shoved even harder. Choking the man and tearing him up on the inside, the invading weapon penetrated further.

Struggling and clutching at Ragnar, the stricken warrior could do nothing.

Ragnar kept up the onslaught, sensing the man's life ebbing fast.

The man's body going limp, Ragnar tore the weapon out, spattering blood and pieces of gore onto the stone beneath his feet.

Giving a dismissive shove, Ragnar tossed the dead body over to the side and looked around.

No celebration of victory awaited Ragnar, or even an acknowledgment of his triumph.

Another opponent stood at the ready, poised at the edge of the circle directly opposite Ragnar. With a headpiece carved in the shape of a leering, demonic face, the next warrior proved a little more difficult to subdue.

Rushing across and swinging his sword-like weapon, the attacker nearly grazed Ragnar with the wickedly-sharp obsidian pieces lining the sides. Shifting fast to the side and swinging his own weapon hard at his oncoming adversary, Ragnar countered.

A loud thwack erupted as the warrior caught the blow squarely on his shield.

Dropping his weapon and closing the space between them fast, Ragnar lunged at the warrior before he could bring his weapon through for another slash. One hand gripping onto his opponent's upraised weapon arm, and the other clutching his throat, Ragnar slid his right leg around and behind the other's right leg.

Driving forward, and keeping his forward leg anchored, he lifted the man off his feet and crashed him into the stone surface.

Knocking the air out from his adversary's chest, Ragnar

raised and slammed the man's right arm into the stone until he dropped his weapon; all the while continuing to choke him in the unrelenting grip of his right hand.

Kicking and flailing, the overpowered warrior strained to free himself, but he could not begin to match Ragnar's raw strength. The fight within the warrior slipped away fast, followed by his life force.

Getting up to his feet, Ragnar could see that yet another opponent had manifested on the platform. This one stood a little taller than the others and had the headdress of an eagle, with the warrior's painted face exposed between an open beak.

Ragnar picked up the sword-weapon that his last opponent had dropped.

"Am I to fight all of you craven worms? Come then, you fool, meet death!"

With a broad sweep of his weapon, Ragnar cut through the tether securing his leg to the timber post

Springing toward Ragnar, the warrior cried out and launched a vicious attack involving many rapid slashes of his weapon.

Ragnar parried one strike, dodged another, and then executed a masterful stroke of his own, landing flush on the side of the man's head. A heavy thud marked the impact and a few of the obsidian segments lodged into the wood of the other warrior's eagle headpiece.

Seeing a chance to control his opponent's movement, Ragnar pulled the warrior toward him and landed a hammer-fist square on top of the man's right shoulder. Ragnar could feel the bone give way at the jarring impact, and the man screamed, dropping his weapon.

Ragnar jerked his sword-weapon free while keeping hold of the man with his left hand. Rearing back, he finished the warrior off with a savage blow of the weapon to the neck, executing a strike that half-severed his adversary's head from his body.

Yet another fighter stood waiting when Ragnar looked up.

The fighting continued until the bodies of ten warriors lay strewn about the edges of the circular platform. Littered with discarded weapons, the stone surface, covered in blood, glistened in the bright sun.

When no more warriors came forth to stand against him, Ragnar slung the last weapon that he had wielded aside; a spear-like weapon fitted with obsidian edge pieces on the blade end. Finding it more conducive to his fighting style, being a long-hafted weapon well-suited for hacking and slashing kinds of attacks, he had taken it up after disarming his ninth opponent.

Stepping down from the platform, Ragnar walked forward. An uneasy silence surrounded him. Nobody moved to stop him.

Catching his breath, Ragnar came to a stop in the open ground at the base of the temple. Sweat dripped from his brow, and blood trickled from the light cuts and scrapes that he had absorbed in the fighting.

The vast assemblage continued to remain steeped in disquiet, with all eyes fixed upon the tall, pale-skinned warrior who had slain ten of their greatest warriors.

A lone voice from high above broke the tense stillness.

"Warrior, come up! The Lord of the Sun calls you to the altar of gods to receive his grace and reward!"

Hearing his own language being spoken, albeit in a thick accent, Ragnar raised his eyes and peered at the man that the words had come from; the same high priest who had presided over the grisly deaths of Grenna and the others.

Straightening up, Ragnar strode to the base of the long flight of steps.

A simmering anger continuing unabated within, Ragnar started upward. Eyeing the blood from his sacrificed companions staining the stone steps provoked his ire further.

Once he had reached the top, Ragnar paused, taking in the

sight that greeted him.

Two rectangular shrines dominated the apex of the temple.

Before the shrine to Ragnar's left stood an even more massive jaguar than the one dripping blood from its tongue near the sacrificial altar. Sculpted from stone, its jaws open in a permanent roar, the creature appeared to be baring its lengthy fangs at Ragnar.

To the right stood a hideous figure. A bizarre mixture of a human and a skeleton, the macabre entity depicted had no natural origin. Bulbous eyes stared at Ragnar just above a nasal cavity bereft of skin.

As if its lips had been cut away, no flesh covered the figures large teeth, bestowing its countenance with a fixed sneer or smile. Ragnar doubted the expression to reflect the latter, unless it reflected the kind of smile bearing a cold, cruel undercurrent.

A human upper chest ended in a midsection that exhibited only rib bones and spine. At the end of its arms, the fingers on each hand ended in sharp, pointed ends, like sets of claws.

Farther down its body, the covering of skin resumed, descending down to the being's feet. Wherever skin covered the figure's body, it had been crafted to look taut on the bones lying underneath.

Each of the shrines distinct in their appearance, their facades displayed an extensive array of carvings.

The shrine behind the jaguar statue exhibited images of war, showing tribal warriors engaged in a timeless battle. Some taking captives, others shedding blood, and still others on the march, the figures represented the full gamut of a war campaign.

Painted in several hues, including blue, yellow, green, and red, the shrine had a vibrant appearance in the open sunlight. A single, rectangular entrance beckoned to the shrine's interior.

The other shrine had human skulls inlaid about the edge of its lone entryway. The carvings rendered upon it included a number of strange and fantastical images. From people being herded by various monsters, to images of bloody sacrifice, to skeletons, the scenes reflected themes of death and fear.

The outer surface of the shrine had been painted in darker colors. Deep crimson hues intertwined with black to give the edifice a brooding, somber aura.

Ragnar found his gaze shifting between the two statues. To his eyes, the air itself appeared to shimmer around edges of the sculptures. Blinking his eyes and wrenching his gaze away from them, he turned his attention to the area closer to him.

In the area between the two shrines, flanked by the statues, a richly-adorned cluster of prominent-looking figures stood, surrounded by many warriors. Wearing headbands of gold or headdresses of long, colorful feathers, displaying an abundance of golden jewelry, some of it inlaid with stones such as jade, and draped in a colorful array of cloaks, the conspicuous group stared at Ragnar with looks ranging from sheer animosity to indifference and suspicion.

On an elevated platform behind them stood a throne, upon which a man in elaborate attire sat. At the center of a magnificent headdress, a transverse crest of solid gold made it appear as if a small sun was rising from behind his head. Framing the man's head and the gleaming crest, a bounty of bright, colorful plumage sprouted from the elaborate headdress.

He wore a cloak of turquoise-hued feathers. Golden bands inlaid with turquoise stones adorned his arms, and an elaborate necklace of small gold pendants rested upon his chest. A gorget of gold, gleaming in the sun's rays, underlay the necklace.

Gold had also been used to fashion a detailed lip-plug ornament, the design of the distinctive piece the visage of a skull.

A narrow face lent the man a hawk-like visage that added further to the intensity of the stare he cast toward Ragnar.

To the right of the group, accompanied by a throng of

armed guards, eight of Ragnar's companions remained bound. All of them looked to him with expressions that conveyed fear and astonishment.

Ragnar gleaned a little relief at the sight. All of the ones who taken up to the temple summit just before he had been made to fight on the platform still possessed hearts and drew breath.

Then, Ragnar took account of the man who had earned his wrath several times over, the figure who had driven obsidian blades into the chests of his comrades.

At first, Ragnar thought the man standing before him to be garbed in raiment reflecting the image of a serpent. Then, he realized the man's attire had been made from the body of some manner of giant snake.

An enormous snake's head had been used for the headpiece. The rest of the man's garb had been covered in genuine serpent scales, presumably from the monster that the head had been taken from.

The high priest took a few steps toward Ragnar. A brawny warrior, taller than all the other native warriors that Ragnar had seen, stood at the high priest's right shoulder. Glowering, the big warrior had the look of a man desiring a fight, from what Ragnar could read within the warrior's cold gaze and stone-rigid expression.

Ragnar held the warrior's gaze for a moment; his own eyes conveying that he had no qualms about meeting the other's unspoken challenge. His response evoked a narrowing of the other's eyes. Ragnar wished that he could fight him right then.

"The Lord of the Sun deems you worthy to receive a high rank in his sacred army," the high priest announced in Ragnar's tongue. "You fought well. You will enjoy great wealth, and you will have command of thousands."

Seeing the words of his own language coming from the man's lips, Ragnar said nothing at first, wondering what kind of magic had been used.

"How do you know my words?" Ragnar asked him, after a few tense moments had passed.

"This is not the first time I have encountered pale-skins, whether here ... or elsewhere," the high priest answered with an enigmatic edge. A mystery coiled within his dark gaze.

"What of my companions?" Ragnar asked, looking aside to the men bound nearby.

"They are to be offerings to Dachtli and Broltec, a great honor for all of them," the high priest replied. "The god of death, and the god of war, who guide us in all things."

Ragnar kept the rage inside him from showing on his face, but his gaze lanced into the other man.

"I saw the abominations you committed," he responded, in a low, rumbling tone. "Your actions condemn you."

The shadow of a smile passed through the other man's eyes and across his lips. "Our ways may be unknown to you, but a god must receive what is demanded."

"Find another god to worship, other than those two scum," Ragnar retorted, casting a glare in the direction of the statues.

He knew his words would have gotten him slain, had the figure on the throne understood them. The high priest tensed, and his face clouded over with ire, but his next words emerged in a calm, authoritative tone.

"You will understand our ways, in time," the high priest told him. "But you must accept the gift of the Lord of the Sun. Do not delay in accepting his generosity."

"What if I do accept? Can I set my companions free?" Ragnar asked, knowing that his comrades would never be let go by their blood-hungering captors.

"You will receive great authority," the high priest answered, evading the question.

Ragnar said nothing in response, letting the impasse

between himself and the high priest grow with every passing moment.

"What else do you wish to ask?" the high priest queried after an extended silence. An undercurrent of impatience ran through his words.

"I desire my weapon," Ragnar told the high priest in a low, firm voice. "I want it to be returned to me. It is the weapon I know and choose to wield."

Saying nothing and looking to be weighing an inner decision, the high priest gazed upon Ragnar for several moments.

Turning, the high priest walked away from Ragnar, heading toward the raised platform and throne set in back of the throng of regal-looking figures.

When he drew nearer, the high priest drew to a halt and bowed low to the man seated upon the throne, who had no change of expression. Then, the seated figure beckoned to the high priest.

He approached the throne with his head lowered in a deferential posture. Leaning in, the high priest exchanged some words out of the earshot of any bystanders.

The man on the throne looked up and stared at Ragnar for a few heartbeats, and then returned his attention back to the high priest. His lips moved, imparting words that distance prevented Ragnar from hearing, even if he could understand them.

The high priest bowed low, backed up several paces, and then turned about, before striding back to Ragnar.

"Your weapon is here, with us," the high priest announced to him. "Taken to be presented as a gift. But in his generosity, the Lord of the Sun returns it back to you. Your request has been granted, if you accept what has been offered to you."

The high priest then faced the group of prominent-looking figures and warriors. In a louder, commanding tone, he called out some words in his own language.

One of the warriors stepped forward. In his hands, the warrior gripped Raven Caller. The sight of an enemy warrior handling his weapon infuriated Ragnar even further.

"Then I accept it," Ragnar said, keeping his tone even and stifling the emotions churning inside him.

Tromping over toward the warrior holding his axe, Ragnar drew to a halt a couple of paces before the grim-faced man.

"Your weapon must be presented to you before the Lord of the Sun, after you have given oath to take the rank offered you," the high priest declared.

"I would rather take my axe back, right now," Ragnar said, the words rumbling from his mouth like the ripple of thunder before a great downpour.

Left arm darting forward, Ragnar gripped the haft of Raven Caller. Evoking a volcanic fury within Ragnar, the tribal warrior held onto the axe and refused to release the weapon to him.

A swift, right uppercut from Ragnar launched the warrior off his feet, releasing the hold on his weapon and casting the other man into an unconscious heap.

Everything that Ragnar had been holding back inside burst forth like a torrent of thunder, lightning, wind, and rain. Bellowing a war cry, Ragnar hacked into the warriors nearest him, felling three in moments.

The other warriors fell back from the martial tempest besetting them.

Lunging forward, Ragnar yanked a javelin away from another warrior. Farther ahead of him, he could see the warriors' ruler trying to get down from the raised platform with the throne.

Without hesitation, Ragnar reared back and hurled the javelin, putting tremendous force into the throw. The missile streaked toward its target.

A cry of pain burst from the ruler as the javelin struck him in the upper arm, causing the man to crumple to the ground.

The abrupt development had an immediate effect on the tribal warriors. All of them hurried back to surround the stricken ruler.

The haughty looks on the faces of the prominent-looking men around the throne had vanished and been replaced with expressions of shock and terror. Like the warriors, they moved back, converging about the wounded ruler.

Ragnar did not waste an instant. Springing forward, he bounded toward the priests who had been involved in the bloody ritual inflicted upon Grenna and the others who had been sacrificed.

Like animals of prey scattering before a great predator, the priests strove to evade his onslaught. One lost their elaborate headdress, the abundance of bright, colorful feathers toppling from the priest's head to the ground. Another tripped, falling to the ground, right in the path of Ragnar.

Using his left arm Ragnar snatched up the lower-ranking priest. Keeping hold of his axe, he hooked his right arm between the priest's legs. Hoisting the man overhead with little trouble, Ragnar carried the figure over to the edge of the long staircase facing the massed crowd far below.

"You take pleasure in casting bodies down these stairs?" Ragnar shouted in anger to the priest, now wriggling and crying out in a tone that could only be taken as stark terror and desperation. "I will show you what it was like for all of them!"

With a prodigious heave, Ragnar sent the man hurtling down the stone steps. Striking edge after edge, the fall hammered the priest without respite, leaving his body broken and lifeless when he reached the bottom.

Ragnar hurried over to his companions, who had been left to themselves during the tumult.

Clutching Raven Caller at the base of its broad head, Ragnar used the weapon like a knife, cutting the bindings from the wrists of his fellow northerners.

"Praise all the gods for you, Stormbringer," Freyyar exclaimed, rubbing at his wrists once he had been freed.

"Grab up any weapons you can find!" Ragnar shouted to Freyyar and the others. "We must get free of this accursed place!"

A short distance away from them, a few of the tribal warriors had begun to regroup. Others escorted the ruler and the group of well-dressed figures toward the mouth of the shrine dedicated to Dachtli, the death god.

Notably, the high priest remained, standing with the warriors forming up to confront Ragnar and the freed men with him. At the forefront of the tribal warriors stood the large, brawny warrior who Ragnar had locked eyes with.

An icy grin came to his face. The warrior would get his wish to engage Ragnar in battle.

Ragnar strode right at him.

The high priest called out from the back of the line of warriors. The words caused the big warrior to look back.

A moment later, the warrior turned his head to face Ragnar again.

Sounding angered and insistent, the high priest shouted again. Once more, the warrior looked back to the high priest.

An irritated look rushing into the warrior's face, he glanced back toward the still-advancing Ragnar. His face a mask of frustration and ire, he remained in place for a moment, before turning to start back toward the high priest.

Not to be denied his quarry, Ragnar leaped forward, swinging his axe in a great arc that caused the warriors before him to dodge and duck. Stepping into a gap created through his attack and reaching out, he grabbed at the big warrior, who had begun to turn back toward him after sensing Ragnar's close presence.

Ragnar's fingers closed on the back of a necklace. Yanking

his arm back, Ragnar pulled the necklace free, intact. Using one arm, he swung his axe.

Crouching and tucking his head against his thick chest, the warrior moved to evade the axe's path. The blade passed within less than the span of Ragnar's hand from removing the scalp of the warrior.

Ragnar kicked upward, catching the warrior solid in the chest and knocking him back.

Other warriors moving in from the sides prevented Ragnar from pressing the attack further. Stepping back, he swatted their strikes aside, leaving a couple more of them dead after delivering short counter-slashes.

The enemy warriors shifted back a few paces, forming another line.

Ragnar glanced down long enough to see that the necklace gripped in his left hand displayed a wide number of claws, like those from the large hunting cats prowling the nearby forests and edified in the statues placed on the temple.

The warrior that he had taken the necklace from had now taken up a position at the side of the high priest.

A few other warriors had since emerged from the entrance to Dachtli's shrine, joining the others in a human bulwark two lines thick that blocked Ragnar from reaching the high priest.

Stymied for the moment, Ragnar glared at the high priest and the huge warrior at his side.

"A pair of sniveling cowards! Craven fools, the both of you!" Ragnar shouted at them, shaking his war axe. "You prey upon the weaker! Come, test yourself against one who is strong!"

Erupting into a barrage of mocking laughter, Ragnar locked his eyes on the both of them, while spitting toward the ground in a derisive manner.

Raising up the claw-necklace that he had taken from the large warrior, he tore it to pieces in plain view and scattered the contents to the ground. Adding further to his display, he stomped on the remnants of the necklace, before all of their eyes.

His actions provoked an immediate response.

Casting a baleful look toward Ragnar, the warrior's face contorted with an expression of malice and something else.

Breaking into a chant, the warrior closed his eyes and began swaying in place, as if falling into a trance. The warriors standing nearest to him backed away, giving him a wide berth.

Only the high priest remained in place, looking undeterred by the warrior's actions.

An even stranger phenomenon occurred at that moment. The shimmering that Ragnar had perceived around the statues when first looking upon them, intensified around the one shaped like a huge jaguar.

After the distortion in the air took place, what looked to be a dark mist in a shape echoing that of the statue rose up from the stone figure. Drifting over to the muscular warrior, the vaporous form seeped into his body until all of it had departed from sight.

The warrior then emerged from his trance-like state and opened his eyes, looking straight at Ragnar.

Eyes filling with a golden hue, and round pupils turning into slits, the warrior grimaced, clenching his teeth.

Lips dripping blood, the tips of fangs appeared, growing and extending downward. The substance of the man's face then began to change, darkening and taking on a malleable, viscous appearance.

"We must go! More warriors are coming!" Freyyar called out, looking out from the perimeter of the temple's summit. "They will soon have us surrounded!"

Scowling at the transforming warrior and the wicked high priest that he protected, Ragnar gripped the haft of his axe tight and gritted his teeth in anger. Every part of him wanted to charge forward and cut his way through the wall of fighters to reach the high priest and the warrior at his side.

"We need you Ragnar! Let us go now!" another of Ragnar's freed comrades called out.

Brandishing his axe toward the enemy warriors before him and releasing his burning frustration through a primal cry at the top of his lungs, Ragnar turned away from his prey. Hurrying over, he joined the others as they left the summit behind, descending the steps and making their way to the bottom.

The sight of the escaping captives sent a great panic throughout the crowds filling the areas before the temple. A chaotic mayhem broke out with people of all status levels seeking to get away from the temple area as fast as possible.

Many fell and became trampled underfoot, littering the open spaces with a large number of wounded and dead individuals.

Once he had reached the ground, Ragnar loped straight for the batch of cages set near to the towering racks of skulls.

"Get these stones off, and free them, now!" he shouted to the eight with him, while grabbing at one of the large stones weighing down the top of a cage.

With the help of the others, Ragnar saw to it that the stones were cleared in swift fashion and the cages removed to set the other captives free.

"What now?" Ursalka asked him, getting to her feet after being released from one of the cages. Wincing, while stretching her limbs, she looked around. "We have no weapons at hand."

"Run now! Your lives depend on it!" Ragnar shouted at her and the others. "Follow me!"

Having borne witness to part of the blood-soaked rituals of their captors, in seeing the mutilated corpses of their comrades landing at the base of the temple stairs, the freed warriors needed little encouragement. Falling in with the others, they hurried after Ragnar, who had taken the lead of the survivors.

The cries and shouts of a great number of tribal warriors

carried to them from the vicinity of the temple.

Legs churning, propelling him fast across the open ground, Ragnar set his mind on a single thought; reaching the edge of the vile city and continuing into the dense wilderness beyond.

***

Behind them, the enemy warriors atop the temple summit began crowding the top of the flight of steps. Jeering and brandishing their weapons, they could do nothing to stop the captives being set free right before their eyes.

Seeing Ragnar and the others setting off at a full run, heading away from the temple grounds, a couple of the higher-ranking warriors among them called for a pursuit.

A few of the warriors had already started down the main flight of stairs when a bestial roar flooded the air surrounding the temple heights. Freezing in place, and fear clouding their faces, the warriors ceased in their descent.

Knocking into each other with an air of desperation, the warriors gathered along the top and those on the first few stairs divided apart, clearing a broad channel at their center.

A towering form covered in black fur, and brimming with muscle, leaped onto the steps. Bounding down them, the creature demonstrated a level of agility and balance far surpassing any man.

When it reached the bottom, the black-furred beast raced forward, heading in the direction of the foreign escapees.

Making no move to follow it, the warriors on the temple watched the creature in a hushed, reverend silence.

Farther ahead of the beast, Ragnar and the other recent captives reached the edge of the city, and then disappeared into the lush foliage of the surrounding forest.

***

Leaving the blood-soaked temple, its maniacal high priest, and the frenzied populace behind, Ragnar and his companions sprinted into the forest. Showing no mercy to their plight, and slowing their pace to a considerable degree, the dense undergrowth lashed into their skin.

On a few occasions, one of Ragnar's companions lost their footing on slick patches of ground, tumbling down hard. To their good fortune, none of those who slipped incurred serious injury. Scrambling back to their feet, they hastened after their fleeing companions.

Suddenly, the damp, unforgiving forest filled with a diabolical roar.

Save for Ragnar, all of the other warriors strained to run faster at the sonorous eruption.

None of the others had viable weapons. Only Ragnar held the means to fight back against any significant threat.

Slowing down to a halt and turning around, Ragnar tried to gauge the direction of the inhuman cry. Having more than a small inkling as to what had made it, he made a quick determination.

When some of the others neared from behind, he shouted to them, "Run! Keep going! Do not stop. Not for anything!"

Following his directive, the warriors hurried by him. Seeing him trudging in the other direction, heading toward the horrid place that they had just escaped, a few of the men cast incredulous looks at him.

"Show yourself, you bastard!" Ragnar muttered in a low voice, eyeing the dense masses of growth around him.

A human cry broke out ahead of Ragnar, followed by the unmistakable growl of a great cat.

Ragnar adjusted his path and hastened toward the sound. Hurdling over a fallen tree with a prodigious leap, Ragnar drove his body through the undergrowth.

Cuts and scrapes accumulated from the thick foliage, but

he did not slow, pushing the pain from the outskirts of his mind.

Bursting out from the undergrowth into a stretch of more open ground, he charged forward even faster.

Only great reflexes and the fact that Ragnar had only set one foot down near its outer edge had prevented him from putting his full weight onto a well-camouflaged hunting trap.

Having pulled his foot back at the sudden give in the surface, Ragnar cursed his foolishness in taking such a reckless approach. Had he been running just a stride or two's distance to his right, he would have fallen straight through the trap's carefully disguised covering.

After taking a brief moment to assess the outlines of the hunting pit, Ragnar continued forward.

Proceeding a few hundred strides beyond the location of the pit trap, Ragnar came to the edge of an extensive, circular depression in the ground, as if a great bowl had been pressed into the soil to shape the land itself.

Farther down the slope, near the heart of the basin, a grisly scene unfolded.

Ragnar set his eyes upon a large, dark form hunched over the still body of one of his companions, a younger, fair-haired warrior named Harradan. Rearing up, and standing on two legs, the creature's movements laid bare to Ragnar's eyes the savage wounds that the beast had just inflicted upon the fallen warrior.

The northerner's throat had been torn out, and his torso had been subjected to a grotesque mauling that left his innards splayed all around his body. One glance told Ragnar that the hunter's intent roved far beyond that of a natural wilderness predator.

What he saw in the basin reflected a punitive execution, not the chasing down of prey.

A lethal intent forming in his own mind, Ragnar locked his gaze on the killer.

Reflecting the form of the god that it served, Broltec, the creature had the head of a large panther. Its entire body coated in sleek, black fur, the creature possessed long limbs ending in broad appendages. Those on the arms blending the forms of a human hand and a jaguar's paw, and those on the legs more elongated in the manner of feet, all of the appendages exhibited pronounced sets of claws; of a kind that shredded flesh to bloody ribbons in swift fashion.

The beast met Ragnar's gaze. Setting loose another extended roar, the creature exposed a glistening set of large, sharp fangs. Pure malice flowed through the smoldering look cradled within the beast's eyes.

Holding the beast's gaze without blinking, an idea formed within Ragnar's mind.

Drawing fury at the sight of his mutilated companion, Ragnar erupted with a loud bellow. "Come and get me, you furry pile of dung!"

He did not wait for a response from the creature. Turning, he ran back in the direction he had come from.

***

Black fur melding with the deep shadows beneath the tree canopy, the beast was all but invisible, save for its eyes; a pair of golden pools simmering with a murderous intent.

Standing in the open ground, Ragnar caught sight of the beast's eyes at the last instant.

Propelling toward Ragnar from the undergrowth, the creature rushed him from the side, taking him by surprise. Striking at the incoming creature with a short back swing of his axe, Ragnar sought to disrupt its attack.

Dodging the path of his axe strike with ease, the beast raked the tips of its upper, right set of claws across Ragnar's chest and right arm, drawing thin trails of blood through his skin.

Ragnar did not have time to bring the axe through for another strike. Jaws opening and white fangs gleaming bright, the beast lunged straight at him.

Thrusting the haft of his axe into the jaws of the panther-man, Ragnar pressed forward against the beast, seeking to negate its ability to swipe at him. With a powerful jerk of its head, the creature wrenched the axe free of Ragnar's hands and tossed it back. Landing far out of his reach, the axe thudded to the ground.

Giving the creature a hard, backward shove, Ragnar kept his body squared toward the beast. Shuffling back several paces, he stayed wary of the location of the concealed hunting trap he had identified, judging his position to be a couple of strides away.

Ragnar's plan now remained his only chance to survive the encounter.

The beast stood between Ragnar and his axe. Faster, stronger, and possessed of an arsenal of claws, each of them as sharp as a well-honed blade, in addition to its set of dagger-like fangs, the creature held every conceivable advantage.

Ragnar had slain ten opponents who held advantages over him on the circular, stone platform before the temple. He would have to slay an eleventh, one far more formidable than the rest.

Bleeding from his multiple wounds, Ragnar held to the one gambit left to him with a fierce determination.

Flashing its lengthy fangs, the creature roared again. Springing forward, and bounding across the ground, the beast charged Ragnar.

Lunging at Ragnar when it had drawn close, the creature stretched its forward claws out wide, readying to tear Ragnar's body to shreds.

Falling backward, Ragnar reached forward at the moment when the creature crossed over him. Grabbing onto the creature's arms and using its own forward momentum to his advantage, Ragnar threw its body overhead, holding on just long enough to guide the creature into a sharper, downward arc.

The creature sailed head-first into the wood and foliage masking the hunting pit. Shattering the covering, the beast plunged into the dark maw beneath.

High-pitched, grating cries erupted from within the pit, the eerie sounds reflecting unmistakable anguish.

Hurrying, Ragnar ran across the ground to the spot where his war axe had fallen. Bending down, he took up Raven Caller, rotated, and hustled back over toward the pit and its new captive.

Impaled on a few sharp wooden stakes, the creature writhed and twisted, screeching and struggling to free its body.

Gnashing its teeth at Ragnar, the beast growled and thrashed, but it could not dislodge itself from the stakes.

Lowering his two-handed grip on Raven Caller, Ragnar brought the axe overhead and chopped down hard, burying the blade deep into the beast's skull and splitting its head wide open.

With a gurgling, dissipating exhalation, the creature's entire body went slack. A moment later, the spark of life within its eyes dulled.

Ragnar ripped his axe free and prepared to leave the creature on the cluster of stakes embedded within its body. Then, a nagging thought tugged at him.

Though the creature appeared to be dead, it had an unnatural origin. Having fought many times against humans that took the shape of beasts, Ragnar knew that he could not assume anything about the creature that he had just felled. Whether or not it could return to life, he had to take one more precaution.

Lifting his axe one more time, he severed the beast's head, sending it to the bottom of the pit. The headless body remained above, impaled on the stakes.

After staring at the body of his vanquished foe for a moment, Ragnar walked onward, leaving the pit behind.

***

Ragnar caught up with the others at the approach of dusk. In their haste, the fleeing northerners had left a trail behind that would be easy for a tracker possessed of even modest skills to follow.

The recognition did not worry him. Ragnar fathomed that further pursuit on the part of their former captors would not begin immediately.

The big warrior that had transformed into a beast would not be returning to the high priest. It would be some time before their enemies learned of that, which served to buy the northerners a little additional time.

Looks of wonder and curiosity showing on their faces, Ursalka, Freyyar, and the others gathered close around him. Though caked in sweat and looking exhausted, Ragnar's companions demonstrated elation at his return through words, smiles, and even a few cheers.

A grin on his face, Ragnar chuckled, and said to them in a raised voice, "You should not act so surprised or relieved to see me! It was just a wild beast that needed to be slain. That damnable high priest has lost his guardian."

Ragnar then informed them of everything that had happened, before insisting that they press onward with every last shred of strength they had left within them. Despite their advanced state of weariness, none of the others argued with his order.

Ragnar could tell well enough that leaving behind a city that rejoiced in ripping out the hearts of captives, in sacrificial rituals dedicated to death and war gods, remained the sole priority for all of those with him.

Stopping only for a little water from a narrow stream, to drink and use for washing clean any cuts, gashes, and scrapes incurred in their escape, Ragnar and the northerners trudged throughout the night and continued deep into the next day. No signs of pursuit manifested, but neither did any of them have so much as an inkling of a destination, including Ragnar himself.

Beyond the matter of escaping the bloodthirsty city with its diabolical priests, the larger matter of finding their way home loomed. With no ships at their disposal, and no idea of how far off course they had been taken by the second great storm, the only consolation remaining to them lay in the fact that the legendary explorer Gardas had somehow found his way back home after facing a similar dilemma.

Pushing the oppressive heat and thick, humid air from his thoughts, Ragnar pressed forward alongside the others, though his body ran slick with a clammy sweat that had him longing for the crisp, biting air of a northern winter. Having had far enough of slithering, crawling, biting, and stinging things, he wished to walk on pristine, snow-draped slopes, savor the scent of towering pines, and feel the wind whipping through his hair.

The forest surrounding them ran rife with sounds, from the howls and hoots of monkeys to the shrill cries of birds. More than once, his companions found themselves startled, whether from walking face-first into a spider web or flushing out a snake from where it had been slumbering in the undergrowth.

Even Ragnar tensed at one point, when his footfalls disturbed a very large specimen of one of the elongated insects that possessed a vast multitude of legs. Moving with great speed, the creature scurried off into the forest, though it had not been lost on him that the thing was of a size to wrap around his neck more than once, with ease.

His only solace coming from the feel of Raven Caller in his hands once more, Ragnar brooded in silence, ignoring the brief exchanges between the others as they continued through the dense forest growths.

Heading east, he could only hope that it would not be too

much longer before they reached the coastline.

From there, they could head due north or south, until they encountered seafaring people. When they did find such a people, perhaps the northerners could find a way to gain control of some manner of ocean-worthy vessels.

Then, they could take to the sea and an environment more familiar to them than the surroundings they now marched through.

***

After organizing a watch, the northern warriors settled in for the remainder of the night. A luminous crescent moon had long-since crossed the point of midnight.

Dawn's first rays would be arriving far too soon for many of the weary northerners. Nevertheless, despite their deep fatigue, many had voiced a desire to keep pressing onward.

Ragnar commanded the halt, knowing that it could not be avoided. The northerners could simply advance no farther, without incurring severe, detrimental consequences.

Sheer exhaustion overcoming them, those that had not been assigned to a watch fell asleep in moments. Counted among the warriors in the first watch, Ragnar took up a position near a tree, keeping Raven Caller at hand.

The eerie, haunting cry in the distance of a large forest cat, most likely that of a jaguar, reminded Ragnar of the shape-shifting figure that he had fought and slain. He recognized the distinctive sound, marking a fresh kill somewhere in the night, and doubted that the creature making it was anything other than a part of the area's natural order.

Nevertheless, Ragnar knew better than to lower his guard, even a little.

The only disturbance that transpired during his watch involved one of the furry, hand-sized spiders that dwelled in the forest. He had just happened to glance down to look at his axe blade when taking notice of the shadowy form of the spider walking along the ground right toward him. Before the bulbous thing crawled onto his foot, he flicked the creature far away from him using the flat part of his axe blade.

Contending with an extreme degree of fatigue, he could not deny a wave of a relief when finally rousing Freyyar to take his turn in the watch.

"Too soon," Freyyar grumbled, getting up from where he had been curled up on a makeshift bedding of large leaves that he had arranged. "I barely shut my eyes."

"I let you sleep longer than all the others," Ragnar replied. A grin coming to his lips, he continued, "This may be a surprise to you, Freyyar, but I am no god. I need a little rest too."

Freyyar shook his head. "No god would be stupid enough to go on these reckless journeys."

"At the moment, I agree with you," Ragnar said, the grin remaining on his face. He yawned a moment later.

"I warmed up the bedding for you already, if you wish to take this spot," Freyyar said, gesturing to the place where he had been resting.

"I will take it," Ragnar said, lowering his body down to the ground. A host of aches rippled through his body. "See you when dawn breaks. Let me sleep, unless it is an army advancing on us."

"I think we should be able to handle most anything else, Stormbringer," Freyyar replied, rubbing at his eyes and giving Ragnar a nod, before shuffling away.

Though the circumstances stood far less than ideal, Ragnar had no trouble sliding into an unconsciousness state after he shut his eyes.

***

Resuming their eastward trek shortly after dawn, the northerners marched in a long, loose column. By then, most of them had fashioned makeshift weapons out of tree branches, with a few showing some further ingenuity using vines and rocks.

Setting a quicker gait, Ragnar sought to cover as much of a distance as they could that day. Every step took them farther from the city and closer to the coastline.

Enduring a few hunger pangs, Ragnar pondered their situation. He estimated that they had already put a great distance between themselves and the city, but no time could be spared for the period of hunting and foraging needed to feed almost fifty warriors.

At the moment, they could persist a while longer without food, but eventually hunger would become a growing, relentless adversary.

Finding food would not be problematic, whether hunting in the forest, teeming with an abundance of life forms, or fishing at the sea, with its varied bounty. Once they reached the coastline, Ragnar knew that some additional time would have to be taken to rest, eat, and regain strength.

Thinking upon the distance they had walked before being taken captive in the meadow, Ragnar did not think that it would be too much farther until they reached the sea. But he could not deny the greater burdens incurred while traveling within an unfamiliar land. Every moment held the prospect of an unpleasant surprise, and the specter of the unknown hounded them at every turn.

Sending a wave of caution through Ragnar around midday, the forest came to an abrupt end, opening onto a broad field where high green stalks rose from the summits of low dirt mounds. Arranged in rows and set at even intervals, the mounds had not been formed through natural means.

While it did not take an experienced farmer to recognize the cultivated nature of the field, no sign of those who had labored to form the mounds and plant the crop could be seen anywhere that

Ragnar looked.

Ragnar brought the group to a halt at the edge of the high stalks. Not wanting to blunder into another ambush, he refrained from crossing through the stalks.

Wondering about the nature of the crop in the field, Ragnar looked at the nearest stalks. Each of them displayed an elongated, oblong kind of growth ensconced within a sheathing of leaves.

Tearing one of them free and peeling the leaves away, Ranger looked upon tightly-packed rows of a lighter-hued, larger kind of seed or grain. A few of the others followed Ragnar's example and inspected the unfamiliar crop.

Shortly afterward, a voice that did not come from any of the northerners rang out across the field.

"You wish life? Follow me!"

Following the sound of the accented voice, Ragnar took in the sight of an older-looking man with a wispy beard, calling to him and the others from the top of a rise in the ground on the far side of the field.

Bare of chest and wearing nothing more than a simple loincloth, the lean, old man wore multiple necklaces, threaded with a variety of shells and small stones. A little matted and scraggly, his shoulder-length gray hair extended to just below his shoulders.

Hearing the words of his own tongue spoken aloud by one of the native inhabitants for the second time since coming ashore, Ragnar called back to the old man. "Who are you? And how do you know our tongue?"

"I am Arutochtli. Enemy of Mazayin," he replied. "I learn. I know of pale-skins."

Ragnar rolled his eyes and muttered to himself. "Wonderful. A crazy old priest or sorcerer."

"Follow now!" the old man called again. "I am friend. Have been friend of pale-skin ... in time before!"

"You can come over here!" Ragnar shouted back. "We are

not going to cross this ground."

"I will!" Arutochtli shouted back.

Starting toward them, the old man began crossing through the center of the field, disappearing from sight several times as he moved through the high stalks.

By then, the rest of the northerners had come up from behind and gathered around Ragnar. All of them eyed the field with great wariness and weapons at hand.

"The old man knows our language," Freyyar stated, his chest heaving with deep breaths.

"We cannot ... run blind forever," Ursalka added, also sounding winded from the great exertion that all of them had been enduring.

"We must learn something of where we are, " Freyyar said, his breath steadying.

"I agree," Ursalka said, wiping sweat from her brow.

"To learn more about this land, we will need to give our trust to him," Ragnar said, watching the high stalks moving where the old man crossed midpoint of the field. "There is no other way at this moment. Are you ready to do that?"

"He could be loyal to them, or he could despise them," Ursalka said.

"If he tries to betray us, we can cut him wide open," Freyyar added, an edge to his voice.

The old man drew nearer.

"We have a chance to learn something," Ragnar said. "Whether by magic or not, he does know our tongue. We have had no one to speak with other than that accursed high priest."

"I say we take advantage of this chance," Ursalka said. "He does not look like a man who would be in the company of the high priest."

The old man reached them and slowed to a stop. His dark-eyed gaze drifted across the throng of warriors.

"I remember ... pale-skins," the old man said, before looking back to Ragnar.

"Sorcerer, or priest, how can we trust you?" Ragnar asked him.

"Not sorcerer. Or priest," the old man answered. "I see much. Live many years. Years teach much."

"I do not care what you are, or how long you have lived," Freyyar said. "I will kill you myself if you seek to turn us over to those bastards who took the heart of my friend."

"No to Mazayin," the old man said, a stern look coming to his face at the word. "Mazayin is enemy. They fight war. Against Tetucoatl. My people. Make us give food. Give cloth. To live."

"The Mazayin ... that is what the people of that city are called?" Ragnar asked him. "The place with the great temple."

"Mazayin build Mixatoplec," the old man answered, nodding. "Take many of here ... offer to Dachtli ... and Broltec."

Ragnar saw an unmistakable flicker of anger within the old man's eyes. Nothing about the old man hinted at treachery.

"Where would you take us?" Ragnar asked.

"To place ... safe ... away from Mazayin," the old man answered him, continuing to speak in a stilted manner.

"Why do you seek to help us?" Ragnar queried.

"You ... enemy of Mazayin," the old man said, pointing at Ragnar. He then pointed at himself. "Me, enemy of Mazayin. Pale-skin of time before ... a friend."

The reference to a possible northerner in the old man's past piqued Ragnar's curiosity, but he could not pursue the matter at the moment. A general decision had to be made first.

He looked to the others. "We either trust him, or we do not."

Freyyar shrugged. "He looks harmless enough. I say we trust him. We need to know more, and his life will be forfeit if he tries anything against us."

Ursalka nodded. "I am in agreement with Freyyar. We must

try to learn more of these lands."

Ragnar looked to the two of them, and then turned back to face the old man.

"We will go with you," he told him. "But do not try and deceive us."

"Follow me," Arutochtli replied in a solemn tone. "I speak true."

The old man led Ragnar and the others from the field of crops and back into the forest. Seeing that he guided them in a more northern direction, instead of continuing eastward, Ragnar had to force some ensuing unease back from his thoughts.

Ragnar could not deny that he found the old man and his references to a "pale-skin" from before to be more than a little intriguing. Neither could he deny the risk involved in placing their fates in the old man's hands.

Keeping close to the old man and maintaining wariness, he marched onward.

Only time would tell whether he had been wise or a fool to accept the offer of Arutochtli.

***

A golden vessel navigating an azure sea, the sun crossed the blue skies far above the dense tree canopy. Below, in pools of deep shadow and vibrant light, Ragnar and the others continued following Arutochtli north through the forest.

Despite his advanced age, the old man exhibited a limber step and exceptional endurance, pushing the foreigners to the limits of what they could handle traversing the thicker undergrowth. Using their weapons, they swept aside leaves, branches, and other obstacles.

Close to dusk, they reached a village consisting of several thatch-roofed huts and a few other smaller buildings. The sight of habitation sent a surge of relief running through the weary, famished northerners.

Slowing down at last, and staying close to Arutochtli, Ragnar looked around and took in the unfurling scene with an edge of scrutiny.

A large crowd of men, women and children gathered at their arrival, eyeing the newcomers with expressions ranging from fear, to curiosity, to anxiety. The men were clad in little more than loincloths, and the women, in ankle-length, skirt like garments tied about the waist with narrow, cloth belts, like those he had seen in the city of the Mazayin. Ragnar could tell at once that they were simple peasants and nothing like the ones in elaborate attire atop the massive temple.

After addressing the villagers in their own tongue for a few moments, Arutochtli turned to Ragnar.

"Take rest, here," the old man said. "Places for all ... pale-skins."

"Answer me now, and do not lie," Ragnar replied, looking the old man direct in the eyes. "I must know before we take another step. How do you know our words? What sorcery do you use?"

"Learn from pale-skin ... name Gardar ... when he here," the old man said. "Not sorcerer. Many year ... I live."

A hush fell across Ragnar's companions at the mention of the legendary explorer's name.

Arutochtli then reached up to his chest and brought out a pendant that had been hidden beneath the other necklaces draping from his neck. A silver brooch, suited to pin a cloak, and unmistakable in its northern origin, lay exhibited within the old man's palm for all eyes to see.

Many eyes widened among Ragnar's companions at the sight.

"That was so long ago," Ragnar said in a low voice, astonished at the revelation. "Stories told even to my father's father."

"Many year ... can live ... here in land," Arutochtli replied. He did not elaborate further, prompting Ragnar to ponder just how old the man standing before him was.

"You knew Gardar?" Ragnar asked, incredulous at the thought.

"Yes ... for many year," the old man replied. "Gardar live here ... teach me your words. Long since spoke them."

From his expression, to tone of voice, and the steady look in his eyes, Arutochtli showed no trace of lying. Everything about him resonated in a sincere manner.

"It is good that you found us," Ragnar said. "We would have marched until we reached the ocean, and still we would know nothing of these lands."

"You bring hope ... for Tetucoatl ... my people," the old man said, glancing toward the small throng quietly listening to an exchange that none of them could understand. He looked Ragnar in the eyes. "For me ... bring peace. Defeat Mazayin. Make Tetucoatl free."

"How? What can we do?" Ragnar asked. "We are not an army."

"Mazayin conquer people ... take many warriors ... offer to gods," the old man said, a faraway look of sadness coming into his eyes. "Three sons taken ... to altar of gods."

"Say nothing further," Ragnar told the old man in a softer tone, understanding Arutochtli's meaning at once.

The old man did not say anything more for a few heartbeats, but the sorrow finally ebbed from his eyes.

"All stay ... rest ... eat," the old man said, looking around to Ragnar's companions. "Guests of Tetucoatl people."

"We accept, and let us begin a friendship with the Tetucoatl," Ragnar answered, pronouncing the name of Arutochtli's people with great care. His words invoked a hearty cheer from Ursalka, Freyyar, and the other northerners, the boisterous response drawing a number of strange looks from the villagers observing them from a short distance away.

"Yes ... pale-skins friends of Tetucoatl," Arutochtli responded, a warm smile spreading upon his face.

"We must think more on what can be done," Ragnar told him, in a tone of reassurance. "Though I do not know where we can get an army."

"May ... be way," the old man said, with an enigmatic air. Then, he stated, in a more direct manner, "Rest now. Eat now. You must."

"Tell us where we must go to do these things," Ragnar replied.

The old man's suggestion sounded good enough to him for the moment, and from the looks of his companions they shared his sentiments. His stomach growling, the promise of food outweighed all other things occupying his mind.

"Wait ... people will help," Arutochtli then said. "I will talk."

The old man turned to his people and addressed them once more. While he spoke, many among the villagers cast nervous glances in the direction of the northerners. After he had finished, the northerners were divided and sent with various men and women from the village.

Ragnar nodded and smiled in greeting to the hosts given to him and three other northern warriors. A younger man and woman, the new hosts did not look as if they been married long.

He suspected they harbored worries, but he could say nothing that they would understand. Remaining calm and quiet, and gesturing as best he could, would be the best that he could do.

When the young man gestured for Ragnar to come with him, he cast more than one fearful glance toward his axe. Turning, with his wife keeping close to his side, he started walking away.

Striding a couple paces behind, Ragnar followed him into the village.

∗∗∗

Restoring their strength and energies, Rangar and his companions found succor and repose in abundance among the tribal villagers during the next few days. The mood of the villagers eased fast when they realized that the northerners would not harm them.

The peasants lived in a simple manner. Their thatch-roofed huts contained one room with a beaten earth floor and were bordered with sides built out of wattle and daub. The huts served as the location where everything from cooking to sleeping took place, though the people spent most of their time outside.

As he had done on every day since their arrival, Ragnar kept to himself for the most part and remained content to observe the ways of the villagers. He found a little comfort in their consistent routines, a stark contrast to the sheer chaos that he had endured since the first storm at sea had taken hold of their fleet.

Seated on a mat fashioned of reeds, Ragnar stared at the circular plate of clay resting upon a triad of stones. A fire underneath the clay plate heated the surface to where flat, round discs made of a fine-ground dough, the latter made from the seeds produced by the tall plants he had seen in the large field, were prepared by the young woman in whose hut they slept at night.

Ragnar had learned more about the crop and its great importance to the Tetucoatl. Called corn, the crop held a pivotal place in their daily food consumption. They made use of corn every day and kept great quantities of it in storage structures crafted of wickerwork and plaster.

Ragnar had come to like the corn meal discs, made before every meal by the village women. Learning that he could wrap beans and many other kinds of food items within them, he enjoyed coming up with different combinations, some of which proved wondrous to his tastes. From bits of meat or fish, to mushrooms, fruits, a vegetable called peppers, and other food items, a number of delectable mixtures could be made and eaten at meals.

After eating another hearty repast, involving many wrapped

combinations, Ragnar took his leave of his hosts and the smoke-filled space within the hut. After stripping down outside, he then sought to cleanse himself off in the enclosed steam chamber located outside of the hut.

A hemispherical clay structure, with a fire-place set against the exterior, the enclosure generated a great amount of steam once it had been heated and water had been splashed on the inside surface.

Ragnar had to enter the small chamber carefully to avoid contact with the heated sides. The moisture and heat washed his skin and called sweat forth, and he also made use of a unique root that produced a lather that he rubbed over his body and then rinsed off.

Emerging from the chamber, he relished the cooling touch of the outside air upon his skin. He imagined a dip into a stream or lake would feel incredible, and he tested the idea by taking a bucket of water and pouring it over himself.

The sensation proved to be incredible, and Ragnar then decided to follow every such bath in the future with a thorough dousing of cold water.

After finishing with the steam bath, Ragnar made his way out to the fields where a ripening field of corn swayed and whispered in the light air currents. The tranquil sight had a rapid calming effect on him.

Ragnar became so relaxed and immersed in the moment that he almost did not hear the approach of Arutochtli coming up from behind him.

"Ragnar," the old man said, announcing his presence.

"It is good to see you, Arutochtli," Ragnar replied, turning his head toward the old man.

"If no big rain ... then many crop," the old man said, looking out over the field of corn stalks. "If big rain ... people will starve."

"We are always at the mercy of the whims of the wind, rain,

and sun," Ragnar replied, understanding Arutochtli's meaning concerning the dangers of too much rain on a crop. "It is that way in all lands where people live, and things grow."

"But no more be at mercy ... of Mazayin," Arutochtli said, glancing over to him with a hardened look in his eyes.

"I do not imagine many wish to be ruled by those devils," Ragnar said, thinking of the blood-soaked hand of the high priest holding the heart of Grenna aloft.

"Pale-skins ... come to fight with us," the old man said, looking to Ragnar and pointing to him. "You fight ... Mazayin. Many fight Mazayin."

"Who is going to fight?" Ragnar asked, perceiving something more within the old man's tone. "I do not have an army with me. We are barely fifty in number. You are speaking of something more, are you not?"

"Many more come ... people like Tetucoatl," the old man replied. "People listen. They know. Pale-skins stop sacrifice. Great warrior throws priest. Strikes emperor to ground! Sign of gods. Time is now. Fight Mazayin."

"A rebellion?" Ragnar said after a pause, raising his eyebrows.

"Towns. Villages. Many. Break free of Mazayin" the old man said, nodding to him. "Mazayin army ... will come ... to fight people."

"Will the enemy come if their emperor is too wounded?" Ragnar said.

"Yes. High priest lead army ... if no emperor," the old man said. "I know ... emperor will come."

The words landed upon Ragnar's ears like soft raindrops pattering onto the surface of parched soil. His mind had been so fixed upon helping his comrades escape from the Mazayin that no thought of gaining an opportunity for vengeance upon the vile high priest had tempted him; until that moment.

"I made a promise to that high priest," Ragnar said. "I would drag him into the abyss if I could."

"Is way ... will tell story," the old man said, showing no hint of jest. "Now ... fight Mazayin ... Tetucoatl and pale-skins together."

"The warriors with me do not have the weapons they are used to wielding," Ragnar said, speaking slowly and hoping that the old man understood enough of his words. "This would put them at a disadvantage in any battle, against warriors using the weapons they have been trained to wield."

The old man stared at him for a moment. Just when Ragnar began to think that he had not comprehended his meaning, the old man nodded his head.

"We can bring weapons ... to pale-skins," Arutochtli said. "You fight. With us. We take weapons ... from Mazayin. Bring pale-skins weapons ... to you."

"How are you going to do that?' Ragnar asked.

"Many Tetucoatl ... slave to Mazayin," Arutochtli replid. "Will help."

"If there is a way to get the weapons we know, then we would be able to fight for you in a much stronger way," Ragnar said.

"We bring weapons," the old man said. "You fight Mazayin?"

"If my companions get their weapons back, I think they will all agree to fight the Mazayin," Ragnar stated, a smirk cropping up on his face. "And you already know that I will send as many of the bastards to hell as I can."

***

Ragnar looked around at the somber faces of his companions illuminated in the firelight.

"Each one of you has a choice. Stand in battle against those who spilled the blood of our comrades to satisfy their feckless gods, or continue on our way," Ragnar said. "I shall not stand in the way of any of you ... nor shall I regard you any less if you choose not to fight with the Tetucoatl against the Mazayin."

"I want to split them all wide open and leave them to rot for what they did to Grenna," Ursalka stated, anger coursing through her tone. "But I no longer have my sword."

"Nor I," added another warrior.

"You were the only one able to regain your own weapon," Ursalka said. A smirk formed upon her lips. "You more than earned it back, slaying ten of those scum's best warriors."

Murmurs of approval and commendation rippled through the gathered warriors.

"I wish I could have slain all of them," Ragnar said, looking to Ursalka, and then sweeping his gaze across the rest. "But we may yet get our chance. I have more to tell you."

A hopeful look sprang upon Freyyar's face. "What do you mean?"

"Arutochtli's people and other tribes are gathering for war," Ragnar replied. "They all have some help in the city of Mixatoplec, as many of their people are now slaves to the Mazayin. Arutochtli has told me that he has a way of getting your weapons and returning them to you."

Many smiles and exclamations met Ragnar's words at the tidings.

"What about the chance to slay the bastards?" Freyyar asked.

"We have been asked to join the Tetucoatl in open battle against the Mazayin. Our escape from the city has led to an uprising. The choice of standing with them in this coming battle has been left to us."

"An easy choice to make," Ursalka replied, a broad smile spreading on her face.

Murmurs of agreement broke out all around her, turning into jubilant shouts and cheers.

Ragnar shared their exuberance.

From everything that he had learned about the wicked

Mazayin and what they had done to people like the Tetucoatl, a reckoning day was long overdue.

***

Ragnar had never seen a more colorful battle array than the one massed across the field from the Tetucoatl warriors and those of two other rebellious tribes. Holding an advantage in numbers over the rebels, several thousand Mazayin warriors stood in orderly ranks beneath a host of ornate standards and awaited the signal to begin the fighting.

Warriors in full, body-covering garments of varying solid colors, including blue, red, yellow, black, and green, along with a great number of warriors bare of chest with distinctive, high tufts of hair, were mixed together all throughout the Mazayin ranks.

Following a blaring wave of conch-shell blasts and a booming cascade of drum beats, the fighting began with a downpour of missiles. Arrows and javelins rained thick upon both sides, claiming many lives at the outset.

The Mazayin, Tetucoatl, and other tribes had an ingenious method of launching javelins far distances. Fitting the javelins in grooves carved into the wooden spear-throwing devices and executing the launch with a whipping motion of their arms, the warriors could put great force into a javelin throw.

Ragnar and the northerners took shelter where they could behind upraised shields held by the rebel warriors. The hard thuds and thumps of arrows and javelins striking wood and the ground accompanied the cries where missiles had found targets of flesh.

After the massive, initial volley, a new torrent of signals reverberated across the battlefield and the two sides surged toward each other. Warriors came together in a tremendous collision, filling the skies with their war cries and the clashing of weapons and shields.

Ragnar and the northerners, fighting at the center of the broad line, waded into the thick of the fighting. In moments, the Mazayin began paying a steep price in blood for what they had done to the northerner's companions.

The battle extended for a long while. The rebel tribes fought off multiple attempts by the larger Mazayin force to turn their flanks. At the center, Ragnar and the northerners drove deeper into the enemy ranks, creating an expanding wedge.

Recognizing the development, Mazayin commanders reacted by pulling back their warriors to form a new line. The Tetucoatl and their allies, invigorated at the retreat, advanced with a storm of war cries.

Witnessing the shifts in the enemy ranks and the importance of the warriors who had high banners secured to their backs and shoulders, Ragnar directed his comrades to strike the banner-carriers wherever they could be reached. Toppling banners to the ground had a swift effect on the movements of the enemy at the center.

Confusion began to spread and the Mazayin's previous cohesion began slogging down. Seeing the effects of bringing down the banner carriers, Ragnar redoubled his efforts to strike at them.

Then, a bevy of conch-shell blasts broke out in the distance, from beyond the Mazayin ranks. At first, thinking that the signals indicated the arrival of Mazayin reinforcements, Ragnar did not understand the distressed looks sprouting on many enemy faces at the sonorous outbreak.

The blasts indicated the arrival of forces from two other rebelling tribes. Already pressed back, the Mazayin warriors suddenly found themselves caught within the jaws of a deadly trap.

Hewing one enemy warrior after another down, Ragnar paid little heed to the momentous swing in the battle, until his eyes set upon a hawk-like visage that he could never have forgotten.

Fear gleamed in the eyes of the Mazayin ruler at the sight of Ragnar carving his way toward him, and he called out at once to the warriors around him, all of them in wooden headpieces crafted in the forms of eagles, wolves, demons, jaguars, snakes and other creatures.

The veteran Mazayin warriors formed a living shield around their emperor and fought back with courage, but they could not stop Ragnar and the frenzied northerners fighting at his side.

Those in his path fell swiftly as he hacked his way closer and closer to the now-trapped emperor.

All around them, the fighting turned into a slaughter as the incoming rebel warriors engulfed and overwhelmed the Mazayin ranks.

After killing the last of the elite warriors protecting the emperor, Ragnar faced the reward he had set his sights on.

Not wasting a moment, he had no care for any formalities. Trudging forward, he tore the headdress with the golden, horizontal crest off the head of the emperor and hurled it to the ground.

Devoid of the elaborate piece, the emperor looked weak and ordinary to the eyes. He began talking and held his hands out to Ragnar. Likely blubbering some desperate plea, the Mazayin emperor shed all pretenses of his former state.

Reaching out, Ragnar clamped his right hand about the back of the emperor's neck and forced him to his knees.

"You spared no one, and now you will not be spared," Ragnar told the once-haughty Mazayin ruler. Then, in a low voice simmering with anger he added, "You will experience one more sacrifice."

Ragnar then had Arutochtli summoned to him. Holding his grip firm on the emperor, he did not have to wait long for the Tetucoatl to fetch the old man, who had been standing at the back of the mass of rebel warriors.

When the old man arrived in the escort of a pair of Tetucoatl warriors, Ragnar told him what he needed to find.

Arutochtli gave him a perplexed look, perhaps wondering at his intent, but nodded and proceeded to speak with a few of the victorious Tetucoatl warriors.

One of them nodded back to the old man. Turning to Ragnar, the warrior beckoned for him to follow.

Showing no concern for the emperor's comfort, Ragnar dragged the man unceremoniously across the ground behind him as he followed the Tetucoatl warrior. Rebel warriors cleared back to create a channel for their passage, while gazing upon the humiliated Mazayin ruler with looks of disdain, hatred, and astonishment.

The Mazayin emperor whimpered and cried, but the only thought that came to Ragnar's mind was imagining the look of rapture on the man's face as he watched daggers plunging into the bodies of terrified men and women. The thought spurred Ragnar forward in a state of full conviction. The emperor had to reap what he had sowed.

In his wake, many of the northerners and warriors of the rebellious tribes followed. They entered the forest beyond the field of battle and continued for a little while until Ragnar had what he sought.

By the time the Tetucoatl warrior had guided Ragnar to the site he had wanted to be taken to, the emperor had been reduced to a battered, dirty, pitiful state. His fine cloaks had been torn and streaked with dirt, and grime covered his body, now covered in scrapes and cuts.

"Your evil consumed countless lives," Ragnar proclaimed, his face akin to a snarl. "Now, be consumed, and be given over to ruin."

The emperor offered almost no resistance as Ragnar pulled

him forward and shoved him face-first into a conspicuous hole in the ground; above which a broad, flat growth remained poised.

Closing its trap, the lethal plant muffled the emperor's shrill cries.

"A grisly way to die," Freyyar remarked, having come up to join Ragnar and eyeing the closed-top of of the carnivorous plant.

"Not grisly enough, for the things that worm is guilty of," Ragnar replied, grim-faced, listening to faint, anguished cries from within the living trap.

Ragnar did not leave the area until long after the emperor's cries had fallen into silence. Around him, a throng stood in silent vigil to the justice that had been meted out to the wicked ruler.

Taking no joy from the destruction of the emperor, he left the site close to sunset

One more figure among the Mazayin still burned within his memory.

***

After resting through the night and part of the next day, Ragnar finally celebrated the battlefield victory in his own way. He needed to be far removed from blood and war, and he knew well the one thing that would take him away for awhile.

The intense look conveyed in the dark eyes of the long-haired, beautiful young woman said everything that Ragnar needed to know. He could not speak her tongue, and she did not speak a word of his, but the invitation remained clear.

Similar invitations had come from many during the time that he had stayed in the village but knowing the young woman to be unmarried helped facilitate his acceptance, now that he needed to avail himself of such an offer.

Guiding him a short distance into the forest, her barefooted stride slow and graceful, the young woman took him to the side of a small pool filled with crystalline waters. Untying her cloth belt and removing her skirt-garment, she presented a body supple and smooth to Ragnar's eyes.

Wearing no tunic, he had only to loosen his belt and shed his tattered breeches to uncover his own body.

Leading him into the cool, soothing waters, she wasted little time in running her hands over his skin, summoning a rising heat from within him. Locking his lips with hers, Ragnar took her in the water, giving release to all of the pent-up tensions that he had accumulated since the first storm had taken their fleet off course.

Before finishing, he guided her over to the side of the pool.

Lifting her out of the water, he set her down slow, onto her knees, and positioned himself behind her. Taking up a fistful of her luxuriant black hair, and holding to her locks firm, he began taking her from behind. Accelerating until he arched his back in one final, heated thrust, an explosion of euphoria rewarded him for the finish of the act.

The woman's legs quivered, and she looked a little unsteady when she got back up to her feet, but Ragnar reached out to brace her with a gentle touch, keeping her from falling. Catching his eyes, she gave him a smile, though her eyes now reflected more than a little weariness.

After the two of them took a brief dip into the pool to cleanse off the sweat beading all over them, they took up their clothes, donned them, and started back for the village.

To Ragnar, the return seemed more like floating than walking.

***

"You look relaxed, Stormbringer," Ursalka greeted him, where she stood in front of one of the thatch-roofed tribal houses. She extended the cup that she held in her hand to him. "Try this."

Ragnar accepted the vessel from her and took a drink. He paused, adjusting to the unfamiliar taste, but found it to his liking.

"What is it?" he asked.

"It took me many hand gestures, but I think I know," Ursalka said. "It is made from sap, from the flower stem of that cactus they make much use of."

"It is not good northern mead, but I can drink it," Ragnar declared with a mischievous grin.

Around them, an air of merriment coursed through the tribal people and the foreigners that they hosted.

"This is a much-needed evening," Ragnar said. He caught the eyes of another attractive young tribal woman that he knew was unmarried, gazing at him from where she stood with some others. He could see the aching hunger with her look. "And I am not done with it ... but there is a task that yet remains."

Following his eyes, Ursalka saw the woman, and grinned. "No, it seems your night is not done. Before the night is through, you may have increased the tribe's numbers."

"I do not think that would be well-received by their fathers," Ragnar said.

"You will have given them some great warriors, if they are born of your seed, Ragnar," Ursalka said. Though spoken in levity, a deep level of respect flowed through her words.

He acknowledged her comment with a bow of his head. Then he grinned, "It is probably better if we are well away from here if any seed takes root."

"Yes, probably wise," Ursalka said, laughing. After a few moments had passed, she asked him, "What is the task that you spoke of?"

"A promise to be kept," Ragnar said, an iron glint in his eyes. "For me to do alone."

***

Ragnar and the northerners accompanied the Tetucoatl and other tribes into the city of Mixatoplec. He had a promise to fill and the allied tribes were all too eager to assist him.

They met no resistance. With the destruction of the Mazayin army and the execution of the emperor, a cloud of fear and disarray had permeated the vast city.

While many warriors with him headed to loot the emperor's palace and the homes of the wealthy Mazayin, Ragnar, the other northerners, and a small band of Tetucoatl warriors headed straight for the great temple.

Deep within the shrine of Broltec, hiding within a concealed chamber betrayed by a former Tetucoatl slave, they found the high priest.

Dragging him from the shrine and down the steps of the temple, Ragnar already knew the destination.

Arutochtli had shared a story with him about the beliefs of his people and a place that none of them dared to tread.

In Ragnar's eyes, he could not think of a better place to take the high priest.

***

"I stay," Arutochtli said, looking grim. "Walk no more."

Ragnar gazed at the dark maw leading into the depths of the world.

Raven Caller rested in the grip of his right hand. His left hand held onto the vines binding the man that he had carried and dragged through the dense foliage for almost an entire day. Though dazed and exhausted, the high priest's eyes grew wide with terror at the sight of the cave.

Making whining noises and biting on the vine gagging his mouth, the high priest made no attempt to mask his raw fear.

"You know this place," Ragnar stated, a cold grin forming on his face. He turned back toward Arutochtli. "Wait for me. I will return."

"I wish that," Arutochtli replied.

Ragnar slipped his axe back into the loop at his belt. Lighting a pinewood torch, he held it up and forward of his body, pulling the frightened high priest along with him.

The air of the cave grew warmer the deeper Ragnar proceeded.

The light of the torch did not reach as far as he thought it should. The dark of the cave appeared to be confining the light in some way, forcing it close to Ragnar and his captive.

A suffocating silence pervaded the air. No drips of water, echoes from footsteps, whispers from a flowing air current, or any other kinds of sounds encountered within a cave environment broke the stillness.

Sweeping the torch to the left and right, illuminating as much of the ground as he could, Ragnar kept a constant watch on the footing. It remained solid enough for the time being, and the ground had only a slight downward slope.

Sweat began beading on Ragnar's skin, and his breathing became more labored despite the fact that he had not strained his body to any significant degree. The sounds of the high priest breathing hard told him that the changes he had been sensing were not figments of his mind.

The air had grown thicker to the lungs, and if the trend continued Ragnar judged that it would not be long before it became impossible to breathe. Continuing forward, he pulled the high priest through the dark.

A black, glistening liquid revealed in the torchlight halted Ragnar on the brink of stepping into it. A faint mist wafted off the glimmering surface.

Pulling more sweat from Ragnar's pores, a tremendous heat emanated from the dark viscous substance.

The high priest began to jerk and twist about, trying in desperation to break free of Ragnar. Using the arm that gripped him, Ragnar shook the high priest hard, caring not a bit if he jarred the miscreant's bones.

"Cease!" Ragnar ordered the high priest in a whisper that sounded more like a curt hiss. "You will not have to wait long now. I am at the shores."

If the high priest could not understand his words, he did understand the meaning. Like a reflex, he tried to pull away from Ragnar.

Distinct and prominent, the flapping of wings sounded within the dark, from high above.

Ragnar looked upwards, knowing that whatever made the sound was much larger than anything that was usually found within a cave. Furthermore, the sounds were of the type he had expected to hear.

It would not be much longer now.

Also coming from high above, a sequence of piercing, high-pitched noises cleaved the darkness.

Sensing movement in the darkness nearby, Ragnar ducked, stabbing upward with his torch when a massive, black shape passed right over his head.

Making matters worse, he could sense other movements around him, on the ground level. Here and there, his torch caught glimpses of spectral, gray shapes moving within the darkness.

Human in appearance, the naked male and female forms shuffled forward in a listless, sluggish manner, making their way toward the edge of the black liquid. The few whose expressions he could make out appeared solemn, if not forlorn.

Ragnar wondered at the origins of the various phantoms, but he suspected the answers would bring him little sympathy for their dreadful state of being.

Reaching the dark, steaming liquid, the apparitions continued into it without hesitation or reaction.

Ragnar's light reached only far enough to show a couple of the nearest ones immersing to waist-height, before they slipped from his view into an impenetrable black.

The sound of flapping wings approaching drew his eyes away from the ghostly forms. The beats of the wings ceased, and Ragnar swung his torch about to the approximate area where the noises had come from.

Though constrained, the torch cast enough light to reveal the monstrosity standing in the gloom. Twice Ragnar's height, the malefic creature showed no reaction to the light or agitation at his sudden attention toward the thing.

If anything, the creature had the air of something in full confidence of its dominion.

Leathery wings spread wide, body covered in coarse, dark fur, the creature stood upon two legs similar to a human. Two eyes gleamed from behind a broad, upturned nose, the latter having a leaf-shape contour to it.

A pair of large, triangular ears angled toward Ragnar.

Ragnar knew without an inkling of doubt that he did not stand before a natural creature of the world.

Above him, more flapping sounds broke out. Some sounding closer, and a few more distant, the noises heralded others of the ilk of the one standing in front of him.

An image of an obsidian blade held high coalesced within Ragnar's mind. In a surreal, slow manner, he recalled the blade plunging into the chest of Grenna, to a thunderous cheer from teeming masses at the base of the temple.

Last, he saw the blood-soaked hand of the High Priest holding Grenna's heart up for all to see, drawing a surge in the roaring of the frenzied crowd.

Each one brutal and vivid in his memory, the executions of his other comrades paraded through his mind in a like manner.

"Take him to the blackest depths, it is where he belongs!" Ragnar thundered at the bat-like entity. "He is yours to take."

With a hard, forward shove, he sent the priest hurtling

toward the huge, winged beast.

The high priest could not maintain his footing and toppled to the ground. Rolling over, he stared at the monster looming above him. The vine binding his mouth muffled what would have been a scream of horror.

With an ear-splitting shriek that caused Ragnar to wince, the bat-creature leaned forward and took to flight, snatching up the offering before it. In an instant, the huge creature vanished into the darkness, and no trace remained of the high priest; not even a faint sound.

Switching the torch to his left hand, Ragnar took up his axe. Gripping it about mid-shaft, he strode away from the searing, black waters. Heading the other way, he passed by a few more of the gray, ephemeral specters, but paid them little attention other than to avoid letting any part of his body come into contact with one.

The flapping sounds persisted above and around him. Twice, Ragnar braced himself, Raven Caller held at the ready to strike hard, hearing the tell-tale swell of sounds indicating something drawing nearer to him. In both instances, the creatures flying within the darkness shifted direction before reaching him.

In all likelihood, they recognized that he had no place within the horrid gateway to depths unfathomable.

Proceeding forward, with the same caution that he had taken when descending, Ragnar made his way back to the surface. The slight upward grade of the slope told him that he headed in the right direction, as did the gradual thinning and cooling of the air.

At last, he broke free of the cave entrance and found himself under moon and starlight once more.

A look of relief washed across Arutochtli's face at the sight of Ragnar.

Ragnar grinned at the old man. "I told you that I would return. Have more confidence."

"No harm?" Arutochtli asked.

"Not to me," Ragnar said. "And everything is as the story you told me said. I have no wish to return there."

Arutochtli looked to the cave entrance with an expression of fear and amazement.

"Let us get back to the village," Ragnar said. "My task is complete. My promise to the high priest has been kept, and it is time to begin finding my way back to my homelands."

Before the old man could answer, Ragnar strode by him, heading back for the village.

***

To his right, salt-graced breezes wafted in from the sparkling sea reaching to the far horizons.

To his left, the forest stood vigil where the rocky beach met with the tree line.

A new day had arrived, and the time had come for Ragnar to begin the journey to find his way back home.

A small crowd of the Tetucoatl tribe had gathered to see the forty-three light-skinned foreign warriors depart. Ragnar caught a few women among them casting longing glances at particular warriors among his comrades.

More than one of the desirous looks being directed toward himself, the yearning expressions reminded him of the succulent passions that he had engaged in during recent nights. He would have to savor the memories, as it would likely be some time before he could indulge in the company of women again.

A long march to the north along the coastline lay ahead of them, beginning their attempt to return home.

"May good health and good days be ahead of you, Arutochtli" Ragnar said to the old man, who stood in front of the other Tetucoatl.

"You ... also," he replied. "Pale-skins good friends."

"Thank you for all that you have done," Ragnar said. "You are friends and always will be in my heart."

"I thank you ... we are free ... of altar of gods," the old man said, giving Ragnar a bow.

Ragnar nodded, and smiled. "It gladdens me to leave here knowing that you are free of them. But we must leave now. A long journey lies ahead of us, and we are not certain of where our path will lead."

"Go to north ... keep going north ... you will find way," Arutochtli told him.

Ragnar chuckled, understanding the wisdom in the advice. Nodding to Ursalka, Freyyar, Magnolf, and all who had survived the harrowing trial in Mixatoplec and the events following their escape, he proclaimed, "To the north, it is time we get headed home!"

"To the north!" Ursalka responded in a jubilant air.

Looking to Arutochtli one more time and putting to memory the smile resting on the old man's face, Ragnar took a step forward, leading the others with him northward.

About the Author

Stephen Zimmer is an award-winning author and filmmaker based out of Lexington Kentucky. His works include the Rayden Valkyrie novels and Tales (Sword and Sorcery), the Rising Dawn Saga (Cross Genre), the Fires in Eden Series (Epic Fantasy), the Hellscapes short story collections (Horror), the Chronicles of Ave short story collections (Fantasy), the Harvey and Solomon Tales (Steampunk), The Faraway Saga (YA Dystopian/Cross-Genre) and the Ragnar Stormbringer Tales (Sword and Sorcery).

Stephen's visual work includes the feature film Shadows Light, shorts films such as The Sirens and Swordbearer, and the forthcoming Rayden Valkyrie: Saga of a Lionheart TV Pilot.

Stephen is a proud Kentucky Colonel who also enjoys the realms of music, martial arts, good bourbons, and spending time with family.

Find Stephen online at:

Website: www.stephenzimmer.com

Facebook: www.facebook.com/stephenzimmer7

Twitter: @sgzimmer

Instagram: @stephenzimmer7

Heart of a Lion
Softcover ISBN: 978-1-941706-21-3
eBook ISBN: 978-1-941706-23-7

Rayden Valkyrie. She walks alone, serving no king, emperor, or master. Forged in the fires of tragedy, she has no place she truly calls home.

A deadly warrior wielding both blade and axe, Rayden is the bane of the wicked and corrupt. To many others, she is the most loyal and dedicated of friends, an ally who is unyielding in the most dangerous of circumstances.

The people of the far southern lands she has just aided claim that she has the heart of a lion. For Rayden, a long journey to the lands of the far northern tribes who adopted her as a child beckons, with an ocean lying in between.

Her path will lead her once more into the center of a maelstrom, one involving a rising empire that is said to be making use of the darkest kinds of sorcery to grow its power. Making new friends and discoveries amid tremendous peril, Rayden makes her way to the north.

Monstrous beasts, supernatural powers, and the bloody specter of war have been a part of her world for a long time and this journey will be no different. Rayden chooses the battles that she will fight, whether she takes up the cause of one individual or an entire people.

Both friends and enemies alike will swiftly learn that the people of the far southern lands spoke truly. Rayden Valkyrie has the heart of a lion.

Thunder Horizon
Softcover ISBN: 978-1-941706-57-2
eBook ISBN: 978-1-941706-56-5

A deadly menace stalks the shadows of the lands to the north, stirring the winds of war. Farther south, the power of the Teveren Empire spreads with every passing day, empowered by dark sorcery. Formidable legions bent on conquest are on the march, slavery and subjugation following in their wake.

Within the rising maelstrom, Rayden Valkyrie has returned to the Gessa, to stand with the tribe that once took her into their care as a child. No amount of jewels or coin can sway her, nor can the great power of her adversaries intimidate her.

With a sword blade in her right hand and axe in her left, Rayden confronts foes both supernatural and of flesh and blood. Horrific revelations and tremendous risks loom; some that will see Rayden's survival in the gravest of peril.

Even if Rayden and the Gessa survive the trials plaguing their lands, the thunder of an even darker storm booms across the far horizon.

Thunder Horizon is the second book in the Dark Sun Dawn Saga.

www.ingramcontent.com/pod-product-compliance
Lightning Source LLC
Chambersburg PA
CBHW030111260626
47156CB00008B/2611